the crash

lisa drakeford

Chicken House

2 Palmer Street, Frome, Somerset BA11 1DS
www.chickenhousebooks.com

First published in Great Britain in 2017
Chicken House
2 Palmer Street
Frome, Somerset BA11 1DS
United Kingdom
www.chickenhousebooks.com

Cover and interior design and illustration by Helen Crawford-White
Typeset by Dorchester Typesetting Group Ltd
Printed and bound in Great Britain by CPI Group (UK) Ltd, Croydon, CR0 4YY

The paper used in this Chicken House book is made from wood grown in sustainable forests.

1 3 5 7 9 10 8 6 4 2

British Library Cataloguing in Publication data available.

ISBN 978-1-911077-17-6
eISBN 978-1-911077-76-3

To Kate and Owen, with love.

Also by Lisa Drakeford

The Baby

Sophie

'Feed me chocolate.'

'Feed yourself.'

'C'mon, your dad always has chocolate somewhere in this house. Find it, Sophie, and feed me. Think of it as payback. I deserve it. Who else would sit here watching *Eastenders* when they could be rocking it up somewhere else?' Tye shoves her in the ribs. She's lying next to him on the carpet; they've been there since eight o'clock and he's now hit 'pause' on the remote. It's always around this time that he demands snacks. It makes her smile – his propensity for sugar is unbelievable.

'Where exactly were you going to *rock it up*?'

He plants a hand on her ribs to shove or tickle. She braces herself. 'Chocolate!'

She's enjoying it now. 'Who exactly were you going to *rock it up* with?'

'Shut up! I do have other friends, you know! Funnier, more

attractive, cooler friends than you.' His hand squeezes the skin just above her waist. 'Chocolate, Sophe, otherwise I might waste away.'

The bubble in her brain gives a small ping. *This is the moment, this is the time. This is the opportunity you've been waiting for, for three weeks now.*

So she does it. She bloody does it. She lifts her neck, aims for his smile and kisses him quickly, waiting for the enthusiastic return she is sure will come. It's bound to happen, it was always meant to be. This is what their lifelong friendship's been building up to. The new era in the Tye and Sophie saga.

Only it doesn't.

'Um . . .' he mumbles, averting his eyes. Those brown eyes which were usually soft and full of glitter; only right now they look like tombstones; tombstones which want to be anywhere else apart from Sophie's front room.

She pulls away from his chest, feeling the sting of embarrassment on her skin through three layers of clothing. 'Sorry.' She coughs. The words scratch her throat. 'I thought . . .'

Tye grimaces. She can see horror spark in his eyes.

That's not nice to witness in your soul mate.

'Sophe . . .' Tye lifts himself on to an elbow and assembles his more usual expression on his face. But she can see the way he tugs at his T-shirt and runs fingers in his hair. She knows these gestures of old. He's awkward, embarrassed and desperately looking for an escape ticket. Emergency exit routes are flooding behind his eyes. 'Sophie, it's not right . . .'

This is mortifying. How could she have got the signals so wrong? She's messed up. She's messed up big time and if she's not careful she might just be wrecking the best friendship she's ever had. Other than Maisie, she's her oldest friend.

She has to put a smile on her lips, she has to do this quickly or else she's going to ruin everything. She's known Tye from the day he moved into the house next door, and they've been firm friends ever since. He's always round her house. Always sprawled on her floor. Always demanding food. It's a ritual now – something even her dad accepts. The weekly Tesco shop now caters for Tye's daily demands. Nobody minds. Tye's lovely. The whole family approves, even her grandma.

She sniffs, rubs her nose with the back of her hand and speaks louder than she means to. 'Whoops. Sorry about that. Don't know what came over me. Think for a minute I lost myself and forgot you weren't Channing Tatum.'

Tye lifts the sides of his mouth into a sort of smile, but they both know she's lying. He sits up straight against the sofa. 'Easy mistake to make.' He grins, but it's the grin he uses for strangers who he's trying to impress, and that stranger's smile is worse than an insult. Even worse than his knock-back.

Embarrassment singes the wallpaper all around her. It was a stupid idea. A STUPID IDEA. Just because they were both single. Just because he's attractive. Just because she'd had yet another dumping by a lying cheating scumbag three weeks earlier.

But her best friend's made of generous bones; his smile's already becoming easier and his eyes a shade more relaxed. It looks like he's going to help her. He tries a different tack: lies on his front, widens his eyes like a puppy. 'Chocolate, Sophie?

Please? I'll be your best friend. I'll do your hair. I'll introduce you to Ethan Price. I'll get you a part in *Grease*.'

It takes every ounce of courage. Every inch of nerve. She forces her fingernails into the skin of her hand and works at a conversation which she hopes will save a friendship. She shakes her head, rolls her eyes, and shoves him to one side like nothing ever happened. 'OK, OK. But let's make this clear. I am *not* letting you anywhere near my hair and I do *not* want a part in your stupid *Grease*.' As she stands up she feels a slight wobble in her legs, but she hopes this is the only sign that things aren't quite what they should be. She makes her way to the kitchen. The house is unusually quiet as her dad and brother are out. She stops briefly and puts her hands on her hips. 'Ethan Price, on the other hand, is an absolute Love God – so yeah, if you could somehow find a way for me to get my filthy hands on him, then I think it's worth a KitKat.'

She likes Tye's snorts which are muffled into a cushion by his side; maybe things aren't quite as wrecked as she'd thought.

But the next noise isn't Tye, or the TV springing into life. It isn't even the boiler. No. The noise which has her jerking her head back into the room is the most unnatural blast of a noise that she's ever heard in her house.

A second's drop in pressure has her lifting her head. A strange ringing in her ears. It feels like the walls and ceiling are suddenly carpeted. The suck of something in her stomach tells her something's not right. The movement on the floor by the sofa tells her Tye feels it too. The window starts to quiver in its frame. There's a strange clatter of what she thinks might be next door's bin. Then a horrible, blood-curdling screech which prickles the hairs on the back of Sophie's neck. She reaches for the doorframe for support, but finds a vibration humming under her skin where there should only be wood. She yanks her hand away like it burns. Her forehead folds in puzzlement.

All in a split second. No time even for Tye to get up off the floor.

Then comes the loudest boom filling the room; filling her head; filling her stomach and stuffing its way down her throat. A noise so loud it has her gasping for breath. Tye slams his hands over his ears. Yelling something. But she can't hear for the explosion of everything else.

Something hard and huge is smashing its way through the bricks of Sophie's front-room wall.

Her dad's curtains are the first casualty. Floral pink things which Sophie has always hated, they get dragged and snatched from their poles so that one of the hooks catapults through the air and stings Sophie's cheek like a wasp. The pole wrenches chalky plaster through the wallpaper.

Beneath the curtain is a car.

A full-sized revving motor vehicle in her actual front room.

It's not a metre away from Tye, who shouts and yells with his hands on his ears as the car screeches closer. As if he could make it stop.

An armchair cartwheels from one side of the room to the next. A potted plant explodes into the middle of the room, spraying multi-purpose compost like confetti. Sophie can taste the soil. Some airborne flecks land on her lips. The noxious smell of burning rubber and dust. The dangerous stench of diesel. Screams from people she's never met before.

The crumble sound of bricks giving way. Falling like leaves in autumn on to her dad's beige carpet. Thumping down now, like giant concrete hail stones. Like bombs from aeroplanes in World War II.

'Tye!' Sophie screams at him to get up off the carpet, but he seems pinned down by something invisible. Fear or panic, probably, but whatever it is, it looks strong.

His face is aghast. Alarm bathes his skin and eyes.

The wall-lights skew. They hang uncomfortably, their bulbs popping out in a fizz.

Murky grey is dragged over everything like a huge dusty blanket. Maybe it's smoke. Maybe it's dust, maybe it's exhaust fumes. Maybe it's the fact that the lights have gone off.

Sophie peers into the gloom. She needs to see Tye. She needs to see that he's not crushed under the front of this unwelcome mechanical monster which has appeared from nowhere.

She doesn't see him, but that's understandable – she can barely see her hand in front of her face.

There's muffled shouting coming from the inside of the car. A soft crash as a school photograph of her and Sam slides reluctantly down the wall. She takes a step forward and trips on the coffee table, which is now upside down in completely the wrong place. She feels the ooze of spilt liquid seeping through her socks.

'Tye!' she shouts again through the thick grey fog of the room.

The TV gleams through the fog. It is still on pause. Still in the position it always was. She gets distracted at how this can be, when there is carnage everywhere else in this normally organized room.

She feels around with her hands, over the coffee table to where Tye should be. Can sense through her nose that the steaming car is centimetres away. Hates it. Wants Tye.

'Sophie.'

She stops, with her hands gripping the table leg, and feels relief flood through her. His voice is to the right, where the sofa used to be.

'You OK?' His voice has a wobble she's never heard before.

She has to cough. The dust or the fumes scratch at her throat. Swallows. 'Yeah. Where are you?'

'The sofa.'

She nudges with her knee, pushing closer to his voice. Presses down on a piece of broken glass. Feels her skin moisten in pain. This must be how blind people feel. Why aren't they always covered in bruises and cuts?

It's hard to breathe. The air is almost solid with something. But she feels a hand on her arm and recognizes the comforting grip. Tye.

He pulls her towards him so that she knocks into a chair. 'Careful,' he breathes.

She falls on to the sofa, which has strange, smaller objects on its cushions where there should be only softness. A lamp-shade. A couple of chunks of plaster and a mug spilling the coffee which she'd made less than ten minutes ago. At least this is what she thinks the objects are, because still the room is thick with grime.

Tye's fingers grip her shoulders and pull her into a hug. He's shaking. But he's still Tye. Her ear crushes on to his T-shirt and she hears the hammer of his heart.

They make a silent, still huddle in the middle of the chaos.

She looks around her as some dust begins to settle.

The car is more than halfway through the wall. It looks unreal. So alien that it could be a dinosaur sitting there, not two metres away from the sofa. The engine under the bonnet gives off ticks and creaks. It oozes steam and more smoke. She knows there are people inside because there's muffled movement from behind the glass. She supposes she should get up and help, but for this small couple of seconds she needs to get her breath.

Besides, she's not sure if Tye is up to more action yet. His hands are horrible twitches on her arms. And he's not saying very much.

The TV in the corner, oblivious to the chaos, suddenly springs to life with the rest of *Eastenders*. The noise seems too much, because within seconds it plinks and fizzes into nothing. The white gleam fades out.

They're left then with nothing but a steaming, ticking car.

Emergency dawns, quickening her pulse. Don't cars sometimes explode? Isn't there something about leaking fuel? Aren't hard hats meant to be worn in demolition areas? Can't walls just suddenly give way?

Adrenaline, horribly delayed, finally kicks in. And she grabs Tye's arm.

'Tye, we've got to get them out of there.' She yanks his

T-shirt. 'And then we need to get out of here ourselves.'

The hammering on the windscreen springs them both into action. More warm liquid from where she's been sitting, on the back of her leg. Unpleasantly cool now. She grabs Tye's hand.

'C'mon.'

The hammering is muffled, but with a background noise of panic. Words which don't make any sense. Sophie can't make out the detail but gets the gist: these people want to get out, but for some reason they can't.

Spurred on by other human voices, Tye at last shakes himself out of his weird trance and jumps up with Sophie. They step over upturned and broken furniture to get to the passenger door. The foot of the coffee table jabs at Sophie's thigh. There will be a bruise tomorrow which will shock her when she wakes up in the morning.

Something plastic shatters beneath Sophie's foot.

There's a pair of pale faces glimmering through the side window and a darker shadowy one in the back. The faces at the front have mouths like thin lines of string. Their eyes are as wide as duck eggs. Sophie's never seen eyes quite so scared. They make her fingers tremble as she reaches for the door handle.

She's relieved to see Tye's hand shoot out before hers, because she's not good with blood. And there could be lots of it in that car. She can't watch hospital dramas, she can't watch babies being born – once, to her mortification, she fainted all over the boy sitting next to her in a biology lesson when they were watching a film on childbirth. So, the prospect of opening a car door on to what could be a bloodbath stops her in her tracks.

She sidesteps on to more plastic and lets Tye tug at the handle. His body is warm next to hers, and suddenly packed with purpose.

He yanks hard but nothing moves. The hammering and muffled yells get more alarmed. It's like they're under water. He inhales, sticks his chest out, fills his cheeks for more strength and has another go. Still no movement.

The duck eggs get wider. They're in a boy's pale face and a girl's. A remarkable resemblance.

One more go. The strain in Tye's torso starts to look painful. There's some shouting from the shadow in the back. Sophie grimaces; Tye is nothing against this ton of steaming metal, leaking fuel on to her dad's carpet.

He looks around him, searching for an answer. Sophie catches his despair. 'We've got to do something. Quickly.'

He nods and then hurdles over the coffee table, dragging a leg so it grazes his shin. Sophie's left with the car and the glimmering faces looking frantic, their eyes glued to Tye's shoulders. He reaches the standard lamp and lifts it like a javelin. Sophie's reminded of pole-vaulters. He sheds the lampshade, tosses it aside and then returns to the car beside Sophie. They're both breathing heavily. It's difficult not to hear the rush of something from under the bonnet and the fuel which is still trickling underfoot.

'C'mon,' she breathes between locked teeth.

He points at the window, then to the lampshade. It's pretty obvious what he's about to do, but he has to spell it out to the people in the car. They seem rooted to their spots.

'Get away from the window,' he yells above the steam.

The boy in front understands quicker than the girl. He tugs at her shoulder and moves them both with difficulty towards the steering wheel. The boy in the back is now shouting and gesticulating between them. His face has an ugly shine.

Tye uses the opportunity within seconds. He's now packed full of urgency; Sophie's relieved to see it. With a powerful jab running from his shoulder to his fingertips he stabs at the window with the end of the pole. The window, already under a certain amount of strain, crackles up like frost. The noise is like a sparkler on Bonfire Night.

Sophie exhales. Checks the steam from the bonnet. Won't look at the fuel now pouring steadily from under the car.

Tye pulls his hand back for another jab and this time makes a hole in the glass. Then another. Then another, until he's able to weave the pole from side to side, mashing the glass. Clearing a space.

The squeals of panic from inside can be heard properly now. They remind Sophie of frightened animals. There's a horrible yelling from the boy in the back as he pulls and paws at the girl. The noise is raw and frightening and very, very wrong.

Issy

The best place to stand when things are like this is right here. Issy's done it countless times before. It's where she goes.

Standing in the front room between the curtains and the windowsill, with the smell of dust in her nose and a tickle at the back of her throat, she can see but not be seen. If she presses her heels against the skirting board and holds her breath so that her lungs feel fit to burst, she could almost be invisible.

This evening it's especially important for her to hide. It's been brewing for several hours now. She could smell it in the air, and she knew it was only a matter of time before she'd be here. Stuffed between the curtains and the blinds, feeling the cold of the glass against her bum and shoulders as she presses herself out of sight.

It's hard to breathe at times like these.

She can hear her mum and Dave yelling and bashing stuff

in the kitchen. She can hear Polish swear words and she can hear hands slamming on surfaces and against things. She really hopes that the hands aren't slamming on to skin.

There are three more crashes and some loud swear words from the kitchen. Issy presses her lips together and puts a knuckle in each ear. She can feel the blood hum behind her eyes.

She doesn't know what to do. She wishes she was somewhere else. She turns around and makes an eye-hole diamond in the venetian blinds with her fingers. She watches next door steadily. Counting the bricks, picturing what her neighbours are doing. She loves Sophie with a gush. Sophie's the best ever sixteen-year-old Issy knows.

Sophie makes her feel grown-up.

She bets that Sophie's dad doesn't shout in the kitchen with the door firmly closed. She bets that Sophie and her big brother Sam don't have to hide behind a curtain while all the horrible stuff is going on. Issy feels the base of her neck rise with heat as her mum screams Polish swear words, the only Polish words she uses now.

The venetian blinds scratch at the glass of the window as Issy pushes further into them.

Then something catches her eye. She's used to the view from the window of Sycamore Street: two trees; a short path to the battered green gate; old Mrs P's house opposite with dirty grey nets; Sophie's house next door with a perky pot of flowers either side of the gate; Dave's old van sagging at the front on the road; and a free parking space where Sophie's dad usually leaves his car. The road is normally quiet, but right now, with a noise which has Issy's head jerking up in a snap, is a car.

Only this car doesn't belong to any of the residents on Sycamore Street. This car is yellow and fast and incredibly noisy. The engine doesn't sound right to Issy. It screeches like it's being strained. It isn't moving properly either. It veers from one side of the road to the next. Lurching between Dave's van and a lamppost.

Prickles spread over Issy's shoulders.

Things aren't right. Even Issy, who at eleven years old doesn't know much about driving, can tell that the car isn't doing what it should.

There are two people in the front of the car and someone in the back. She sees them as the car just misses her gate. She recognizes in a split second that the ones in the front are both blond and pale. And she can tell that they are scared and that they are shouting. She can see by their mouths, which look twisted knotted up.

There's a splintering sound which makes Issy's eyes spring wide. The car shoots from the road on to the pavement and then through next door's fence. One of the flower pots spins through the air and lands on Issy's front path. There's soil everywhere.

And then, even more alarming, so that the venetian blinds get shoved aside because she has to see more. Issy can't believe her eyes: the car spurts over Sophie's front lawn and slams into the brick of Sophie's house, smashing through the wall.

There's an explosion of dust and powder and soil. And the crashing sound has Issy jamming the heels of her hands up against her ears.

This has to be the most alarming and frightening sight that Issy, in all her eleven years, has ever, ever seen.

At first she's rooted to the spot, staring at the smoking back end of a car sticking out of next door's house. Her heart's beating fast and she imagines it, banging away.

Sophie.

The best ever sixteen-year-old in the whole wide world.

Issy can't stand still any longer.

She rushes to the kitchen door. Not thinking of what's behind. Only imagining Sophie under the wheels of the car. She shoves the door wide, her mind full of images of blood and bones sticking out of skin. She only half sees her mum. Only half sees the way that she's leaning over the cooker. How her body is twisted and strained and how the gas is lit. The way that Dave has her mum's hand forced towards the flame. How her mum's face looks twisted and ugly. The pulse which throbs in Dave's neck.

Only half seeing all this, with half her head already next door, she runs to the back door.

'Issy!' her mum screams.

'Shut up!' Dave hisses through teeth which are clamped shut.

Issy averts her eyes, only thinking of Sophie under the wheels of the car. But she stops short suddenly when the fullness of what's happening finally seeps through.

She won't look at her mum. She won't look at the hand which is centimetres away from the flame. Instead she screws her eyes tightly shut and whispers, 'It's next door. There's been a thing. Something horrible.' She wonders if she might wet her pants. Her knees feel like rubber.

She won't look at Dave, who is white and sweaty. Instead she fumbles for the door handle. She knows she has to shove it with her knee. It's been stuck since the time Dave lost his temper with her for bringing in a frog with a broken leg. She'd wanted to keep it in a box. Dave was having none of it. He'd kicked the back door and told her to get the thing out of his house. She'd wanted to tell him that it wasn't *his* house, but he'd kicked the door so violently that she got scared. Ever since then it gets stuck.

The door gives way after the second shove and she flees into the outside air. Sophie, the best ever sixteen-year-old, probably needs her help, and she's going to be there. Like a superhero on TV.

Running with her hair everywhere she dashes through the gap in the hedge which nobody has bothered to fill. She hopes Sophie's back door is open. It usually is. But even if it isn't, she knows where the key is kept. She's used it before, when she looked after the hamster.

Luckily it's open.

But it's dark inside.

Only then does she falter. Only then does she think of her mum's hand centimetres from the flame. One foot into Sophie's house she feels torn. Should she return?

Her heart beats like a bomb underneath her ribs. She doesn't know what to do.

But strange screams coming from the inside of Sophie's house finally get the better of her and she takes another step. She wishes it wasn't dark. Feels around for the light switch which she knows is next to the door. But when she switches it on nothing happens.

She recognizes Sophie's voice. Feels her own voice scratch in her throat. Something sharp.

There's movement coming from the front room and a horrible smell. Clouds of dust and something else. She walks blindly through the kitchen, her legs like elastic bands.

The voices lead her further into the house. There are lots of them. Some she's not heard before. There's broken glass underfoot and she's glad she's wearing her trainers. The crunch where she's walking doesn't feel very good.

She makes out figures. Sophie. Tye from two doors down, who's nearly always around. He's nice. He has conker-brown skin which she's always thought is the perfect mix of his mum's black skin and his dad's tissue-white. Sometimes Issy feels jealous, though. Sophie and Tye's friendship is one which she can't break into.

There are other figures too. Figures she's never seen. They're being pulled and yanked by Sophie and Tye. Everyone's coughing and nobody's standing straight. Faces are twisted. Hands over mouths. There's a horrible sobbing. It's male.

Someone's yelling swear words. Whoever it is, they're angry and scared, and this in itself is worrying.

The house creaks. It seems to groan like it's alive. One of the blond figures gets shoved into the kitchen. It crouches with hair all over the place. Issy works out that it's the girl. She has her hands over her face and there's blood. Issy has a vague sensation that she's seen her somewhere before, but it's not the right time to think about that.

Tye and Sophie are still in the front room. There are scuffles and groans. She makes out people pulling a figure from the car. This one's the boy. Blond like the girl crouched in the kitchen. The same shade of blond. Only he's more of a mess. He's wearing jeans which have blood on them and his top is all ripped up. He's coughing and Issy can't make out his face, there's too much dust. Tye looks shaky. It seems to be Sophie doing all the pulling.

There's another groan from the ceiling, and both Issy and the girl look up. It doesn't feel safe like a normal ceiling.

'Sophie!' Issy manages to scream. She doesn't like the way the house sounds. She sees Sophie jerk up her head at her name.

'Issy,' Sophie yells, though it's more of a wail. 'Get out of here. I think it's going to collapse.' She speaks through tugs and yanks. The boy falls to his knees and Sophie has to pull him up. Through the dust Issy watches Tye shake some more.

Issy has no intention of leaving, even though her knees are wobbling and her heart is hammering. She's sure that she has to stay. She touches the girl on the floor. The skin on her arm is cold and wet, Issy doesn't know what with. 'Come on,' she says, 'come with me.'

The girl looks up at Issy and even in the dust, even in the fumes and the chaos, Issy can see that she's beautiful. She has the bluest eyes Issy has ever seen. And her nails are painted a pale green. Issy has always wanted nails like this.

It's funny what people think in the middle of an accident.

The girl gets up like Issy is in charge. Issy feels important and strong. Not many people in Issy's life do what she says, but this girl moves with her into the back garden and is happy to be led to the patio-set by the door.

'Stay here,' Issy says. She likes saying this. It feels like she's in the films.

The girl nods and leans forward so her head is on the iron table. But then she lifts it in a jolt and looks behind her. There's a panic in her eyes. 'Don't let him come here. Don't let him out!'

It's confusing. Issy isn't sure what she means. She's not sure if it's shock.

Sophie and Tye are now in the kitchen. They are all coughing horribly. Old-man coughs. And both boys are kind of staggering. It's Sophie doing all the pushing.

'Get out!' she yells.

Issy stretches out her arms to help pull the blond boy. He's gasping for breath and making strange sounds. Issy spots tears and snot and blood. He's also very damp under her fingers. She doesn't want to think what with.

One last push and they're out of the back door. Someone steps on Issy's toe, but she manages not to cry out. Being brave right now is far more important. These people are all hurt and she's the only one who isn't.

There's more dragging of chairs and the blond boy slumps down, almost missing the seat. Tye's not far behind. He can't seem to bend very well. Issy watches Sophie glance over nervously. She has worry lines on her forehead.

The blonde girl is looking behind her, her neck in an ugly twist. 'Deano,' she spits. 'Where is he?' She shoots panicky looks at the blond boy. 'Don't let him near me, Harry, please don't let him near me.'

But the blond boy has something wrong with him and his eyes aren't taking things in.

Tye lifts his gaze, as if he's seeing Issy for the first time. 'Ambulance,' he gasps. Issy feels around in her pocket for her phone, but then remembers that Dave confiscated it when it was ringing at dinnertime.

She hates Dave more at that moment than she's ever done before.

But the girl with the beautiful eyes has a phone. A posh one. She fumbles around, tapping in a code. Her fingers are trembling. All four of them watch as she shakes the phone to her ear, her eyes constantly skittering to the door.

'What about the other one?'

'No!' shouts the girl.

'We need to get him out.' Sophie tries to be calm but Issy can hear the fear.

Tye stands up, staring at the girl. 'We have to get him out. We can't leave him there.'

'Please!' says the girl.

Sophie, who looks so droopy and thin like she might fold over any minute, shakes her head. 'We have to.'

Tye nods quickly. 'I'll go. You lot stay here.'

They all eye the ceiling, which gives another creak.

Sophie quivers. 'Tye – I—'

But he starts to run back. Back into the darkness, back into the fog. Issy wraps her fingers around herself, feeling sick. Sophie starts to cry.

For two horrible minutes everything is silent. The people around the table are barely breathing. Just the sound of

Sophie's sobs. Then what seems like a scuffle and an awful thick crash brings two figures to the doorway, but they don't make much sense through the murk. One of them is slammed against a doorway so he slithers to the ground, while the other uses the opportunity to peer into the outside and make a run for it. He's dark and tall and stares quickly at the blonde girl, who turns away with a squeal. The boy grunts some twisted words and limps quickly past the table, squeezes through the gap in the hedge and runs off in a funny lopsided way, clutching at his stomach.

A flash of realization: Issy knows where she's seen them, the blonde beautiful girl and the darker boy – by the post office last year, his hands in the blonde hair and his cigarette so close to the girl's cheeks that Issy hadn't known where to look.

Everyone's attention is quickly diverted when the phone in the girl's hand beeps into life.

The blonde girl lifts the phone to her face. Her voice is wobbly, but confident all the same. 'Ambulance . . . yes . . . there's been an accident.' She quickly looks up at Sophie, who is standing trembling next to Issy. 'Where the hell are we?'

Sophie gives the address, her voice ending in a screech as she sees Tye's form on the floor squirm and slither out of the darkness and curl up in a ball of pain at their feet. Seconds later the blond boy's head crashes on to the table in what Issy hopes is just a faint.

She had good news. It was like a firework in her pocket. She had good news.

She never had good news compared to her brother. This must be how he walked home every day; full of the bubbling and pop of good information to impart. She can picture her mum's face, and how her dad might open his arms wide and let her slide into the satin of his suit jacket where she could inhale his warmth and enjoy his pride. She loved her dad so much, it would be good to make him proud. It didn't happen often, it was usually her brother. Pride.

It's good to suck on that word as you walk home from school. It's been so horrid recently, now that she's been thrown out of Stephanie's group. Miserable and lonely. Nobody to talk to other than her brother. She hadn't realized how completely dependent she'd become on Stephanie and her friends. How everybody else had stopped existing. And how, now that they'd all turned against her, she was entirely on her own. It's hard to take when you used to be so popular.

So today's good news; well, it warms up places which had started to be cold.

And another thing: good news like this brings power. She speeds up her steps at the very thought. This might be the way to put forward her suggestion. The first step towards her future. Katy Stewart, her neighbour who's in the year above, knowing how she'd wanted this for a long time now, has found her a job at the NEC. Nothing very big, but a part-time job in the cloakroom where she can look out on to all the people, maybe meet some celebrities and begin the first fairy step towards her career. She's going to manage bands and live an important life looking after celebrities. And she knows exactly how she's going to do it. She's not her dad's daughter for nothing; she knows she has to start at the bottom and she's prepared to do it anyhow. She doesn't need Stephanie, or her friends. Just her sixteenth birthday in two weeks' time, and her parents' permission.

And this kind of good news might just pave the way.

An A in science is pretty good news. It's never happened before, and she had to ask Mr Johnson to repeat it. So she stuck that A in her pocket, walked round with it all day and imagined her parents' reaction. Maybe a celebratory ice cream in the new cafe after the orthodontist tomorrow. Maybe a mocktail. Maybe some underwear shopping with her mum. It's time. She wonders if her mum has noticed.

The firework in her pocket fizzes happily at the sight of both her mum's and dad's cars in the driveway. Perfect timing.

She plans the conversation. She won't bring up the job thing, not straight away. She'll leave that until the A has sunk in and she's maybe helped with tea.

In the house there's a strange silence. No clattering in the kitchen, no music anywhere. Maybe they're outside.

It's only when she steps into the kitchen that she finds her mother with her face in a tea towel and her dad's shadow through the kitchen window outside. It gives her jagged edges, the first since she's had the A that morning.

'Mum?'

Her mum puts down the towel in a small swift movement. But it doesn't hide the redness of her eyes or the shake in her fingers.

'Are you OK?'

Her mum brushes fingers through her fringe and looks around her like she doesn't know where she is. 'I'm fine . . . Just . . . um, a bit tired.'

As Gemma grabs a glass from the cupboard and opens up the fridge she thinks about her news. It'd be nice to say it to them both together. She's waited all afternoon. She can wait a few more minutes until her dad comes back in.

'What's for tea?'

Her mum looks alarmed at the question, as if it's not been on her mind. She searches the counters for inspiration and sees a pack of prawns leaking wetness on the surface. 'Um . . .'

But then her dad shoulders in through the door, his finger wagging. It flares poison across the kitchen. 'And another thing . . .'

'Your daughter . . .' Her mum shakes her head frantically,

sending 'not now' signals. But her dad seems to have missed them because he's raising his voice, his eyes thick with anger.

'What right did you have looking through my credit card statements anyway?'

Her mum's neck is pink and disturbing. 'We're married, for God's sake. "For richer, for poorer", remember?'

Gemma places the drink back into the fridge. She's not thirsty any more. There are stings of worry at the back of her throat instead.

'Dad?' Her voice is a wobble.

He ignores her. So does her mum. They're wrapped up in a tangle of an argument. Gemma picks at the braces on her teeth, which have been annoying her all day, but she's only just noticed.

Her dad bangs his fist down hard on the counter, making them both jump. Stars shimmer behind Gemma's eyes. 'The envelope's marked confidential. The woman I married would never have done such a thing.'

'Things change.' Her mum's words are miserable.

Another thump. 'You're telling me.'

Gemma's been learning about World War I at school. Right now it's easy to think what it might have been like in No Man's Land.

Frantic. 'I have some good news.' Her words are a jumble and nothing like how she'd rehearsed them. Maybe she won't mention the job offer tonight after all.

'NOT NOW!' Her dad doesn't even look at her.

'Don't,' says her mum.

'You started this with your dirty little detective skills.' He moves closer to Gemma's mum so his finger is centimetres from her nose.

Her mum's eyes bulge in an ugly way. 'No, *you* started this with your clandestine affairs.'

'Shut up!'

'No, *you* shut up!'

'My news . . .' It's a whisper. Gemma finds she's backing into the pantry. She hears the rattle of the car keys. Her dad scrapes his nails against the surface as he drags the keys on to a finger.

Her mum sees too. 'Where are you going?'

'Out!'

'With her?'

He rolls his eyes and shakes his head in a weary, angry way. Jabs his fingers in the air, his car keys dangling from them. 'Fuck you!'

In her room, twenty minutes later, with the thrumming, vibrating cat, she sits on an empty square of carpet and strokes and strokes and strokes. Sid arches his back and bats against her face with a fierce and powerful jaw.

'I got an A,' she whispers to him. 'I got a bloody A.'

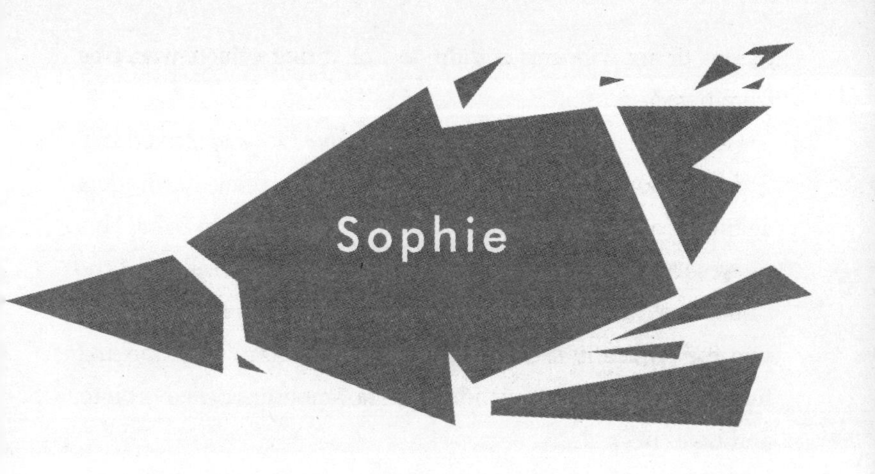

Sophie

Sophie hates the ward. It's got a sticky plastic antiseptic feel about it which makes her shudder every time she comes in. She hates how Tye doesn't have any edge, any depth, any angle. He's just a flat, silent body under a hospital sheet.

He's been like this for three days now and it's like visiting the ghost of her best friend.

The breathing equipment is the only sound in the room. It's mechanical and artificial and about as opposite from Tye as you can get. Sophie hates how it doesn't matter what time of day she visits, the sun never reaches him; the bed's in just the wrong place. She'd like to see sunshine fingers rest healing hands on his body through the giant window. He'd enjoy that. He's always had a thing about the sun. While everyone else shoves on hats, shades and sunscreen, Tye uses the opportunity to strip off as many clothes as is decent and lay his skin bare.

The thought brings a gulp to her throat which won't be swallowed.

What if Tye never feels the sun ever again?

Today Sophie hovers in the doorway, grazing her fingers against the doorframe watching a nurse check him over. This nurse is Sophie's favourite, and she's sure Tye would feel the same. She's Welsh and pretty with skin which is so flawless you can virtually see through it. She has long, cool-looking fingers which Tye would adore as she smoothes down his hair and takes his pulse.

Wake up, Tye. Wake up so you can go on and on about this nurse. Wake up so you can go into gory detail about how every time she takes your pulse it's actually code for wanting to get inside your jeans.

The nurse isn't the only other person in the room. She never is. Aside from Tye, there is always a member of his family there. It's a vigil which they haven't broken in three days. Tye's mum, dad or brother; they're always there. Perched on a hard plastic chair tensely staring, or curled uncomfortably in the chair in the corner, in grey, crumpled-looking sleep. They're a surprise, this family. Sophie's never seen them so complete. Normally his brother's at uni having the time of his life, and his dad's on business somewhere exotic in a suit and a scowl of rushing. It's very rare that Sophie's seen him without a lanyard or a label. Without one, he doesn't look entirely himself, like perhaps he shouldn't even be there.

But today it's his mum. She's sitting fretting on the edge of the chair, looking dreary and old, with lines on her face which have appeared from nowhere. She has on an odd outfit of a smart blouse with a pair of jeans which look like they're usually worn for gardening. Her jet-black hair is normally shiny and styled with something bright on the side, and she always wears lipstick. Today there's no sign of a lipstick and her hair is untouched. She looks a ghostly version of herself. But when your son's been in a coma for three days, having suffered a car accident and then a blow to the head which should have sucked his life away, there's not much time for costume coordination or hairstyling.

Sophie coughs to show herself at the doorway. The grief and strain in Tye's mum's face is too personal to butt in on. It's better to look like she's just got there.

Tye's mum shifts and gives a little jump of the shoulders. 'Oh, Sophie.'

The nurse looks up from her clipboard and gives a soothing smile.

Sophie takes a step in, trying not to breathe too much. 'Hi.' She nods at the flatness that is Tye. 'How is he?'

Tye's mum hisses out a sigh from the bottom of her lungs. 'Oh, much the same.'

There's a chair on the other side of the bed which Sophie takes silent steps towards, skirting the nurse, who looks like she's almost finished. Sophie touches Tye's wrist, which is too cool and still. It's hard not to recoil. 'Hello, Tye,' she whispers, feeling slightly awkward in front of the two women. She prefers her one-way conversations without an audience.

Tye doesn't answer. Of course.

Tye's mum peers at her over his bed, as if she's not seen her in ages, even though it was only yesterday. 'How are you,

Sophie? What's the hotel like? It must be strange living there.'

Sophie shrugs. 'It's all right, I s'pose. Nice breakfasts but no privacy.' She begins to play with Tye's lifeless fingers, hoping he can hear. 'There aren't enough rooms at the moment so I have to share a room with Sam, which is an absolute nightmare.'

'Oh dear.'

Sophie nods. 'He hates it as much as me. And they still won't let me go back into the house to get my stuff. They say it's structurally unsafe or something. I've worn these jeans for three days now.'

Tye's mum nods. 'You just have to look out of our bathroom window to see that. The whole house looks like it might collapse any minute.' She frowns again and knots her fingers. 'Poor you.'

Sophie grimaces; she could kick herself. It's ridiculous moaning about wearing a pair of jeans for three days when Tye's lying there facing death at any second. She makes her voice gentle. 'Do you want a break? I bet you could do with a drink, or maybe some breakfast. I'll sit with Tye. I've got all morning.'

There are several minutes while Tye's mum fusses with his sheets and gathers together her stuff. 'They say you're going to be interviewed by the police. Apparently there was some confusion over what happened. They need to get to the bottom of it. Tye too, when he wakes up.'

Sophie notes the 'when' and feels grateful. She nods. 'I know. There's not much I can say, though. Just that a car smashed its way through our front room and that there were three people in the car.'

'Did they ever find the third boy?'

Sophie lifts her fingers off Tye's skin. 'Not that I know of. It was all a bit weird.'

Tye's mum lingers by the door. Her shirt's crumpled and the no make-up is distracting. She nods at Tye, her expression an open wound. 'Talk to him, Sophie. He loves you, he always has. They say he can hear us. That he'll take comfort from our voices, that we act as stimulation. Apparently I've got to bring in his music and other personal stuff to stimulate his brain.'

Sophie nods. 'I'll do my best.'

In the end she doesn't say much. She's already said it all. Instead she sucks in some breath, trying hard not to cry, shifts the chair so it sits in a pool of sunshine and holds on to his hand like the warmth can pass through. It's awkward talking to someone who doesn't answer, so she tells him about *Grease* in a burst of words; how they're going to use someone else to play Kenickie, but should he wake up in time, then he'll be allowed to take that person's place. She hopes, if he really can hear her, that this hasn't gutted him, but that it might act instead as an incentive. Tye has been dreaming of this part since Year 8. So then she ends up singing *Summer Nights*. He'd crack up at her singing, if only he could. She's tone deaf; Tye and Maisie have always found this a huge source of humour.

Then that thought makes her cry.

She fiddles with her bracelet, the one with the dangling heart, the one her mum bought for her the day before she left. She wears it all the time. Sometimes it would be good to see her mum more often. She allows herself to cry even more.

When Tye's mum returns and it's time for Sophie to go back to the hotel, she kisses him on the cheek, wincing again at how he doesn't smell like Tye and how his skin is too cold under her lips. 'Bye, Tye,' she whispers. 'See you tomorrow.'

Tye's mum nods and settles down to her plastic-chair vigil. They share a sad smile and Sophie walks down the corridor where the silence of the room begins to fade.

After an hour and a half in this sterile building the need for fresh air is extreme. But as she reaches the end of the corridor, ready to take a left for the stairs to the exit, something distracts her. Something more important than fresh air.

In front of her, less than two metres away with her back to her, is a girl around her age. A girl swinging quickly through the throngs. A girl on a mission – at a guess she's probably visiting. She has an unusual hair colour: a pale shade of blonde Sophie's not seen before – except that now she has. Because not three days ago, a girl and a boy with exactly that shade of hair colour were ploughing their way through her front-room window, slamming their way in, causing havoc, chaos and disaster.

Fresh air can wait. Sophie decides to follow. It's almost certain that this girl will lead her to the boy who nearly killed Tye. It feels important to see his face.

At sixteen she noticed that boys started looking at her. Maybe it was her hair. It was an unusual colour and she wore it long, but backcombed it sometimes, so it looked fuller and wilder. A little bit like how she was feeling.

The braces were taken off her teeth, the spots stopped appearing, she got a taste for fashion and she found a new way of walking. It seemed to fit how her mind was working.

It would be a lie to say that she didn't like the looks.

And it was the older, braver boys who caught her eye. So it was only natural to enjoy the talk and the looks and the low whistles when she passed Deano and his mates at the bus stop. She made it her daily ritual to saunter past the gang of lads at exactly the same time every day before school. Deano was the ringleader. The cool one. The good-looking one. The one who was always in trouble. Her mum and dad knew who Deano was. Everyone in town knew. He'd been in the local paper after getting done for anti-social behaviour and GBH.

It was good to annoy her parents. Even if they didn't know about it. It was good to have Deano's admiring nod, and some of the words he said to her, fizzing away under her skin when her mum and dad were arguing. These days they never noticed her, they were far too distracted by their messed-up marriage; besides, if they were going to notice anyone, it would be her brother and his genius-level art. Sometimes it felt like she was invisible. She'd sit on her bedroom floor above the kitchen as they argued, picking away at the rips in her jeans, listening to her mum swear at her dad, and her dad accuse her mum, and she'd remember how Deano told her she had a nice arse, that her legs looked good, that her hair looked like a she-devil.

Even at sixteen.

'What's your name?' Deano asked one day when she slunk past the bus stop and caught his eye in a long hard stare which she'd learnt off *Hollyoaks*.

He flicked his fag to one side on the pavement and took a long stride to where she was standing. This had never happened before. He'd always been in the thick of his gang. Today though, he was up for it. Today he was taking steps towards her, shrugging off his friends like a snake sheds a skin.

In the sunlight she could see that he was even better looking. His hair was glossy like a chestnut. He was tall and his chest was as wide and as flat as a small table.

'Tess.' She swallowed. She had no idea why she lied, but it felt important. And she'd always liked the name Tessa.

'Nice.' He rubbed his nose with the flat of his hand so that she could see the three dark cross tattoos on the middle knuckles of his left hand. They were thrilling, those tattoos.

She didn't know what to say.

Deano inhaled through his nose and lifted his chin. He had a small chip in one of his front teeth which fascinated her when he spoke. He tapped his foot. 'Wanna come with us, Tess?'

Gemma heard the low jeer of his mates under the bus shelter. Saw him flick the Vs behind his back.

She swallowed again and found that her foot was tapping as well.

She fancied a skive off school. She'd never done it before. It sounded wild and exciting and how she was feeling right now. Her brother would cover for her. And besides . . . it would serve her parents right.

'OK.'

She remembered to keep her eyes on his. She remembered how to walk again. She remembered that she was now called Tess and that if anyone asked, she was eighteen.

It was a derelict mill in the woods by the next village. It smelt musty, of rotten leaves and mud, but she quite liked the smell. It was very different from her house, which smelt of scented candles all the time.

They'd set up a kind of den. There was an old armchair in the corner which someone had dragged up the open steps; some cardboard for people to sit on; two wooden crates which served as tables; an upturned bucket and a stained, damp-looking mattress which was propped up against the wall. All this was messily surrounding a pile of ashes in the middle of the room. The floor was bare; it looked blotted and scarred like a giant stain of vomit from where the fire had been lit and relit.

Today the fire was the first thing that one of Deano's mates went at. He crouched down with his lighter, some wood that he'd picked up on the way and an expression that twisted his face like a corkscrew. His name was Tam.

Gemma stood at the top of the stairs feeling stupid in her school uniform. She was conscious of a breeze lifting the hem of her skirt, pushing it back against her thighs. Then she remembered that she was called Tess, that she was eighteen and that girls like that didn't mind a breeze. Sometimes they even encouraged it. So she lifted her chin and smiled a bit.

Deano caught her eye as he sank into the armchair in the corner. He winked, patted the arm of the chair with his tattoos. 'C'm'ere, Tess. Chair like this – it's big enough for two.'

So she did.

She spent most of the day there. And then the next and the next. It was fun. It was exciting and she could forget about the other things in her life. They were nice to her, these boys. Gave her sausage rolls, crisps and lager which they produced from plastic carrier bags every day. And Deano? Well, they were nice to her because he was. Tapped the arm of the chair every day. Told her she looked like a devil with an arse like hers in a school uniform and hair that was wild like a lion. No one had ever spoken to her like this before and it felt good as it fizzed away in her belly. He'd look at her through the smoke from his cigarette, over the tattoos on his knuckles, with a slow, knowing grin. Like he knew exactly what was going on under her ribs. The chipped tooth gave her goosebumps.

Deano didn't touch her. But he made it clear that one day he might. He also made it clear that nobody else should. Tam tried once, when she was sitting at the fire twisting up wrappers to feed the flames. Deano had been off somewhere and it didn't feel right. Tam put his fist on her thigh and leered in. It didn't feel good underneath her ribs, but Deano had swanked up the stairs several minutes later and swore some words at Tam who immediately lifted his hand away, leaving a small charcoal stain. And straight away she felt better. Tam never did that again.

In a weird way it made her feel safe.

As safe as she could feel in a derelict mill, away from school with a handful of boys who played with fire, knives and lager.

On the fourth day there were bottles. Not cans. Cheap vodka from the Co-op. Tam shrieked with laughter when Deano peeled them from his pocket next to where she was sitting. She felt his elbow brush against her thigh as Tam rubbed his hands through the thick smoke from the fire.

'Happy Christmas!' sniggered Deano.

'Happy Easter!' laughed Tam.

'Happy Birthday, T!' Deano knocked the bottles against her knee so they chinked like champagne glasses. She didn't know what made her legs frost up with goosebumps. But they did.

(Her birthday wasn't for seven months.)

She liked the vodka less than the lager. But now she's Tess. She's eighteen years old and she can slump on the arm of Deano's chair and feel his elbow on the fleshy part of her thigh.

There was some messing around. Some fighting and laughing and shouting over speakers. She was dancing with two boys right by the fire. Dancing like she'd seen on YouTube. Sandwiched between their faces. Breath in her eyes and breath at the back of her hair. Dancing, so her legs wound round like she'd seen on TV. (She wasn't stupid. She knew what to do. She was Tess. She was eighteen and the music was good; it invaded her skin and got into her bones.)

Deano watched from the armchair. His slow grin followed her everywhere, the chipped tooth glinting.

She wound her legs even more.

But then, embarrassingly, she wasn't on the arm of the chair any more. And she wasn't dancing. She was curled in a heap on the cardboard in the corner. There was an awkward pool of drool by the side of her face, staining the cardboard; her head felt swollen and throbbing. If she opened her eyes the fire and the wall and the boys swerved to the left in a lurch. So she closed them again quickly, although she moved her hand so it covered the wet patch by her face. She stayed like this for a while. She thought she'd probably been asleep judging by the way the darkness of the afternoon had crept into the mill, and by the fact that the boys were quieter.

She heard the clatter of their voices through the fug in her head.

'We'll need to get her back, won't we?' one of the voices

questioned. 'Rich bitch like her – there'll be a mummy and daddy asking questions.'

'Fuck 'em.' Then a cough and a laugh. She thought it was from Tam. It made her squirm. But even squirming hurt her head.

A silence and a rustle. Some laughter and more coughing.

Her school skirt was caught between her thighs. She shifted a bit but kept her eyes tightly shut.

'Whatcha gonna do with her, Deano?'

She heard his voice from over by the fire. She tried to focus. Tried to reach for a memory which wasn't quite in reach. Nothing seemed to get to them.

Deano laughed. It was a dark laugh which came from deep within his throat. He sniffed. 'Don't need t'do anythin'. Th'way I see it she'll walk in this fire if I tell her to.'

There was a cloud of laughter and somebody joked, 'fattening her up for Christmas.'

The words dropped in her like hard, heavy stones into a very deep lake. *She'll walk in this fire if I tell her to.*

She drew her knees into her chest and tried to use every available inch of strength not to cry.

(It was ten more months until Christmas.)

When darkness fell – she could feel it on her skin – the shivering got the better of her and she started to move. To scratch at her arms and to sit up in spite of a head which pounded horribly. She ignored the sniggering and the harsher laughter and remembered that she was still Tess.

'I'm going,' she mumbled into the collar of her school

blouse, which was now too thin in the brittleness of the evening. She staggered to a stand and had to hold on to the wall. Her fingers were like pliers, but they kept her upright.

'You off, T?'

She hoped to find some kindness in Deano's words. But it was difficult.

'Mm,' she managed.

She swayed a bit and wouldn't look at them.

'See you next week?'

'Maybe.' Fighting back a gag.

He stood up. She sensed it. Despite herself she felt warm as he approached. He placed a finger under her chin. She could imagine the tattoo.

'You had fun. We all did.' It was a statement. A fact right in her face.

She wished she could remember if she had.

Issy

This isn't hiding. This is worse. There's a smell of dark and of cobwebs. Issy hates spiders. She doesn't like to think of them crawling in her hair. Sophie once told her that on average, a human eats approximately eight spiders in their lifetime. The thought makes her shudder, which reminds her that she's cold.

Her mum couldn't get a blanket in time.

She's only got her One Direction T-shirt which is really for summer, not February. She draws her knees up tighter into her chest, closes her eyes and hums. That way she can't hear. Screwing up her eyes tight she can see pinprick stars. She's hungry. She's not had any tea.

Her mum couldn't get her anything in time.

Her arms are sore where Dave grabbed her. Issy places her fingers on the soreness and presses. She holds her breath. Feels the tears swell. She squeezes her eyes tight. Dave doesn't like cry-babies. And he doesn't like bruises. She'll have to wear her H&M long-sleeved hoodie tomorrow.

If she's allowed out.

Because this isn't hiding. This is worse.

It started yesterday. She could feel it looming in the walls of the house. But her mum didn't seem to be able to. They were helping Sophie's dad. It was nice. Sophie's family still weren't allowed in their house, but they could go in the garden now that the car was removed. For two days afterwards there'd been blue striped tape all around the fence. But yesterday someone had come to remove it, which meant they could enter the garden.

It felt good. Mum and Sophie's dad, their hair whipping their faces as they tried to straighten the place up. Mum had a broom and was sweeping all the stuff out of the way. And Sophie's dad was propping up the fence, which was all wilting and limp where the car had crashed through. Putting on a tatty sweatshirt, Issy joined them, enjoying the smiles and chat between Sophie's dad and her mum. Their voices were musical in the breeze.

She'd got the dustpan and brush from under the sink and started sweeping the path. Neighbours stopped to chat, shaking their heads at the accident, saying how amazing it was that nobody got killed. Even old Mrs P – who never normally says anything, just bangs on her window with a stick – even she came out in a headscarf and asked after Sophie.

Issy felt important. Part of a team, helping out. Like when the whole village made the bonfire on the park for Bonfire Night.

But she'd forgotten about the looming feeling she'd had all morning. How Dave was sulking and her mum didn't seem to realize.

After an hour, when Mum said they should stop soon for a drink, she heard Mum's bedroom window bang open. She lifted her eyes and saw Dave's face peer out. She recognized the red blotches on the tops of his cheeks. They weren't good signs.

'Nina!'

All faces in the garden lifted towards the voice. Sophie's dad looked interested, like he thought Dave might be offering tea. Issy's mum put on a blank face, but Issy recognized the small movement in her lips.

'Yes, love?'

His eyes skittered towards Sophie's dad, then narrowed towards Issy's mum. 'Can I borrow you for a minute?' There was a grating sound in his voice. Issy held her breath. The dustpan dangled in her hand.

Issy's mum gave a quick smile. She touched Issy's shoulder as she walked past.

Sophie's dad smiled and got back to tying a fence post.

Issy didn't have the heart to carry on with the sweeping. Her breathing was short and she wanted to go into the house after her mum, but didn't want to seem rude. She stood still and stared at the door her mum had walked through.

It felt important to follow. So she plucked up the courage and found some words. 'I'm just going to the toilet, Mr Dukes.'

'All right, love.'

*

When she got into the kitchen there was a full-scale shouting match going on. Issy shut the door quickly. She didn't want people to hear. She stood at the door, her hands holding the handle behind her, her eyes wide.

'It's not like *he* does anything for *us*. Watcha go skivvying around there for? Making yourself look like a mug.'

Issy's mum was wringing her hands. Her neck was all strained. 'He's a friend, Dave. He's been my neighbour for years now. They've had an awful accident and I wanted to help. It's nice.'

Dave's head jerked up. He laughed. Unkind. 'Nice! Don't make me laugh. You're making a bloody fool of yourself. Since when has he been in this house and helped us? This floor,' he gestured towards the kitchen floor where there were a few crumbs by the bin, 'it's a bloody disgrace. Since when has that man been in here and so much as picked up a mop?' He took a step towards Issy's mum. Issy winced as her mum cringed against the cooker. 'He's never so much as set foot in here.'

Issy remembered times when he had. When Sophie's dad used to pop in the house for a cup of tea quite regularly. Issy's mum would teach him Polish swear words and they'd laugh for ages over the tea. But that all stopped once Dave moved in. Issy knew better than to say this. Thankfully, so did Issy's mum.

Dave took another step and Issy's mum looked quickly at Issy. 'Issy, love,' her voice was strained, like a knife on glass, 'off you go, love. Go and watch some TV.'

Issy widened her eyes. Her heart hammered. Her fingers squeezed the door handle so hard it started to hurt. 'No, Mum,' she mumbled. 'I'm staying here.'

Dave jerked his neck round. The red was even higher in his cheeks now. 'What did you say? You cheeky little—' he blustered, and moved away from Issy's mum towards Issy. She didn't like how much her wrists were wobbling. He had her hands on her arms before Issy could even wince. He grabbed hold and pressed so her skin felt like plasticine. 'Don't you talk to your mother like that!'

'Dave – leave her alone.' Her mum's voice was tight and high. She clung on to his free arm. He shook her off like a dog. A grunt from his throat made it sound like he was satisfied. He yanked Issy so her feet tripped on the floor. She stumbled but he lifted her arm so it hurt her shoulder joint. Pulled. Issy heard a clicking sound from somewhere in her body. She saw her mum in a heap on the floor. She was crying.

'Dave!'

Issy's teeth chattered. He yanked her from the kitchen, stood looking around him in the front room, his grip still tight on her arm.

It was the not knowing that was worst.

She didn't know what he was going to do to her, but she knew it wasn't going to be nice.

If he wasn't holding her upright, Issy was sure her legs wouldn't be supporting her. He exhaled. She smelt old beer. Her eyes followed where he was looking.

It was under the stairs. With the old coats, the deckchairs, the Hoover, some boxes and a stepladder . . . and the spiders.

He grunted as he shoved wide the triangle door. Kicked her bum and pushed her inside.

She fell on top of the Hoover. Heard the stepladder rattle as her foot got caught up and her mum screaming and sobbing in the kitchen.

The door was slammed shut.

It hadn't always been like this. Her mum had met Dave on the internet three years ago, when Issy was eight. Her mum had been lonely after Issy's dad had died when she was little. Issy's parents had come over from Poland, for a new adventure in England. Issy had been born and then, not much later, her dad had died. That hadn't been part of the plan, and it took Issy's mum a long time to move on. Then she met Dave. He didn't remind Issy of a rat then. And he made them both laugh. He took Issy's mum out every week to the cinema or to the carvery, and once to see a group in Derby who used to be famous. Sophie next door babysat, and Issy loved this. She enjoyed the way they'd sit on the sofa, shoulders gently pushed together, sharing a bowl of popcorn, watching *X Factor* with Sophie's mobile phone flashing every couple of minutes. Sophie was a popular girl. Everybody knew that. Sophie was brilliant.

Then Dave moved in. And for a while things were fine. She was allowed to go to the carvery with them sometimes. Dave would watch her pile her plate full of gravy and potatoes and vegetables. He'd smile and tell her he was putting meat on her bones. Once he even came back from Asda with a large cardboard box for her. Inside was a television which he said she could have for her room. He told her she wouldn't need to keep disturbing him and her mum that way. He even wired it up and tuned it in. It's still there now.

Then Dave lost his job at the printers', some accusation about stealing money. He didn't go into detail.

Though her mum got a cigarette stubbed out on her neck for asking.

Much later, when it's gone very quiet. When all the screaming and the shouting and the crying and the swearing has finished. When there's not the TV sound and she's not even sure if anyone is left in the house, she finally hears someone come down the stairs above her.

They're soft steps. The steps of a woman trying to be quiet.

The door opens and a triangle of light hurts Issy's eyes. Her mum's silhouette is in the gap. Issy can't see her features but she can tell, by the way her head's tilted, that she's probably trying to smile.

Brave, considering what Issy has heard in the last four hours.

She stumbles in. Stifles a sob. Issy's not sure who is comforting who. Her mum lowers herself on to the floor. She does it warily, like she's hurting. They hug. A damp, hot-cheeked hug. Issy smells metal and a bit of BO. But she nuzzles into her mum's T-shirt like she can't get enough.

They spend ages like this. Not saying anything. Just stroking and holding. A whimper now and again.

Eventually Issy's mum pulls down some coats. They make a sort of nest. And it's much warmer anyway. Two people in a storage space.

'Like two little Harry Potters,' her mum laughs against Issy's neck.

They sleep in the end, curled up in their nest like mice. Her mum's hair is tangled and itches against her nose. But Issy doesn't mind. She wouldn't have it any other way.

Just Issy and her mum. In a dark, small space with love and unhappiness coming up through her mum's T-shirt.

Gemma two years ago

Another time he took her to some different woods. All alone this time. Without Tam or any of the others. It felt good to be singled out. Deano had his favourites and she was one of them. It wasn't very often that she was a favourite. Not when she had a brother like hers.

The woods were just at the back of the housing estate, and they skirted all the way up the side of the quarry. It was a damp soggy day. Deano strode on ahead of her, whistling under his breath, lighting up a cigarette so that she inhaled his smoke behind him.

They frightened a wood pigeon, which made a clumsy clattering escape through the branches of a tree. A blackbird made a brave series of alarm calls as Deano led the way, bashing away at some saplings with the palm of his tattooed hand.

He stopped suddenly, 'Wanna know a secret, Tess?'

She shivered at the thought. She nodded, eyes widening. (She'd seen that on *Hollyoaks* too.)

He turned round then and placed a hand on her shoulders. It felt good to feel the notorious Deano's hands on her. She wondered what her dad would say.

Deano looked down on her and breathed nicotine. 'I'll show you something I've got hidden in this place. Nobody knows about it – 'cept you. Only you'll have t'do something in return.' He nodded down at her with expectant eyes. She felt them linger on her chest, then stomach, then skirt.

It was hard to breathe with Deano's hands pushing on her shoulders and his eyes painting her body. So she didn't breathe. She didn't speak. Just a small nod.

Deano moved into the thicker part of the wood, skidding on some mud. He swore under his breath and stopped by a tree, an old oak with a V-shaped cleft in its gnarled-up trunk. He stood against it and looked at her, his hair glistening under a soft ray of sunshine. 'You sure you want to see it?'

'Yes,' she breathed, certainty bristling up the skin at the back of her neck.

'Can I trust you?'

'Yes.' She felt important and much older than sixteen.

With his eyes on hers he reached into the cleft. Deep down into the trunk. Then drew something out. It rustled in a breeze which whipped up her hair. He was grinning at her, daring her to move her eyes away. She was proud that she didn't. He dangled the bag in front of her face.

A Morrisons bag with something heavy in the bottom.

'Take a look.' He opened it wide.

At last she moved her eyes away. She stood on tiptoe and peered into the bag. What she saw made her open her eyes wide and jerk her head away. She'd never seen one before. Even plastic ones were banned in her house.

It was a gun. A black, heavy-looking, cold thing with a brown mottled handle.

'Is it real?' she gabbled.

''Course it fucking is.' He laughed and reached down into the bag, lifting it out. He held it carefully in the palm of his right hand, stroking it like a baby with his left.

'Where'd you get it?' She hated how posh she sounded.

He snorted, still stroking it. 'Wouldn't you like to know?'

No, she wouldn't, actually. She wasn't sure why she'd asked. 'Does it work?' She didn't like the way he was holding it now. There was a tangle of fear at the back of her throat. She was in the woods with a stranger. It was nine-fifteen in the morning when she should have been at school. It was cold and wet and nobody knew where she was.

He lifted his eyes to hers. She didn't like the look. ''Course it works. Want me to prove it?'

'No – it's OK.' She stepped back, leaning into a bush.

He laughed. It was ugly. He stopped being good-looking then. She felt younger than sixteen now. This had been a bad idea.

He held the gun in his right hand and put his index finger around the trigger.

She heard herself whimper.

He pointed it at something behind her right shoulder, then waved it around to his right. He was sniggering, it sounded watery in his throat. The laugh echoed up to where more pigeons were roosting. There was a clattering up high.

'Want me to use it?'

'No,' she said quickly. 'No, it's OK.' Her thighs were wobbling but she hoped the bush was hiding it.

He waved it in front of her face then, so that flashes of heavy black and brown blurred before her eyes.

'Stop it.' It was a whisper.

He laughed again and jabbed at her shoulder with it. 'You sure you don't want me to use it?'

'No. Please.'

He looked at her carefully. 'How old are you?'

'E-eighteen.'

He smirked, then put the gun back into his left hand. 'Waste of a bullet, I s'pose.'

'Yes. Why don't you put it back? I won't tell anybody.' She knew she was babbling.

Deano shrugged, then reached down for the bag, which had fallen by his feet. He let the gun dangle by the trigger for a few seconds, then dropped it to the bottom of the bag. It rustled. Gemma let her breath fall into a sigh. Folding the bag over twice, he moved back to the tree, where he manoeuvred it into the cleft. She was shaking all over now. Her teeth chattered.

He turned back round and grinned, a horrid smirk. 'Your turn now.'

'What?'

'Your turn for your part of the bargain. Remember?' He rubbed his hands horribly.

She couldn't step back further into the bush. 'What do you want?'

He didn't answer, but moved a step closer so that his face

was nearer to hers. 'C'mon, Tess, you know what I want.'

He smelt of nicotine and matches. She jammed her head against something when he placed his hands on her school shirt, rummaging against the cotton. He found a button with his tattoo fingers and slid his hand underneath.

Alarm trickled up her spine. No one had done this before. It felt wrong and horrid. His fingers wound round her right breast. She thought she might be sick. He pushed. Her whole back was against the thin trunk of the bush now.

'No,' she managed to say when his fingers slipped inside the padding, searching.

He laughed. He took no notice.

And then suddenly it was too much, in this bush, in the cold with this stranger's fingers in her bra. Especially after the gun. Tears sprang up her throat so that words jammed themselves in her mouth, scrabbling to be heard.

She pushed his hand away and burst into tears. 'No. No. Sorry . . . only . . . I think my dad might be leaving my mum.' The words surprised her.

She collapsed into a heap at the bottom of the bush because her legs wouldn't hold her up any more. Deano stepped back, his hands in the air like he was a surrendering soldier. He reached in his pocket for his cigarettes; laughed an ugly laugh when he'd lit one, and looked down at her from where he stood. 'I ain't no attacker.' He shrugged, his cigarette still in his mouth. 'But I'll tell you something for nothing.'

She looked up at him miserably, through tear-soaked fingers. She waited.

'You're a fucking prick-tease, you.'

She could feel the mud seep through her skirt. 'Sorry,' she gasped.

'And you ain't eighteen, are ya?'

She shook her head miserably.

He laughed another watery laugh, shook his head and turned to go. 'A fucking prick-tease.' Then he started to walk off. Stopped three trees away and seemed to be thinking. She watched, from under the branches, hoping and praying that he wasn't going to come back. He turned around with his eyes scrunched up. 'But I'm sorry 'bout your mum and dad.'

She was left then, in the bush which shuddered and bristled with the sobbing that now broke free from her. It pushed through her skin, through her school uniform and through the throb of pain from her mum and dad's late-night argument.

Sophie

Every day is the same now. Every single day. Fitting everything in. Juggling small tasks so she can do all the things that need doing.

She finally has her own room. It was killing her having no space. Having to share with her eighteen-year-old brother was ridiculous and inhuman. All they did was fight over the space in the room, and the noise and the smells which filled it. It was impossible.

She has to go to school again now. It seems that having your house knocked down and your best friend in a coma isn't enough to stop the texts and phone calls from your head of year to remind your dad how important this year is.

But she still sees Tye. She still finds the time. That will always happen – she has made this promise to herself and nothing anybody says will change it. So she's started to drop into the hospital on the way home from school. It's on the way, now that her home is a scruffy hotel.

And she has lots more to tell him now, which is a bonus. School, as ever is brimming with gossip and activity and she finds that she can prattle about inconsequential things for the best part of an hour, as long as nobody else is in the room.

His room is still horribly silent. Just the machine and the noise of all the activity out in the corridor. Tye is always too flat, too lifeless and too still; Sophie will never, ever get used to this. He lies there in bad pyjamas, breathing sterile air, taking in everything she says but giving nothing back. Sometimes it's hard to concentrate because it's almost as if it's not Tye. Tye would never take her sarcasm, Tye would never wear those pyjamas, and Tye would always twitch a smile when she said something stupid.

Leaving him is difficult. It's always the hardest part. The sadness usually swoops into her throat and bumps under her ribs. What if this was the last time she saw him? What if he was all alone when he opened his eyes and saw nobody, then died feeling alone and unloved? What if he needed something? What if he had a nightmare? What if he was hurting and couldn't say? What if he was about to take only eight more breaths and she wasn't there to hold his hand for them?

When she eventually drags her feet through the doorway, saying bye to Tye's mum, dad or grandmother, she doesn't go home. Not straight away.

No. She finds it comforting and a little bit interesting and now strangely compelling, that she walks the long way round. Back through the corridors of misery and illness. She takes a left towards another ward: the ward where she followed the blonde girl on that third day. And there she has to look. She has to hide by the wall so that she can't be seen, where she can stare at the boy with the pale blond hair, sitting in his bed, biting his nails, talking to his visitors or staring into space, the boy who nearly killed her best friend.

It's him; she's one hundred per cent sure. There can't be any other twins in the county with shared hair like that. The same twins who crashed their way through her front room. The same twins who bashed the life out of her best friend and sent Sophie's own life into smithereens.

It's an odd feeling staring through the glass. His profile doesn't look violent, his hair doesn't look like a monster's, and his long sleek fingers, which are never still on his sheet, don't look like those of a murderer. But he almost is, and that's a fact.

On another day, after school, she decides that she wants to go home. Just for a look; just for old times' sake; just because she can't quite face the smell of the hotel. So she does, with Maisie for company.

They turn into the road and she feels a thrumming behind her ears. This was where the car must have spun out of control. There are still skid marks on the road. They etch out an urgent collision course in tarred-up black writing. She has to avert her eyes.

And then when they near the house they stop. She can't take her eyes off it.

Her house. The house where she's spent so much time in the last few years. The house where she's sat gossiping with Tye, doing homework, eating and drinking, planning a future, learning lines and generally dossing; now with a gaping hole the size of a bus in its front. It's boarded up with some flimsy-looking hardboard, but it's scarred and ugly and gives her a lump in her throat.

'Shit,' says Maisie.

And then, from nowhere, Sophie's aware of Tye's dad standing behind the hedge. His presence is spooky and sad, an odd concoction. She's never been comfortable in Tye's dad's company. He's too clever, successful and strict. His mum is much easier to be near – and to be fair, his dad is often away on business.

He stands by Maisie, nodding. He has grey flecks in his hair, which Sophie's never noticed before. 'I know. Horrible, isn't it? I don't like looking, to be honest.'

There's work noise coming from inside. Banging and scraping. Sophie shuffles her feet, trying to dredge up something to say. 'I wonder if they'll let me in today. I really need some more clothes.'

Maisie looks at the garden. Someone has tied up the fence, but there are giant skid marks across the lawn. 'I can't believe you all survived.'

Tye's dad bristles on the other side of the gate. 'Someone needs to arrest whoever did that. It's nothing other than dangerous driving. He must've had his foot on the accelerator until he bashed through the wall.'

Sophie ducks her head. Mumbles. 'Maybe it was just an accident . . .'

Tye's dad tuts and gives his head an angry shake. 'An accident, my arse. That's either driving under the influence of something very strong, or a suicide attempt.'

It's strange how Sophie feels defensive. She breathes careful, controlled words. 'Tye's going to wake up, I'm sure of it.'

'Hmm.' His dad jabs at the gate.

Sophie's front door opens and a man in a high-vis jacket and a hard hat stands on her front step. He reaches in his pocket for a cigarette. The radio blares behind him. It feels wrong.

'God, I hope they hurry up.' She throws death stares at the builder. She didn't know the sight of her home like this would be so difficult. She glances over at Tye's dad, wanting to draw him out of his desperate son-filled gaze. 'I keep looking at the size of the hole.'

Tye's dad shakes himself out of his trance. 'Hmm.'

A pale glimmer on the other side of the house catches Sophie's eye. A small movement, mouse-like, from the house next door. Sun glints off the back door as it opens. A flash.

The girl. Issy.

Sophie's shoulders relax; she sticks up her hand in a wave. 'Issy!'

She's a quiet little thing, her neighbour. Quieter than a mouse. Too skinny. Pale as a ghost. Sophie used to babysit for her – they were always nice evenings.

Issy stands at the back door. Nervous-looking. Worry all over her forehead. She turns her head to check for something, then makes hesitant steps forward.

Sophie strides towards her, enthusiasm in her legs. She opens her arms when she's closer to the girl. Laughs a bit, watching a shy smile spread over Issy's cheeks.

'Hiya, Issy. How are you? I've not seen you since . . .' she lets her hand move towards the hole in the house, '. . . all this.'

Issy's voice is quiet. Eyes which don't leave Sophie's face. 'I'm OK. I saw you from the window. I was looking for you. Are you coming back for good? I miss you.' She pulls her sleeves over her hands. Her fingers curl around the cuff. She's a bit shabby-looking today.

Sophie shakes her head. 'Not yet.' She nods towards Tye's dad. 'I've just come to take a look.' There's a pause of awkwardness as they watch Tye's dad turn into the grey staring figure again. Sophie smiles at Issy because she looks too anxious. 'I'm in a hotel in town. It's a bit grim, but at least it's not going to fall in on me.'

Issy's eyes widen and move towards the house. 'Is it going to fall down?'

Sophie shakes her head and puts her hand on Issy's shoulder. She feels a surprising flinch. Strange kid.

'No,' she laughs, 'they're making it safe. It's going to take a bit of time.' She flicks a lock of Issy's brown hair off her shoulder. 'You know, you were so brave, Issy. We might not have made it in time if you hadn't come along to help.'

Issy ducks her head. Her sweatshirt looks too big and there's a grease stain on her shoulder. 'Will Tye come out of his coma?'

The question makes Tye's dad flex his fingers.

'He will, I'm sure of it.' Sophie crouches in front of her, cocks her head to one side. 'You OK, Issy? You look knackered.'

There's a flicker of movement in Issy's eyes, then a sudden glaze. She lifts her head. Smiles a bit. Shakes her shoulders.

'I'm OK, thanks. What about you?'

Sophie stands up again, speaks quietly so that Tye's dad can't hear. 'I'm fine. Not even a graze. It's just Tye and the boy in the car who ended up with injuries.'

A movement behind the window at Issy's house makes her suddenly ramrod tense. 'Gotta go!' she says in a tight high voice.

Sophie nods. 'See you around, yeah? I'll give you a shout when I next come round. Maybe we can go to the Rose Cup for a milkshake?'

Pink happiness fills Issy's cheeks. She nods. 'OK.' She turns to her house. 'Better go.'

Sophie watches as she runs in a darting jerk towards her house. She's an odd one, that's for sure.

Tye's mum comes into the hospital room bringing with her the scent of rain and her citrus perfume. Sophie's glad she's started to dress like she used to; her hair is piled high and fastened with a bright blue flower bobble. If Tye's sense of smell is still around then it should act as a comfort. His mum's got red cheeks under her brown skin from rushing, and she's clutching a jaded old CD player. She's an unusual sight in this antiseptic room.

'God, sorry, Sophie. Thanks for waiting.'

Sophie shrugs, she hadn't noticed the time. She'd been too busy relating the gossip of the day and stealing all Tye's liquorice. She knows for a fact that if he was awake he'd take the piss and tell her she had black teeth.

God, how much she wants him back.

'No worries, I've got nothing to hurry back for.'

'I thought I could play this in the room.' His mum holds up a *Grease* CD. 'The nurses asked me to look for things which might trigger memories.' She shakes her head. 'And this was definitely his latest obsession. He'd learnt all his lines before everybody else.' She looks stricken and has to flop on the plastic chair. 'Oh, God. I don't think I can cope if he's still unconscious when it's on.'

There's an awkward ticking in the room, from the machine. It's unbearable when adults crumble like this. Sophie doesn't know where to look, so she fiddles with Tye's hospital bracelet and blurts something out which surprises her.

'Was Tye all right, Mrs Stanley? – you know, before the accident? Only . . .' She watches his mum's head lift in a frowned-up question, '. . . only, he was acting kind of strange with me . . . sort of distant . . . a little bit distracted?'

That's very difficult to admit to. She can't quite believe she's said it. But the question has been nagging behind her eyes for some time now.

Tye's mum rises from her chair and begins to fiddle with the CD player. 'He was very busy, maybe it was that. Rehearsals were in full swing, and he was working on some coursework.' Her back is narrow and bony. Even more bony since the crash. There are pale nubs of spine sticking out like knuckles at the base of her neck. She looks sad, even from behind.

'Maybe.' But it wasn't that. It was something else. Something Sophie had been hoping to talk about on the night of the crash.

'Tye,' she whispers, 'please wake up. Please.' She lifts his horribly limp wrist with its bracelet. A bit louder: 'Your mum is now going to drown out the hospital with uncivilized music. It is your public responsibility to wake up so you can tell her to turn it down.' She drops his arm back on to the sheet. 'Now is not a good time to go quiet on me.'

She watches his unresponsive face and if she didn't love him so much she'd hate him.

Tye's mum takes a couple of steps towards her. Her face is a cloud of mystery; importance fills her lips. 'Did he tell you he was in love?'

Sophie feels her eyes widen as she bats away the awkward memory of her failed kiss.

'No. My God!' She won't feel cross with someone in a coma. She won't let herself. But it's hard to think he hid this from her. They were normally so open. 'Who with?'

Tye's mum waves an arm vaguely. 'Oh, someone from *Grease*, I think.'

Sophie sits swiftly on to the bed, surprise weakening her knees. 'I didn't know . . . why didn't he say?'

A layer of softness glows in Tye's mum's eyes. 'I think he was trying to find the right moment.'

Sophie balls her fist, letting in the embarrassment. *And while he was looking for the right moment, she was trying to kiss him.* She's not sure she can bear the shame.

'Oh, Tye,' she whispers. The words sound like the saddest two words ever spoken. They seep round the room filling every crease and hollow.

*

Even after that curveball, she still walks to the blond boy's room – it's a habit now. It's a sick compulsion that she doesn't understand. But she's tired of trying to work it out, so she lets her legs do the walking while she thinks about Tye's news.

She feels strangely let down when she sees an empty room. It's alarming, like she'd not thought about it before. He won't always be here; he might leave the hospital before Tye wakes up.

If Tye wakes up.

The seep of panic is chemical.

Sophie's fingers trace the yellow line on the wall, thinking of the hundreds of thousands of people who've done the same. She misses the blond boy. She was enjoying the way his fingers were never still, she was enjoying the shade of blond, she was enjoying watching somebody who had no idea she existed.

All this against the solid, horrible fact that he was technically responsible for causing her best ever friend to be lifeless and flat in a hospital room. The thought makes her cough and brings a ringing to the space behind her ears. It's important that she hates him.

Metres before the door – before the trigger point, so they're still firmly shut – she catches a glimpse of a shade of hair which stops her in his tracks. She slows down. Feels a cluster of nerves.

They're together, the boy and the girl. The twins. He's hobbling on crutches in a dressing gown which is miles too big for him. She's scowling and hissing at him. He's got a determined set to his mouth. It seems like he's in pain.

The girl looks up first and sees Sophie. Her lips form into a twist of recognition. 'Hello.' Her voice is clear and a bit posh. Like a smooth pebble, dropped cleanly into a pool.

'Um, hello.' She watches the boy look up with interest. She reminds herself that it's as a result of him that Tye is lying in the coma.

The girl nods towards the boy. 'Thought it was time he got a bit of exercise.'

The boy lifts his head. He's pale, with dark smudges under his eyes. Eyes the same shade as the girl. Hair exactly the same blond.

'Do you remember me?' says Sophie.

The boy lifts one side of his mouth into a tired, confused smile. His nose crinkles and his eyebrows knot together. 'I know you. You come to my room. You hide, but I've seen you,' he mutters. Unlike his sister, his voice is a low mumble.

Sophie feels an embarrassed brittleness in her shoulders. She nods. 'Yes,' she admits. 'I've been watching you. Um . . . should you be doing this? It looks painful.'

The boy slides his eyes across to the girl. 'Nurse Gemma here reckons she knows best. Reckons I'll never get out if I don't push myself.'

Sophie sees an irritation in the twitch of the girl's lips. 'Don't be soft. I thought you hated all the fuss.' She nudges him with her shoulder, trying to be playful. 'Anyone would think you enjoyed being trapped in here.'

Sophie stands still, tapping her foot gently. Wondering when one of them will mention it: the reason why they're all there.

It works. The boy looks at her and blushes. It makes her wonder.

'I'm not sure who you are, though.'

There's a high-pitched wail as an ambulance swings into the parking space outside. The whole corridor bursts with it. There's no point in trying to speak until the noise dies down. Instead, they stand awkwardly in the corridor, a hotchpotch of discomfort. Sophie's blush rises high on to her cheeks. The boy turns back to looking at the floor and the girl starts to stare at Sophie, chin high.

The siren stops abruptly and the girl uses the moment to stick her hand out at Sophie. 'Hi,' she says. 'I'm Gemma.'

Sophie nods. Glances at the boy. 'Not a nurse, then?' Gemma's hand is cool under her fingers.

There's a hint of a smile. 'Don't think I've got the personality.' Her eyes are strained and deep and there's stuff behind them which Sophie can't quite get.

The boy snorts. A proper smile now, reaching his lips. He looks up to Sophie. 'And I'm Harry.'

'And I'm the girl who lived in the house that your car crashed into. Sophie.' She blurts her words, making them lifeless and hollow. She wants them to hurt.

She watches the colour drain from the boy's face. 'God, I'm sorry.'

'It was an accident.' Gemma's voice is clear and smooth.

Harry droops on his crutches. 'Even so . . .' He looks around him. 'What about the others? There were other people, right? It's all a bit . . . hazy.'

Flashes of Tye lying lifeless under the sheet. 'There was Tye

– my best friend. He's who I come here to visit. He's . . .' she feels a grimace form on her face, '. . . he's in a coma, I'm afraid. He's not woken up since the crash.'

Harry lifts his hand to his mouth. 'Shit, the police said someone was still unconscious – but he's your best friend. God, Sophie, I'm so, so sorry.'

Gemma has a hard mouth. 'I'm sure he'll wake up.'

This gives Sophie a liquid shot of anger. 'No one knows for sure.'

Harry droops back on his crutches, his face miserable. His sister glances around the room looking like she needs an escape route.

'What about you?' Sophie asks, despite herself. 'When can you get out?'

Harry shrugs and Gemma speaks quietly. 'Not yet. Harry's been bleeding internally and he's dislocated his knee.'

'There were more people,' says Harry. 'I'm certain there were.'

Sophie nods. 'There was that boy in the back of your car. He ran off – nobody knows where he is.' She senses a tension between the twins which she stores up to think about later. 'And then there was my next-door neighbour, Issy. If it wasn't for her, I don't think we'd have got out in time.'

'God. What about the house?'

'Unliveable. They're still making it safe. They reckon it'll be OK in about a fortnight.'

The boy's face has gone from white to grey. The girl looks jerky. She grabs Harry's arm and pulls him. 'Come on, we'd better go. I've got work in an hour.'

Harry twists a look over his shoulder as his sister continues tugging. 'Will you come and see me, next time you visit your friend? Properly, though. So I can apologize?'

Sophie flushes again. 'I might do.' There's an odd sensation in her forehead where she should feel anger. For Tye's sake.

Gemma rolls her eyes. They're lagoon-blue. She tousles her hair which springs all over her shoulders. She looks complicated. One minute sure of herself, the next a bit tense.

Just as Sophie's leaving, as she moves towards the door, she witnesses something odd. Two boys, a couple of years older, wander into the building. They have hoodies and trainers on, like her. One of them is holding a giant chocolate bar, like they're on their way to visit someone. Nothing very different there; but it's when they catch sight of Harry and his sister that things turn unpleasant.

One of the boys prods the other and points at Harry. They lock eyes and start to snigger and whisper. It's obvious they know him. Sophie can't make out the words exactly. But whatever's been said has caused Harry to flush red and Gemma's backbone to snap straight with anger. She bristles and stares at both boys.

Harry looks awkward. He pokes Gemma with his crutch and says something under his breath. It's plain to see he wants to get away, and on this occasion Gemma seems to agree. They move up the corridor swiftly – as swiftly as possible when one of them's on crutches.

For the most part she stayed away from the bus stop after that. She took the shortcut with her brother and tried not to think of Deano. And generally it worked, until the council decided to dig up the road along the shortcut.

She could tell Deano was in the bus shelter by the plumes of smoke. She'd have to walk past him alone, because Harry wasn't well.

He saw her as she rounded the bend. Gemma could feel his eyes like lasers. She felt the sniggering of his friends and smelt the cigarettes in the chill of the morning air.

'Tess!'

It was a soft word. The softest she'd ever heard from him. It made her lift her head in surprise.

He was good.

He stepped out from the shelter, a glow in his eye. 'Tess.' A tattoo finger slicking back his hair. His good looks swiped at her stomach and she thought she saw a blur of kindness behind his eyes. It gave her a jolt; a nudge of something nice, something hopeful.

'Yes?'

He bent his head towards her so his mates couldn't see or hear. 'You OK, T? Long time, no see.'

'I – I'm OK.' She wouldn't stutter any more in front of him. She wouldn't give him the satisfaction. 'I've been going to school. My parents . . . they were getting phone calls home.'

He grinned then, so that she found herself staring at the chip in his tooth. Strange stirrings in her stomach began to get the better of her.

Then he hung his head. *He actually hung his head*. She couldn't be more surprised. 'Sorry about last time – I was a bit . . . um . . . off my face. I'd taken something, see, taken something I shouldn't, if you get what I mean?'

And this made sense. It explained the manic waving of the gun.

'Oh.' The word fell out, surprising her. A small bead of optimism began to glow. Had she got him all wrong?

'Look, I'm really sorry, yeah? It was a crazy thing to do.' He looked awkward for the first time ever. The hope began to burn brighter. 'I didn't hurt you, did I? You weren't harmed or anythin', were you?'

She shook her head, remembering the way she'd crumbled to the floor. She looked away. 'No, not by you.'

'And your mum and dad? How's things there?' He sounded interested – something she'd never heard from him before. It was nice. Nice to have a boy like Deano show concern. It was difficult not to feel flattered.

'Still arguing.'

He scratched his chin and left a few seconds for her to stare at his face. 'Feel like coming to the mill today? Have a laugh? Get back at your parents? Tam made a fire last night like it's Bonfire Night. Fuckin' massive, it is.'

He tilted his head hopefully and it almost made her laugh. He *wanted* her to come. Someone like Deano wanted her to spend some time with him, even though she'd cried like a baby when he last saw her. Even though she didn't let him get very far in her bra; even though he knew her age; even though he'd called her a prick-tease. He didn't think she was a kid; he still liked her. Someone like Deano still liked her!

'Not sure.'

He took a step closer so she could smell his smell of bonfires and cigarette smoke. So his face was close to hers. 'C'mon, T. We need someone fit like you. It's no fun watching twats like them all day long.' He jerked his head towards his mates behind him. He rolled his eyes and it made her giggle. 'You add something. It's good to have you around. I need a distraction.' He looked her over quickly so the fine hairs on her skin stood quickly to attention; so that she had to swallow quietly. 'C'mon, Tess. You're good to have around. There's something about you. Something good.' He pulled the tattoo fingers through his fringe and lifted a lopsided smile. 'You can tell us all about that posh school you go to with all them rich kids.'

She frowned. 'It's just a normal comprehensive.'

He laughed and stepped gently on her toe. 'But it's full of kids from the right side of town, Tess. And you're not like them, are you? You're funny and fit and clever. C'mon, Tess.

Give a bloke a break.'

The temptation was there all over again. To sit next to someone like Deano. Someone good-looking and powerful who sucked up admiration from his mates. Who'd singled her out and made her feel special; she wasn't special to anyone else, even her brother was distracted these days.

Quietly, in that soft tone again: 'I'll not touch ya. And I won't let them either.' Another jerk of the head.

Sighing and feeling a weak sunshine smile break on her lips. 'No vodka, though.'

He grinned. 'No vodka.'

Like it was the easiest thing in the world. Just a small dip of her head. 'OK.'

Issy

Issy is allowed back to school on the Wednesday. Her mum says the bruises and swellings have died down and as long as she keeps her sweatshirt on and doesn't roll up her sleeves, then she is all right to go.

Issy's relieved. She likes school and gets on OK there. She keeps her head down and doesn't say much to anyone, but she likes the smell of the art room; she likes the feel of her new trainers when she slides in her feet for netball; and she likes her form tutor, Mrs Peters, who always asks Issy to take the register back to the office because she knows she'll be quick. And more than anything, she gets to see her friend.

Briony has been her friend since the first day at secondary. They're both quiet, hardworking girls who enjoy sinking their teeth into a complicated maths sum, or smoothing down a new page in their English exercise books to write. Some of the other girls tend to tease Issy and Briony about their hard work. But they've both found that if they ignore the comments and hide their eyes in their hair, the other girls get bored very quickly and move on to other people who might start to cry or blush red – or even, in the case of Bridget Stevens, start to shake and stammer with rage and embarrassment.

Briony's eyes light up when Issy walks through the tutor-room door. She smiles, smears her hair behind her ears and pushes her glasses back up her nose. She wriggles in her seat. 'Where have you been? It's been so boring.'

Issy lowers herself into her chair, careful to move her bag strap away from the bruise on her left upper arm. She sighs. 'Sickness and diarrhoea. Yuck, it was horrid.'

Briony looks at Issy, a sympathetic expression on her face. She has tumbles of curls which fizz everywhere and can never be tamed, and Issy rather likes this. 'You poor thing. Joseph had that at Christmas – his nappies were disgusting. The smell was all over the house.' She wrinkles her nose.

Joseph is Briony's baby brother and the reason why Issy rarely goes to her house. Apparently Briony's mum suffers with postnatal depression and the baby screams and screams, so Briony tends to go to Issy's.

Mrs Peters clears her throat and opens the register. Both girls look up expectantly, waiting to answer their names and start the day.

Issy doesn't have time to think too much about her mum. There's a geography test which she didn't know about for first lesson and then gymnastics before break. Issy's quite good at floorwork but hideous at vaulting. And vaulting is what they do today. She doesn't seem to have the strength in her arms, and her run-ups aren't fast enough. She has to wear a long-sleeved T-shirt to cover the bruises, and her PE teacher sniffs and looks cross when Issy walks in.

'Where's your PE shirt, Issy?'

'In the wash, miss – sorry.'

Miss Stevens is new and young, so she rolls her eyes and sighs but doesn't do anything else. 'Make sure it's clean and dry by Friday, please.' And she fills her cheeks to blow the whistle.

Issy nervously eyes the girls to her side, who nudge each other and giggle behind hands.

There's a bit of bother at the end of the lesson when somebody hides Briony's shoes. The changing rooms smell hot and rubbery and there's bright chatter in the air. Issy and Briony are in the corner by the pipework, where they always go. It's quiet over there and they usually put their school shirts over the pipes so that when they get changed back into them they're warm and comforting, if a bit dusty-smelling. Briony notices about halfway through changing that her shoes are missing. She buttons up her top button and squeezes her eyes tight shut. She does this when she's nervous. And it means that Issy sometimes has to talk to closed eyelids, which can be a bit off-putting.

'Have you seen my shoes?'

Issy looks under the bench, pulls a puzzled look. 'No. Where did you leave them?'

Briony points. 'Just there.'

Issy tucks her shirt into her skirt and sighs. She knows what's happened, they both do. And judging by the quietening changing room, so does everyone else. She can feel darts of inquisitive looks peppering her back; she can hear stifled laughter. She ducks her head like Briony and sits down on the bench to do her own shoes. Briony, she notices, has gone bright red.

'Sit down,' she hisses. 'We'll find them when the bell goes.'

Briony wobbles on to the bench and pretends to find something very important in her PE bag.

Squirts of deodorant, more stifled giggles, and finally the bell goes for break. Neither Issy nor Briony move from their seats. They're both a bit pink and Briony is frowning terribly, fiddling with her curls. They both stare at the floor in front of them and wait for the room to empty. It seems like a long time. It's cold and wet outside, so nobody feels in a rush to leave the warmth of the room. Briony's feet twist in their socks on the floor.

Taylor Padgett and her friend Katy are eventually the last to leave. They look at Briony and laugh. They both wear their ties like fat rats under their collar. They'll be told to tie them properly by third lesson. Taylor looks over her shoulder as she walks out of the changing room.

'No shoes, Briony?'

Briony shakes her head, her cheeks now flame red, her curls even frizzier than usual.

Katy joins her friend's laughter. 'Have you looked everywhere?'

Briony's eyes are squeezed shut, but she nods her head all the same.

'Absolutely everywhere?' Katy and Taylor burst into laughter as they look at each other.

Issy nods for Briony now because she's gone very still, although from where Issy's sitting she can see her fingers trembling.

Then Taylor looks over to the corner, hooting with uncontrolled laughter. 'Perhaps they needed airing. Maybe they smell a bit. Maybe someone was doing you a favour.'

Briony grimaces. Issy follows Taylor's look, hating her stupid, laughing face. In the top corner of the room, above coat racks and lockers, is an air vent. And there, wedged in the small rectangle in the wall, are Briony's school shoes.

They can hear Taylor's laughter echo up the corridor.

It doesn't take them long. Maybe two or three minutes. And it's only break they're missing. They have to climb on the bench and then reach with a tennis racquet to unbalance, then catch each shoe. There's a technique involved, because if they push too far the shoe gets shoved further into the air vent. But Issy does the first one and Briony the second.

They manage the procedure in less than four minutes. And it wouldn't have been a problem. Except that as Briony's standing on the bench – tennis racquet in hand, one shoe on, the other in her other hand – Miss Stevens walks in with her keys jingling, ready to lock up.

She scowls at them. Issy knows they look guilty standing on the bench, still flushed and a bit wobbly.

'What on earth are you doing?' Miss Stevens shouts so that some of the corridor outside can hear.

Issy swallows and Briony closes her eyes. The tennis racquet slides from Briony's hand and clatters on to the floor, making an even louder noise.

*

They get an orange slip each. Issy's first ever. The slips are put in Mrs Peters' pigeonhole over lunch and she flaps them around at afternoon registration. Her eyebrows meet in the middle. Her mouth pinches tight.

'What are these?' she says, straight after taking the register.

In the corner of her eye Issy sees Briony's chin hit her chest and a bright red blush spill on to her cheeks. It looks like her glasses are misting up. Issy feels weak. There are titters of laughter behind her. She can imagine the sparks of amusement glittering the classroom.

'Girls?'

'Sorry, miss.'

'I should think so too. I don't expect this kind of thing from you two.'

There's a humming behind Issy's ears. She'd like to jam the heels of her hands against them. Instead she grits her teeth.

'What exactly happened?' Mrs Peters has now walked in front of her desk and towers over the girls. Standing like this she has a bit of a stoop. She reaches for her glasses and perches them on the end of her nose. She reads aloud. '"Dancing with a tennis racquet on the benches in the changing rooms, during break."'

Issy can feel the class inhale in anticipation. It doesn't feel like there's any air left in the classroom. Everything is silent. Then someone giggles.

She can feel Briony collecting words and thoughts together, and this worries Issy. She's not sure what Briony will say. So quickly, interrupting the clearing of Briony's throat, she blurts, 'We were messing around in the changing rooms, miss. We didn't want to go outside.'

Briony flicks a glance at Issy.

'We have wet rooms at break for bad weather. You know that.' Mrs Peters flaps the orange slips again. Issy can feel the ripple of air on her nose. 'I am very disappointed.'

Issy senses a bubble of something horrid rising up her throat. She sees Mrs Peters look at her closely, her head to one side. Thankfully the bell goes for fifth lesson. Issy itches to escape.

Mrs Peters addresses the room. 'OK, class, off you go.' But then she presses her fingers gently on Issy's shoulder, just above the worst bruise – though Mrs Peters doesn't know it – and speaks softly. 'Issy, can you stay here for a minute, please?'

Confused, Issy wonders if she'll be asked to take back the register. But the register is pushed aside on Mrs Peters' desk. The teacher stands in front of Issy, her face grimacing at the noise as chairs get dragged out, then pushed back under desks.

Briony pulls an apologetic face and dashes after the rest of the class.

There's a hum of silence. Mrs Peters drums her fingers on Issy's desk. Issy watches them. She has a wedding ring and an engagement ring which has lots of diamonds. They glitter.

'Are you all right, Issy?'

Issy nods to the hands.

'Only you look a bit pale. A bit thin.'

'Sickness and diarrhoea, miss.'

Mrs Peters nods. There's some shouting in the corridor by a very angry male teacher. 'Yes, but I was thinking . . . you haven't looked very well for a while now.'

Issy's back teeth ache with awkwardness. Her ears buzz again.

She knows.

She knows.

She knows about Dave.

About Mum.

There's a horrible lick of shame which bleeds up her back. It's hard to swallow. There aren't any words yet.

'Is everything all right at home? Only, I didn't see your mum at parents' evening last week. She normally comes, doesn't she?'

Issy *thinks* she nods.

Her mum couldn't come to the parents' evening. She'd intended to. She'd filled in the slip and made all the appointments, but at the last minute Dave told her she was being neurotic. That only over-fussy Polish parents go to parents' evenings. That it was up to the school to tell the parents if there was a problem. And besides, he needed her to go to Aldi with him because there was no food in the house. Issy's mum argued and said they could do the shopping on the way home. So Dave punched her in the eye three times, which then made parents' evening impossible.

'Issy?'

Issy has to look up then; Mrs Peters' voice signals that she must. She has nice eyes. Lots of mascara. Issy imagines the colour of the bruises on her arm and thinks that they might be the same shade as Mrs Peters' eye shadow. She thinks of Dave's bulging eyes. Of the purple colour in his cheeks when he's angry.

Issy swallows. She knows her teacher won't be happy until she says something. She won't be able to leave until she does.

She takes a breath. Feels the tremble in her throat. 'Yes, miss. Everything's all right at home. Mum got the bug too.'

There's a knock on the door and an impatient-looking supply teacher raises his eyebrows. 'We OK to come in yet?' He nods towards the queue of noisy kids behind him.

Mrs Peters looks doubtfully at Issy and leans back against the desk. 'Yes, OK.'

Issy gets up quickly. Relief washes over her like a wave.

Mrs Peters stops her, though. 'Oh, Issy.'

'Yes?'

'Can you take this as you go, please?'

She hands Issy the register. Issy hugs it to her chest.

On the way home from school, she hears a shout.

'Issy!'

Her head swivels round. It's Tye's brother, Emiel, back from university. He's holding a packet of two pork pies in one hand and a half-eaten one in the other. His skin is exactly the same conker shade as his brother's. He wanders up to Issy and stops.

'You OK? Just got back from school?' He nods towards Sophie's scarred house, not waiting for an answer. 'What do you reckon, then? Sophie thinks they'll be finished in a fortnight. Do *you* think so?'

He takes another bite of his pork pie and looks back at Issy. His eyebrows are high with questions. Issy swallows, not sure which question to answer. She's always been a bit in awe of Tye's brother. He's very good-looking. And old.

'Um . . .' Her fingers etch at the damp wood of the gate post.

Emiel grins again, shoves the packet of pork pies near her face. 'Want one?'

She realizes she's starving. She's eaten nothing apart from half a sandwich all day. Nobody suggested breakfast this morning. And nobody said anything about lunch – neither dinner money *nor* sandwiches. Issy didn't like to ask. She was grateful that she was able to leave the house. Briony felt sorry for her at lunchtime and shared her sandwiches, but now she's famished.

She looks doubtfully at the pork pie, though. She's not sure how to eat it. There are crumbs all over Emiel's chest and flecks of pastry at the side of his mouth. She can't imagine eating one in front of anyone, especially Tye's brother.

She shakes her head. 'No, thanks. I don't like the pastry. Anyway, Mum says she's cooking my favourite tonight.' Her heart leaps at the lie. 'How's Tye?'

Emiel wipes his mouth with his hand and looks over to the house again. 'Still the same. Mum and Dad are worried to death. That's why I'm home – to do my share of visiting.' He shrugs. 'He's strong, though, is Tye. I'll bet you any money he'll come round smiling and ask for Mum's shepherd's pie within seconds.'

'Really?'

'Reckon so.' He screws the pork pie wrapping into a tight

ball and shoves it into his pocket, gazing at the tyre track marks on the lawn. 'That driver did some serious shit damage. They reckon he was speeding like a maniac.'

Despite what's going on and the horror that they're looking at, Issy feels thrilled that he chose to swear in front of her. She nods enthusiastically.

Emiel swallows the last of the pork pie. 'It's weird, though. Whenever anybody asks Sophie about the crash she makes excuses for him. Saying stuff like, it was wet on the road and everyone skids round that corner.' He shakes his head. 'Soft as shite, our Sophie.' He shoves his hands hard into his pockets. 'Well, best get in. See you around, Shorty.'

Issy nods again, feeling eleven years old once more.

She takes a breath. One last grip of the gate post. She makes a step forward.

It's hunger that gets her to the back door.

But it's only when she has her hand on the door handle that she thinks of something: something Emiel said which wasn't quite right. It nags at her as she steps into the kitchen.

'Tell us about your mates, then. Which one's the richest?'

This was a regular occurrence in the mill. Deano's daily question. He seemed obsessed with her friends as he picked away at the dirt in his nails with a rat-sized army knife.

She dug her hand into a giant bag of crisps. 'Cassie Peterson is pretty loaded. She has a car even though she's too young to drive, and an underground swimming pool which is divine.'

'Divine.' Someone imitated her over the top of the fire in a high-pitched voice. It was Bulldog, her least favourite of the group. He looked like a dark rodent and had a mouth in a permanent smirk. Gemma was glad when Deano chucked a stone at his head.

'Where does she live?'

'Queens Road way. Why?'

'Just wondered. She nice?'

She nodded and licked the crisp flavour from the tips of her fingers. 'Yeah, she's cool. She never rubs it in or anything.'

Deano sniffed, and wandered around the room. From where she was sitting he looked like a tiger. 'Any rich kids you don't like, Tess?'

She shook the dregs of the crisps into a corner of the packet, ready to tip upside down. Not really thinking now. No need. 'Yeah, Stephanie Hughes.'

She had Deano's attention again. He'd stopped prowling, his ears pricked up like a greyhound. 'Why?'

'Because she's a bitch. Because she thinks that just because she has money, she can buy her friends. Every year, at Christmas, she gets her friends a pair of designer jeans each.' She tipped back her neck and poured the crisp crumbs into her mouth. 'All her mates start creeping round her in November.'

'You're not one of them?'

'No. I'm not rich enough any more. Since Dad's business started losing money I can't mix in her circles. I don't shop in the right shops any more. One time she bought me a Burberry bag for my birthday, then asked for it back when I didn't use it for school.'

'Bitch!'

'Yeah. Nobody likes her really. She should go to a private school, only her dad doesn't approve of them.'

'Smug cow.'

She thought about it as she folded the crisp packet in half, then half again, then again. She skimmed it into the flames and it burst into a bright orange light. 'Yeah, smug cow.'

A careful silence which seemed to tick around her.

And then, in a low voice, Deano spoke as he prowled towards her to put a hand on her neck. She felt a buzz from his skin on to hers. It was always like this when he touched her now. 'Maybe she needs to learn a lesson.'

It's rained for the last four days. That's how it seems to Sophie. There's mud everywhere. Filthy walking boots in the hotel foyer. Guests padding around in steaming socks as they walk to the lift. Dirty water along the pavements. Every time a car drives past, when she's walking to school or to the hospital, she runs the risk of a drenching.

Grim February.

But she walks with a spring today. Tucks her hair under her hood as yet more rain threatens from the clouds. Skirts a deep puddle with swirls of purple iridescent oil marks, and marches on.

The hospital grounds come into view as the rain starts to spot down. She speeds up. Weaves around parked cars, around other visitors hunched in the sudden rain, around greasy puddles. She knows the shortcuts now.

Tye. Why didn't he tell her he was in love? They always told each other everything.

She wanders through the familiar corridors. She's been here every day now. It's almost more of a home than the hotel. She walks confidently. Knows exactly where to go.

She spends half an hour with Tye, who's still horribly lifeless. She plays him some music and talks about school. And then she leaves him to find Harry. This is what she does now: she pours her heart out to Tye and then seeks refuge with Harry. It's an interesting feeling. She wonders briefly, as she rounds the corner to his ward, if he really likes her coming. If his invitations are only out of guilt. But Sophie's learning a lot about guilt; it's amazing how you can live with it.

A nurse with hair in a cheerful ponytail smiles at Sophie from her desk and waves her through. 'Hi, Sophie, he's in the TV room today.' She nods to the room opposite.

Sophie fills her cheeks with stale antiseptic air and pushes through the door. Harry's sitting with his back to her, watching a daytime soap. There are flickers on the screen of an Australian beach with kids in their school uniform sitting around on rugs: *Home and Away*. It makes her laugh.

She stands behind him. He's not noticed her come in. Blond fronds of hair stick to the back of his neck. They're a bit messy. She likes that. He's in normal clothes today, the first time since the accident. She'd become used to the dressing gown which was much too big for him. Today he's in grey trackie trousers and a navy hoodie. Good quality, by the looks of things, if a little faded. He's got bare feet, though. Strong, pale feet with straight, long toes, some of which are curled around the edge of the table in front of him. She imagines they'll be warm.

Fights the urge to touch. Forces herself to think of Tye, lifeless under the hospital sheet.

He's chewing his nails. She's noticed this before. She watches as he places one finger after the next into his mouth. Between his lips. Between his teeth. Watches the twist of his wrist under his sleeve. Thinks she can see pale hairs glisten under the lights. Sees the flick of his tongue as he moistens his lips.

There's a glow under her ribs at the sight, which she tries to ignore.

She's sure his twin doesn't bite her nails. She would put her life on it. Gemma's nails are manicured to perfection. Pale green, she seems to remember. Sophie's never seen such faultless nails. Even after a car crash.

She could stand like this, staring, for ever. Taking him in. Fighting the guilt. But he'd know in the end. He'd have heard the doors swing open and she'd be found out. She feels awkward at the thought. So she gives in, grins in anticipation and speaks loudly.

'Didn't know you were a fan.'

His head swings round, his finger held up mid-chew. Surprise morphs into a smile which fills his face, giving colour to the greyness of his skin. He stuffs his hand guiltily between his thighs. 'You came, then?'

Sophie moves round to his side, pulling up a chair to sit on. 'I did.' She nods at the TV. 'And I caught you in the middle of your dirty little secret.'

He laughs. 'There's nothing else to do.'

'That's your story and you're sticking to it?'

His eyes are dragonfly-blue. Every day she's surprised how easy it is to talk to him.

'OK, OK, I admit it. I've got all the box sets at home. I'm Alf Stewart's biggest fan and I stalk all the main characters. I enter all the competitions and I've applied to be an extra.' He waves his hands around in exaggeration. A bubble of laughter rolls off Sophie's tongue. It shouldn't.

He smells of soap.

'I don't know whether to believe you or not!'

He widens his eyes. 'You'll never know.'

They stare at the screen together. She puts her feet next to his on the table, crossing her ankles like his. She looks from the screen to their feet. Puts her left foot against his right. 'Your feet are massive.'

Still staring at the screen, but with glitter in his eyes, he says, 'Big feet, warm heart.'

She scrunches up her nose. 'That's cold hands, you idiot!'

He throws his head back and laughs. She's not heard him laugh properly before. It's like music. 'Is that all you've come here for? To abuse me? I get enough of that off my sister, thank you very much.'

Sophie shrugs, sliding her hands between her knees. 'Where is she, by the way?' She doesn't add how strange but nice it is that Gemma's not there.

He shrugs back, still with his eyes on the screen. 'Dunno – work, I expect.'

'What does she do?'

Harry sighs. 'She has this job at the NEC. She loves it. She gets to help with all the bands and the VIPs and the conferences. It's kind of what she wants to do for real when she leaves school. She wants to go abroad after her A-Levels, I guess she's hoping she'll be spotted by some Simon Cowell type and get swept off her feet into a megabucks job. She's already missed two shifts after the accident, so I think she was determined to go back today.'

Sophie can imagine Gemma working at the NEC. Her hair all tousled, her eyes lagoon-blue and wide, her green finger-nails, talking to important people. Impressing people who matter.

'She's very . . . strong, isn't she?'

He glances at her, his eyelids lowering. 'If you mean she's bossy, then yeah, she's . . . "strong". But actually she's not strong. She's a mess.'

Sophie's careful. 'She does boss you around a bit, doesn't she?'

Harry peers at his nails, which look short and ragged. He laughs, 'Nothing stops Gemma when she puts her mind to something. It drives Mum crazy. She gets into loads of trouble these days, hanging out with the wrong crowd.' He shrugs, shakes his head. 'And yeah, I guess she's bossy with me.'

'Why do you let her?'

Harry rubs his nose again. 'Long story . . .' he inhales, '. . . but basically it's a habit of a lifetime.' He reaches for the remote and snaps off the screen. 'But enough of my screwed-up, assertive sister.' He grins, looking over to Sophie's bag, which she's left on the floor. 'Please tell me you've brought junk food in with you again. I'm actually starving.'

Sophie smiles back, happy despite everything. 'I happened

to stop at Greggs on the way.' She produces a greasy-looking paper bag which radiates a warm pastry smell as she lifts it.

Harry sticks his nose inside. 'Oh my God, you are the devil in disguise, Sophie Dukes. I adore steak bakes. How did you even know?'

Feeling smug, Sophie smiles. 'Just a hunch.'

Later, when the steak bake is devoured, when Sophie's been to the vending machine to get cans of Coke because the pastry made Harry thirsty, when the pale February sunshine has almost faded away, they're quieter. The room is still empty and they've been lucky enough to be able to banter and laugh without other frowning patients to make them awkward.

Sophie's enjoyed herself, and that's not right, but the feeling is so nice amidst all the agony elsewhere. Cheeks flushed from laughing and a smile twitching on her lips, Sophie could stay there for ever. Harry seems to be happy with her company. His skin has lost its greyness and he looks more relaxed than she's seen him before. She wonders if it's because his sister's not there. She doesn't want to ask, though.

She checks the time. She has an essay to write by Monday, and she's promised her dad she'll attack it tonight. Harry sees her looking, and the smile slides from his face.

'You got to be somewhere?'

Sophie nods. 'Psychology homework. I have the strictest teacher. She's a cow.' She pulls a face. 'And the funny thing is, she's called Miss Jersey.'

Harry laughs. 'We have a teacher called Mr Smallman and he's six foot four.'

There's a small throb of silence between them.

'How's Tye?'

Sophie feels a curtain fall behind her eyes. 'The same.' Her voice wobbles. 'I just want him to wake up. I *need* him to wake up.'

'He's in the best place. This place is really good.' Harry's eyes burn on to her face.

'I know, only I feel so bad. Here I am laughing with you and there he is all unconscious and still and unmoving. It's horrible, and besides everything else, I feel guilty.'

A silence rolls through the room like a fireball.

Harry's fingers twitch. 'Because of me?'

'Not just you, but . . .'

'. . . it doesn't help that I'm responsible for him being unconscious?'

Her voice is small. 'Maybe.'

She watches him close his eyes.

Sophie begins to get her bits together. She stuffs the paper bag into a bin in the corner, jams her phone back into her pocket and pulls on the sleeves of her jacket. She can feel him watching her; the thickness in the room is horrid.

Another tick of silence, then Harry clears his throat. He weaves his fingers together. He looks anxious.

'I wanted to say something.'

She looks up from her zip. 'What?'

He gazes towards the blank screen. Sophie sees his Adam's apple move up and down in his throat. She sits down again, suddenly nervous. 'What?' she repeats.

His words shake a bit. 'I wanted to say sorry. For the

accident. All the hassle we caused. You having to live in a hotel. Having your best friend in a coma. Not being able to get all your things. It must be horrible. And it's all our fault.' He frowns. 'That fucking stupid car . . . I don't know what happened. I really don't. I've forgotten everything.' He sighs and his words come out too quickly. 'I told the police that I don't remember, but they don't seem very satisfied. They said we were witnessed driving down your road at a dangerous speed and they want to know why.' He glances quickly at Sophie; his eyes seem to have become paler along with his skin. 'I'm sorry, Sophie. Really sorry. I think the car went out of control. But I can't be sure. I'll say sorry to your dad too, and Tye's parents obviously, if they ever allow me to see them.' He drops his shoulders. 'I can't believe I've actually wrecked a building. Your house. And caused another human to be in a coma.'

Sophie thinks swiftly about Tye's dad. How angry he was. His assumption that the driver had been drinking, or that he'd done it on purpose. She knows that her dad thinks the same.

But looking at Harry now, his cheeks packed full of regret and his mouth so sad, she's sure this can't be the case. Harry's not that kind of person. She can tell.

'Tye's going to wake up, I know it.'

He closes his eyes. Looks suddenly knackered. 'I don't remember very much. Just coming round the corner of your road. We were lost. Then being trapped, and you and Tye getting us out. Then it all goes a bit blank. And a smaller kid scurrying around in all that dust.'

Sophie nods. 'Issy . . . my next-door neighbour. She was brilliant.'

He opens his eyes again. More dragonfly-blue. 'You saved my life. And I trashed your house and nearly killed your best friend. That doesn't seem very fair, does it?'

Sophie smiles over the familiar guilt. She can't stand the downward spiral the conversation's taking. 'You can make it up to me. A shitload of chocolate might do the trick.' She stands up, determined to break the mood. It was nice before, despite everything. 'Now stop being all depressing and start to get better. Because I mean it about the chocolate. You need to earn some serious money to supply me with the amount that I demand.'

He smiles weakly. 'OK.' He reaches for his crutches to stand up with her. She helps him with them, breathing in his warmth as their arms collide.

'Shall I come again tomorrow?' She can feel her heart rumble slightly beneath her ribs.

He smiles properly now, leaning on his crutches. 'If your Mrs Jersey Cow allows the time.'

But then she remembers something. 'I've got to see the police tomorrow, though. So it'll be later.'

Harry's eyes narrow. He shuffles forward. There are deep lines in his forehead. 'You've got to see the police too?'

'Yeah. I'm a witness, apparently.'

Harry grimaces. 'But you didn't see anything till we were in the house.'

'I know. But I'm still needed.'

He slumps back in his chair. He smears his palm across

his eyes.

'Hey,' she says, taking a step back into the room. 'I won't be long. I've got nothing to say. I'll come straight over as soon as I'm done.'

She watches as he nods slowly. His eyes are far away now. 'Yeah, OK. See you then.'

He doesn't seem to be listening when she says that the police station is right next to a Subway, where she can pick up a chicken and bacon ranch melt for him.

There's a fizzing sensation in her stomach as she walks through the corridors, out of the hospital and towards the hotel.

'Where's this Stephanie Hughes live, then?'

They were walking home after a day in the mill. It was one of the other boys – Adam, this time. After Deano, Adam was her favourite. Tall, like her, with jet-black hair and arms that were the longest she'd ever seen. She knew he liked her too, only Deano would never let anything happen.

'Down the Marshlands.'

He whistled through his teeth. 'Swanky!'

She frowned. They all seemed obsessed. 'Yeah – as I said, she's the richest girl in school and she makes sure everyone knows it.'

Adam turned his head, glanced quickly for a nod from Deano. 'What number does she live at?'

She shrugged her shoulders and looked back at Deano; he'd kept to his word. He'd not touched her, other than a couple of carefully planted hands, for three weeks now. She was starting to trust him. Starting to rely on the effect he had on all of them.

'Dunno.'

Adam tilted his head, kicked at a stone. 'But you could take us there?'

She slowed right down then. Stopped on the pavement so that Deano had to join her. Felt the now-familiar mixture of fear and comfort when he got close enough. She watched as a look she couldn't read passed from Deano to Adam.

Adam coughed. 'She was just sayin' about this Stephanie kid. How she's still a bitch. How she lives on the Marshlands.'

She felt Deano's thumb press on her forearm. It made her swallow. 'And do ya reckon she deserves some payback?'

She thought about last week, when she'd been in school and found one of Stephanie's group in the toilet. Red circles round her eyes from crying. How she'd not even asked, because she'd seen it all before. How this was the ceremonial dumping which happened most months. How one of Stephanie's group of 'populars' would say something which Stephanie didn't like. How suddenly, without any warning she'd be picked on and ignored and then replaced so viciously that the girl in question wouldn't have chance to register her isolation until she found herself entirely alone. How this happened again and again and again. There was never a shortage of girls on the waiting list. It was ridiculous. It was sick. It was wrong.

She'd been there herself. She knew what it was like to be on the wrong side of Stephanie.

Swallowing again, she found herself breathing the words. 'Yes, maybe she does.'

*

So, a few days later, when it came to an invitation to join them, she thought she'd have a go. After all, Stephanie Hughes deserved everything coming to her.

'You don't have to, T. We won't mind . . . only this bitch is *your* bitch. Your chance to get back at her.'

She nodded and even gave a smile. It was worth the small sweat which broke out down her spine as he squeezed her arm with his finger and thumb. This was a good answer. This made him proud. And there was something about Deano which made her want him proud.

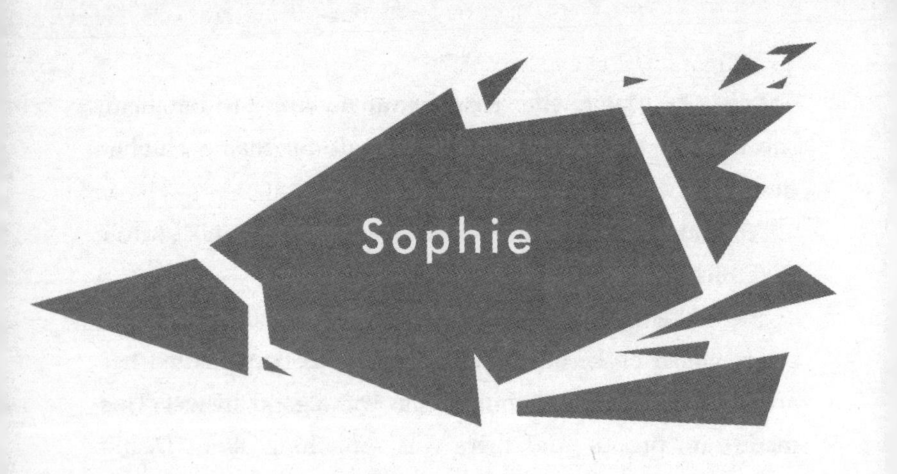

She's standing outside the police station with a scowl on her face. 'That was horrible. I didn't expect to be interrogated.' The interview had been cancelled three times and she'd been hoping that they'd forgotten about it.

Her dad's inside the car, looking through the window, his face a haze of lines as he screws up his eyes. 'What did they ask?'

'About everything. About what I was doing when it happened. What Tye was doing. How we got them out; who was driving; what speed we thought they were doing; who was in the back; what happened to him; who saved who.' She shakes herself. 'It was awful. And to be honest it's all a bit hazy now anyway.'

Her dad nods and inserts the key into the ignition. 'I thought it might be, but in a way that's good. They need to be thorough if they're to get to the bottom of things. Poor Tye's lying there as a result of this. He deserves a proper investigation, don't you think?'

Sophie thinks of her friend, how his pale brown colour against the pillows isn't his real colour any more, there's no shine. She dips a nod at her dad and then thinks about Harry. Flashes of guilt and panic spike through her. 'Well, at least it's over.'

Her dad nods back. 'You sure you don't want a lift?'

She shakes her head. 'No, I'm going to see a friend.'

Her dad nods an OK and starts to fiddle with the radio. 'See you at six.'

Sophie starts walking. She pulls out her phone and starts to key in a postcode. The cold air blasts against her hair. She's not exactly lied to her dad, just omitted to relay all the information. The postcode is Harry's. He was discharged from hospital the day before and he's promised to show her a film they'd been talking about.

She walks to the corner and starts to head off left, then left again, then right. She bats away the flashes of guilt. Out of the hospital this suddenly feels more real, more of a statement, more of a betrayal of Tye. It's difficult to ignore the shame.

She recognizes a smarter side of town, where the posher bars and restaurants begin. She feels a fizz of anxiety. She knew where she was in the hospital.

She crosses the road, skirting two taxis with drivers shouting at each other, then she follows the instructions towards a road lined with trees. She swallows. The cars parked here are impressively large. She looks down at her skinny jeans with rips in the knee and her battered trainers which have seen better days. She slows down, a wary feeling passing over her.

She has a tatty bit of paper with the address on in her left hand. Sophie peers at big houses with fancy names and numbers, then comes to a stop in front of number 28. It has big bay windows, a stone driveway which she crunches over and a front door which you could fit a small car through.

Why were they driving down Sycamore Street? It's nowhere near here.

She slides her phone into her pocket, she fiddles with her hair, trying to tidy it in the March breeze. It doesn't work. The nerves are now ramming up her insides.

Quickly, so that she doesn't chicken out, she puts her finger on the doorbell.

There's about a minute's worth of tension while nothing happens from behind the door. She feels her legs begin to wilt. But then, at last, some movement. A shadow. Some blue. A shimmering figure. It's the girl – Gemma. She opens the door. Lots of blonde hair. Heavily-made-up eyes. They drink in Sophie.

'Hi.' Gemma flicks her hair off her shoulders, winds it round her fingers to let it drape down her left side.

'Hi.'

'Well, this is a surprise.' Gemma has bare feet. Her toes curl round the front step. Her toenails are aubergine.

'Harry said to come.' Sophie waves the paper with the address on it.

'He's not here.' She laughs like shattering glass. It's an unpleasant laugh and it makes Sophie's head fall to her chest. For a second she steps back so that she wobbles on the step behind her. She has to force herself to remember Harry. How he's not like his sister.

'I could wait . . .?'

Gemma pushes her lips together. 'He's only just gone out. But come in anyhow. It's freezing out here.'

She's ushered in through the front door. Warmth and a rich cooking smell hits her hard. The hallway is massive. Stairs in the centre with a sofa at the bottom. Who has sofas in their hall?

Gemma pads along a lush carpet towards the kitchen, gesturing with a hand for Sophie to follow. She trails after her. Gemma's hips sway in black skinnies. It's hard not to look.

The kitchen is space-age. Stainless-steel counters, giant-sized fridges and an island made from marble. There's evidence of food preparation on the island. A sharp purple-handled knife with peppers and cucumber chopped into slivers. A tall glass of something fizzing and popping. Ice and lemon. Gemma leans against a fridge. It towers over her.

'Want a drink?'

Sophie nods. She can't stop staring at everything. It's like a magazine.

Gemma pulls out two bottles of brightly coloured liquid. Nothing like the pop or squash in the fridge at home. 'Fruit juice?' She holds up each bottle. 'Pomegranate and lime, or clementine and juniper?'

Sophie shrugs. 'Clementine, please.' After a torturous minute, 'So where is he?'

Gemma tiptoes up to a high shelf, pulling down two tall glasses. Her legs look like a ballerina's. She laughs the shattering-glass laugh again. It really grates on Sophie. 'Don't know. He didn't say where.' She smiles unpleasantly over her shoulder. 'Have you been stood up by my brother?'

Sophie feels confused. Like a seven-year-old. 'He said to come . . .' Her words trail off uncomfortably.

Gemma rolls her eyes. 'He's a bit crap like that. Don't go relying on Harry. Probably got a better offer.'

Sophie grits her teeth. Gemma's enjoying this. Enjoying seeing someone squirm. It's not nice. A bit cruel. Sophie feels a pop of anger. 'Is everyone in your family so bloody rude?'

There's a flicker of surprise in Gemma's lagoon-blue eyes. She hands her the glass.

Sophie's glass knocks against her teeth. 'I don't get it—'

Gemma sighs. Interrupts. 'Don't worry, I'm sure you'll get an apologetic text.'

She moves towards the island and picks up the knife, begins to slice the flesh of a pepper. The swish of the knife is the first soft sound in the kitchen. It gives Sophie the opportunity to look around.

There are unusual pictures on the wall, framed in Perspex. Some of them massive. Patterns and sketches in bright dazzling colours which transfix and hold the eye. She takes a step closer towards one of them. 'These are brilliant.'

Gemma nods, her knife poised mid-chop. 'Aren't they? They're Harry's, actually. He's good, isn't he?'

Sophie's eyes widen. 'Harry did these?'

'Yes. He's into art in a big way. He's doing it at A-Level. Wants to do it at uni. Only Dad reckons it's not a good degree. He wants Harry to do something boring like accountancy or medicine. They argue all the time over it. My dad's basically the Hitler of this century, but I'm not sure he's going to win this time. Harry's pretty determined.'

Sophie's eyebrows feel high under her fringe.

Gemma continues, slicing and chopping in time to her words. She has fascinating long pale fingers like her brother's. She points her knife at the three paintings opposite. 'Those were all done when Dad left. Our parents split last year. He lives on the other side of town now, with a woman only just older than us. Makes me feel sick, to be honest. He's got no idea she's after his money. But I think it's so bloody obvious.' She stops chopping for a minute and Sophie sees how white her knuckles have become. 'Harry spent weeks in his room creating all this art. Everyone was worried about him. He went all dark and brooding. Typical Harry – to go all arty and anxious.' She slides the blade into the cucumber. 'But I guess he was doing his own form of therapy.'

Sophie's voice is steady. 'What was your therapy?'

She grins and lowers her lashes. 'I found myself what my mum would call a "bad crowd". Lots of unsuitable boys.

'Actually,' Gemma's chin is high, 'thinking about it, that's probably where he is now – Harry, I mean. He's probably with his old art teacher.'

'But it's half-term.'

Gemma shrugs. 'That doesn't seem to matter with Harry. His teacher had this special relationship with him. They talk and stuff, even now that they're not at the same school any more. It's a bit . . .' she searches the walls for the right word, '. . . unusual.'

Sophie lays down her glass noisily. She hasn't finished her

drink. 'I think I'm going to go.' She hears a wobble in her own throat, it makes her angry.

'Yeah?' Gemma's eyes are cold. She's a mixture of cruelty and something else which Sophie can't put her finger on.

'Yes.' Sophie's sleeves are pulled over her hands.

'You're welcome to stay.' There's crazy laughter behind the words.

Sophie shakes her head, more anger in the pit of her stomach.

Bitch.

'No. I'll go.'

'Suit yourself,' says Gemma.

Sophie feels Gemma's eyes burrow deep between her shoulder blades as she follows her into the hall. Gemma leans against the kitchen doorway, her head at an angle. 'How's the house?'

Sophie stands with her hand poised, ready to turn the front-door handle. Her neck is upright and stiff. She doesn't turn round. 'Still standing.'

'And Tye, your friend?'

'Still alive, no thanks to you and your brother.'

She feels a secret thrill at this small amount of courage. She turns to see Gemma's eyes darken slightly. She looks awkward now. Brittle, like if she was pushed she'd shatter.

'Yeah, sorry about that.' She plays with the ends of her hair.

Sophie makes a strange noise with her throat and fumbles furiously with the door catch. It seems to take ages to work out.

She bursts out of the doorway and immediately her hair

whips skyways in a gust of wind. She knows her face is bright red as she fiddles with the buttons on her jacket. 'Bitch,' she says to the wind, to the posh driveway, to nobody, to the brother who wasn't there.

She stomps on the gravel, sending small stones skittering.

Bastard, bastard, bastard. 'Special relationship' with his art teacher. She stamps her feet as she heads back to the hotel. *Bet she's drop-dead gorgeous too.*

Sophie

There's not much she'll miss about this place. The bed wasn't bad and having a toilet to herself was brilliant. But everything else she's really pleased to leave behind. She zips up her bag with a snap.

There's a soft knock at her door. It's Sam. 'Got any deodorant?'

She rolls her eyes at him. 'Not that won't make you smell like a girl.'

Sam sniffs. 'The least girlie-smelling one, then.'

Sophie widens the door and Sam trudges in, yawning. She goes to the bathroom and sifts through her toilet bag, draws out two aerosols. Holds them up. 'Glimmer or Crystal. The choice is yours.'

Sam snorts. 'Not bothered. Just chuck us one.'

She does and he catches it quickly, shoves his hand under his T-shirt and squirts. He looks around him, surprised. 'You're ready. You've packed.'

Another roll of the eyes. 'No shit, Sherlock. Why? Haven't you?'

He pulls his mouth down. 'Naah – what's the rush? I kind of like this place.'

She looks at her bulging, fully packed bag and at the half-packed toiletries. 'I want to get back to normality. You know, seeing my mates at home and cooking and stuff.'

Sam draws the back of his hand across his face in a yawn, already bored. 'Will you still see your "bezzie mate" Tye?' He says this in a horrible squeaky voice with a screwed-up face and fingers which click quotation marks in the air. It always winds Sophie up. She knows there's not much love lost between Tye and Sam, though she's not sure why. She steps towards the door, wanting Sam and his wind-ups to leave. ''Course I will, he's my best friend,' she snarls. 'At least I've got one. The closest thing *you've* got to a friend is the Xbox controller.'

Sam takes wide, bored strides towards the door. He grins, whacking Sophie's shoulder with the palm of his hand. It doesn't hurt, but it's annoying. 'You ever wondered why he was always around? Why he was always hanging round like a bad smell? Why he's not got friends of his own . . . sex?'

Sophie frowns. She hates it when Sam gets cryptic. 'What's that supposed to mean?'

He sniggers and shakes his head. 'Think about it.' He laughs again and walks out of the door.

Sophie sticks her head round the doorframe, not caring who else in the hotel can hear. 'And *you* can talk about bad smells . . . Don't forget to open your window before you leave, else the cleaner might actually pass out.'

She slams the door. God, she hates her brother sometimes. Only *he* can ruin what is supposed to be the best day of the last few weeks.

It doesn't feel the same and it doesn't look the same. But it's home and she's grateful. They each step out of the car, all a bit wary, all a bit hesitant. Sophie's dad opens the boot and sighs at the bags and cases they've collected over the last few weeks. He exhales. Sophie and Sam stand and stare at their house.

The front door is new. So's the front window. The bricks have been patched up around the window frame; they look out of place in the rest of the wall. The fence panel is golden and fresh-looking. The lawn is divided into three ugly curves by deep tyre marks and the front step has a new, pinker-looking slab.

Sam whistles. Their dad shakes his head. 'A good rain shower and everything'll blend in,' he says, too brightly.

Sophie glances at Sam. She hopes he won't contradict him.

Their dad drags a case out of the boot with difficulty. 'Is anyone going to help me here, or what?' His limp, which he's had since his teenage years, seems more pronounced today.

Holding her own purple suitcase, Sophie has a quick look either side of her house. She can feel the twitch of curtains behind her; Mrs P is sure to have her nose pressed against the glass. She looks over to Tye's house – it's blank and empty. And on the other side, where Issy lives, it looks similarly quiet. Kind of dead. For a moment she thinks she sees a tiny movement in the corner of the upstairs window, almost a flicker, but then nothing else. She's surprised: it's the weekend, and surely someone would be around to welcome their return.

Inside, the kitchen isn't that different apart from a layer of filthy dust, but the lounge is completely transformed. Almost all the furniture has gone. The sofa, the coffee table, the TV, the lamp, the shelving unit, the curtains – all gone. Instead it's a shell of a room with fresh plaster on the walls and a smell of dust and damp. Sophie shudders.

'You OK?' Her dad places a hand on Sophie's shoulders.

Sophie gulps, blinking back the flashes of memory from when she was last in this room. 'Yeah – think so. It smells horrible, though.'

Sophie's dad nods. 'That's the wet plaster. It'll look fine once we've got some furniture and put some curtains up.'

Sophie looks around her. At the space. At the bare floor. Strange and terrible to think a car forced its way through the wall. She touches the windowsill. Tests it with her fingers. Wonders if she'll ever be able to trust bricks and mortar again.

'I take it we're having takeaway tonight?' Trust Sam. Even in the tensest of times, he thinks of his stomach.

Her dad smiles. 'I guess so. It's going to take a couple of days to get the kitchen straight.'

Sam grins. Cheerful strides up the stairs. 'Chinese for me.' His words echo up the stairwell.

In her room Sophie sinks on to her bed. It's beautiful, like a fragrant dressing gown, this space which has been hers for years. Nothing much has changed in this room; it's pretty much unaffected. She opens her wardrobe doors, inhaling the scent from her clothes, sifting her fingers through their textures. She makes a starfish on her bed, pulls a finger down the spines of the books on her bedside table, sticks her head under the curtains taking in the familiar view, drags a hand along the radiator enjoying the recognizable vibration. It's lovely. Like treating herself to favourite chocolates. Her room.

She lies back on her bed again and reaches for her phone. A familiar pose: head sunk low in the animal print cushions, feet on the windowsill. The screen is empty.

A slight disappointment.

She hears the sound of muffled grunge coming from Sam's room. Smiles to herself. Her brother's happy.

Checks her phone again. Just in case.

There's been a text from Harry every day since he stood her up. The first, a long rambling apology; some excuse about his art teacher needing him. She'd not texted back. Then the next day another. Less wordy, more blunt and to the point.

Sorry. Really want to see you.

She still didn't reply. She'd been warned, hadn't she? Gemma said he'd text with a rubbish excuse. And he had. She was sick of being treated like that. That evening, as she'd watched *Hollyoaks* and eaten chocolate, she vowed that no boy was going to treat her like that. And so far she'd stuck to her promise.

Besides, it meant she could concentrate on Tye.

She'd not sent one text back. Despite – ten days on – a text every day. Mostly asking to see her. Sometimes apologizing again. Enough was enough. Only today's the first day he hasn't sent one. She supposes he's given up. She shrugs. Didn't take long.

She ignores the bubble of disappointment.

Their first meal back in their kitchen is weird. They're all quiet. None of the usual celebratory jokes over a Chinese. Sam not hogging the prawn crackers. Dad not moaning that they've ordered too much. Instead, muted chat, like they're still in the hotel.

Sophie's dad passes her the special fried rice, his face a bit fake. 'Your favourite.'

Sophie spoons the rice. There's a whiff of wet plaster still in the air, even with the door tightly shut. Her dad keeps glancing over to the lounge. His mouth is a cat's bum of crossness. Sophie pretends not to notice, but there's still a horrid glow in her stomach.

In the end he can't help himself. He shakes his head and snaps the lid back on his curry. 'That boy should be shot.' He glowers at the door leading to the lounge. 'Messing up our lives like this. Nearly killing Tye.'

Sophie widens her eyes. 'That's a bit harsh.'

'OK, then, he should be locked up and they should throw away the key.'

Sophie sighs. 'Maybe it was an accident. Maybe his drink was spiked. Maybe he just got it wrong. Some drinks are stronger than you realize. Perhaps he got the maths all wrong.'

'Just one drink's more than enough. It should be illegal, full stop. All this units business. It's a load of rubbish. The boy needs to take responsibility for taking so much as one sip.' Her dad has ugly purple patches on his cheeks. Sophie groans inwardly and stares at the bean sprouts left on her plate.

Shut up, shut up, shut up!

Sam looks up from where he's shovelling prawn crackers into his mouth, making white powder marks over his lips. Sophie can hear the fizz as they dissolve on his tongue. 'How come you always stick up for him? He nearly killed you, and your best friend's in a coma thanks to him.' A haze of prawn crackers surrounds each word.

Sophie's dad shudders, scowls up his forehead. 'Leave it, Sam. Can we stop talking about it?' He stirs the rice, offering it to Sam. 'Tye's going to wake up and then we'll all be back to normal, once the decorators have been.'

If it was up to Sam, Sophie's sure he'd do a full evaluation of the whole incident. But Sophie's not ready for that; it's difficult enough having to walk through the room to get to the kitchen and the rest of the house. She doesn't want to talk about it any more. Now Harry's out of her life she could do with moving on and concentrating on Tye.

Later, when everything's been eaten and the dregs have been scraped into the bin, Sophie wanders back upstairs. She doesn't have the heart to stay downstairs. The empty lounge feels hollow and loud, and besides, the TV's not arrived yet. Instead, she hovers around in her room picking at her stuff, brushing her fingers on everything, re-feeling its familiarity. It's lovely. She smiles to herself. Thinks about finishing an essay which needs to be handed in in three days' time.

She's standing at the window looking out into the inkiness of the evening, thinking about Tye, about his blank bedroom window. She studies the navy patches of shadow in the garden which glimmer and move as clouds pass over the moon. It's a full one, and she loves the clean white circle suspended over the house.

Something catches her eye. Something which doesn't belong in her garden. Something which really shouldn't be there.

It's down by the greenhouse, in a pool of illumination thrown over by the light coming off next door's kitchen. She peers heavily, leaning her forehead against the glass to get a better look.

And she's sure she's right. It definitely doesn't belong in her garden.

It's a crutch. Made of aluminium. A crutch which people might use if they had a dislocated knee. She feels her heart hammer, bewildered. And right next to the crutch, jammed up against the glass of the greenhouse, is a leg in plaster. Straight and a little bit awkward.

The leg can only belong to one person. A person who dislocated the knee in a car accident. A person who crashed through her lounge wall in a most unwelcome way and who shouldn't dare to make a repeat visit.

Harry. She mouths the word in surprise.

Without thinking, in a purely reflex manner, Sophie pulls back from the window, slides her feet into some trainers and finds herself standing in the middle of the room trembling.

Five seconds later she takes the stairs carefully, avoiding the third one down which has a noisy creak whenever it's stepped on.

She goes through the front door, avoiding the back as her dad's still moving around in the kitchen. The click of the door is quiet. Nobody will hear it.

The garden smells damp and dark. It is silent apart from the muffled grunge from Sam's window. She wonders if anyone can hear her heart battering around underneath her ribs. Her breathing comes in short gasps.

She reaches the greenhouse in five paces across the lawn. It's squelchy under her trainers; there's been a lot of rain. Sophie hears a commotion of movement: the rustle of a coat, some hurried shifting of a crutch, and a stiff leg in plaster. It clashes against the glass. She knows she's taken him by surprise and she's pleased about this. It seems only right that she startle him for a change.

'What the hell are you doing here?' Her words are a hiss and they sound nasty. They surprise her.

He's hunched over, sitting on a crate which her dad uses for potatoes. His face is a mess of concern. 'You wouldn't answer my texts.'

It's freezing. She stands still, facing him, hair flying around in the breeze. She feels goosebumps prickle her wrists. 'How did you know I'd be here?'

He lifts some fingers through his fringe. Nods over to Issy's. 'I came here yesterday. That girl next door, the one with the black eye, she said you were coming home today.'

The black eye distracts Sophie for a minute, but then she

focuses her mind again. 'My dad'll kill you if he sees you.'

He grimaces, then shifts his leg awkwardly. 'Yeah, I was waiting for him to settle down for the night and then I was going to phone you to say I was here.' They both look towards the kitchen, where her dad's still moving around. 'Doesn't he ever sit down and watch TV?'

'He would if we had a lounge to sit in! But some idiot went and ruined that for us.'

He winces. 'Aah. OK, I see what you mean.'

He looks massively awkward. All hemmed in and miserable against the dirty glass of the greenhouse. Something shifts in Sophie's stomach. 'Sorry, I didn't mean to be such a bitch.'

He smiles weakly. 'S'OK. I guess I deserved it.' He moves to one side, trying to make some space on the crate. 'Will you sit down?'

'It's bloody freezing.'

'Tell me about it. I can't actually feel my toes.'

'How long have you been here?'

He leans his head against the glass. 'Long enough to know what you had for tea.'

She smiles. 'Hang on.' She takes some steps towards the greenhouse, where she knows her dad keeps a fleece for when he's pottering about in the garden. It smells dry in there, like hay or straw. She grabs the fleece, which has her dad's fragrance in the folds, and pulls it over her head. All the time she can feel Harry's eyes over her, through the glass.

She joins him; he shuffles up a bit and she sits down next to him. There's still some warmth coming off him. It's a comfort. He nudges her gently, trying to smile. 'You can sulk for

England, can't you?'

She pouts, using it to hide a laugh. 'Apparently I get that off my mum. But I am still mad at you. I can't believe you stood me up like that.'

'I had to see my old art teacher.' His eyes shine in the moonlight. She can't see their colour, but she remembers the blue.

'Yeah, your sister took great delight in telling me all about the "special relationship" you have with her.'

Harry shakes his head, rolling his eyes. 'Gemma's got the biggest mouth when it comes to stirring.' He spreads his hands over his knees. 'I don't s'pose she told you that my art teacher is a bloke and that he's been through a really hard time?'

'Oh.'

Harry nods. 'Yeah, he's a top bloke, and he's been really good to me. Only he's gone through a load of shit and he needed someone to talk to. He's helped me over this last year or so. With my art and then . . . with Mum and Dad's break-up. He's not much older than us, see. In his early twenties. And his parents split up when he was around my age. He kind of knew what I was going through. So we talk and stuff. He's not my teacher any more. He left – some of the kids made his life a misery and the head thought he was a "weak teacher", so he got rid of him. He works in a private school now. But he hates it. So every so often we meet. I moan about Mum and Dad, he rants about his job.'

'In the holidays?'

He sighs. 'I know it sounds stupid and it's a long story.

There's other stuff too. Private stuff about Gemma. She got herself into trouble a while back. He kind of gave me advice. Good advice. I'll maybe tell you sometime, but believe me, I didn't have any choice. Sometimes if good friends need you, you have to drop everything. I did try phoning you – several times, but you didn't pick up.'

'I was being interviewed by the police.'

His face drops and his shoulders sag. 'Oh, that.'

There's a silence then. It's soft and quite nice and is only interrupted when Issy's back door opens and her mum's silhouette fills the space. They both watch her hunched figure as she moves to take something to the bins. She's folded over and seems to be hugging her stomach. She doesn't look quite right.

Harry takes a breath; Sophie senses his chest rising with it. Her arm is resting against his. It feels right. 'I'm sorry, Sophie. I hated standing you up. So when you wouldn't answer my texts I thought I'd have to force you to see me. I didn't want you to think I was messing you around. It felt horrible.'

Some of Sophie's hair whips into his face in a gust of wind. It makes them both smile. She can feel the tug of it as it hits the moisture of his lips. She doesn't know what to say. Her throat feels swollen. He leans into her some more. 'Does your dad hate me that much?'

She nods. 'Yes, at the moment he wants to send you to jail and throw away the key.' She looks at him carefully. 'When my dad was a teenager he got knocked down by a drunk driver. Have you seen how he limps?' Harry winces and drops his eyes in a nod. 'Well, ever since then, drink-driving's been a sore subject, if you see what I mean.'

'Shit.'

'Yes, shit.'

There's a rustle of something in the hedge behind them; they both look round, then back. Tension ripples up Sophie's spine. 'Sam says it's probably going to go to court.' She takes a breath. Feels a pulse in her neck. 'Had you been drinking?'

He closes his eyes. Weaves his fingers together. 'Yeah – a bit.'

'Oh.' The word is a whisper. 'Sometimes drinks are stronger than you think.' The sentence lifts in a question. But Harry shakes his head.

He looks miserable again. Changes the subject. 'What about you?' He pulls his hand over his face. 'Do you hate me, like your dad?'

He's warm. He smells musty like soil. His hair is lifting in the wind. His profile is curved and gentle. She knows she doesn't hate him. Yet she knows she should. Her best friend's lying in a coma thanks to him. She knows that this shimmering feeling between herself and Harry is in the worst possible taste. She knows a lot in the pit of her stomach.

'No, I don't hate you.' The words sigh over her tongue, all guilt-ridden and grey.

He turns to her so she gets the fullness of his eyes. 'That's the best thing I've heard in the last ten days.' His tone is soft, to tell her he means it.

'But I feel shitty for being your friend when Tye's

still unconscious.'

'I can understand that.' His eyes are gentle on hers. 'And I can't defend myself, cos I feel guilty enough as it is.' He lifts a nail to his mouth. 'Would I like him?'

'Definitely.' She has a spark of an image of Tye's laughing face. 'I'm sure you would. He's my best ever friend, and apart from a couple of weeks before the accident we knew everything about each other.'

He lifts his lips into a smile. 'He'll wake up, Sophie. I'm sure he will. I'll help you. We'll research getting people out of comas and we'll spend as long as it takes for it to work. I want you to have your friend back. I want to meet him. I want you to stop feeling guilty.'

She sees a mole to the side of his left eye. She's not noticed it before. It gets hidden under the crinkles of his skin when he smiles. His eyebrows are a shade darker than his hair; even in this evening light she can see this. He parts his lips to press a fingernail between his teeth.

'You bite your nails,' she whispers.

He pulls out the fingernail, cross with himself. 'Yeah, I know. Horrible habit. It's when I'm nervous or bored.'

She stares at the mole slipping in and out of sight. His face is centimetres away. She can feel the wash of his warm breath. It feels good on her cheeks. 'Am I boring you, then?'

He grins, lifting a hand for a strand of hair which is whipping her eyes. He pulls her face closer using gentle tugs on the strand. 'No, but you're making me very nervous.'

Then he places a smile of a kiss on to Sophie's lips and she forgets for a moment that she's in her back garden, sitting on a potato crate, wearing her dad's old gardening fleece. For a moment all she can feel is the kiss sinking inside.

Harry drops the strand and uses his freed-up fingers to sift through her hair, over her scalp. His hand feels lovely and warm and large and comfortable. She could rest her head in that palm if she wanted.

Instead she tilts her chin higher and kisses him back.

They both pull back at the same time. He's laughing, she's smiling. Sophie holds her breath, her lungs buzzing. She straightens her legs, notices that her arms are shivering.

Harry notices too. 'You're cold.'

She crosses her ankles, draws her feet back in. 'And it's not like I can invite you inside.'

He grins, shrugs. 'It would be weird using a door anyhow! My preferred method of entry is crashing through a wall.'

She tries not to laugh. 'That's such bad taste.'

He's serious for a minute. 'Sorry. I know. I've got to go home, anyway.'

She glances at his profile, curious. 'How are you getting home?'

'Gemma said she'd pick me up.'

'Gemma?' Sophie's eyes widen.

He smiles a lopsided smile. 'She's not all bad, you know?' He grimaces as he starts to lever himself up. 'She's just not very good at showing her . . . softer side.'

Sophie gets up quickly and helps him rearrange his crutches. 'You can say that again.' They make their way slowly over the grass, keeping wary eyes on the kitchen, which now seems to be quiet and still. 'Does she even have one? A softer side?'

He laughs. ''Course she does. She gets upset over crazy things. When Rex, our dog, died, she wore black for a whole month. And she's been through some bad stuff in the last couple of years. It sometimes affects how she behaves.' There's the soft ticking of somebody's central heating and an aeroplane pulsing a red dot high in the sky. He looks up and she catches his profile again. 'She's pretty sensitive, only she doesn't want people to know.' The ground makes squelching sounds under Harry's crutches. Sophie decides not to continue with the subject. She can't see this side of Harry's twin. It's hard to imagine the aggressive and spoilt Gemma being anything but that. But she won't say this to Harry; doesn't want to ruin tonight. The taste of their kiss is still fragrant on her lips.

At the side of the house, where there's a wall and no windows, Harry stops. 'What you said back there, about your mum . . . you don't talk about her much.'

She shrugs. 'Not much to say. She had an affair, then she left, that's all there is to it.'

He takes the hint from the shrug; she likes this about him. She can feel him studying her. 'OK.' He leans against the bricks, like he needs the support. 'I said I'd meet Gemma at the end of your road. Seemed safer that way.'

She nods, feeling how close he is to her, by the wall. He rests on one crutch and presses his toe on Sophie's trainer. 'So, if I text you tomorrow will you text back?'

She concentrates on his mouth, which is millimetres away from hers. 'Yes.'

They kiss in the wind, with Sophie's hair wrapping around their heads and Harry's left crutch nudging her elbow.

He leaves gingerly, down the front path. She finds it difficult to breathe standing there. Like she's just run a hundred metres.

It was easy finding the date. Stephanie had been boasting about her weekend trip to New York for the last three weeks. Taking shopping orders from friends like she was going to Tesco.

Gemma had handed this nugget of information to Deano like it was a piece of gold. She'd received a special smile and a hand in her hair which had her glowing for the rest of the day.

Getting out of the house at night was a piece of cake; her parents were too absorbed in hating each other to even notice her absence. They walked in a huddle down the road. A clump of cigarette smoke, swear words and nerves. Deano went over the plans, giving them each a role. It felt good to be a part of the team. Nervy – but good.

The house was swathed in darkness so phones were switched on. Hushed voices now. There was a light rain which shimmered on their foreheads, shining up Deano's good looks. Hard not to stare too much.

She had to give it to him, he was good at this. A master at work. Made her stomach slick like treacle. Tam was given the lookout job, the rest of them crept round the back.

There was a scent of freshly mowed grass which smacked of some gardening work. Probably some member of staff who was paid peanuts. Their feet crunched up some gravel as they tried to move softly. Her heart was quite literally in her mouth. She'd forgotten how to breathe.

'Where's the back door, Tess?'

She'd been here only once before. Some pool party where she'd stuck out like a lemon because she'd worn her school swimming costume instead of a flash new bikini. She'd kicked herself at her stupidity.

'Round there.' She pointed to her left, squeezing out a memory.

Deano led them in single file: Adam second, then her, then Bulldog and Jinx bringing up the rear. It was about one o'clock, with just a sliver of moon for light. Both Deano and Adam kept up with the encouragement in whispers: 'Well done, Tess.' 'Good job.'

She was doing well despite the nerves. They thought she was good.

At the door, Deano and Jinx got to work. She didn't see what with. But there was a scramble of something metallic and lots of soft swear words.

And in thirty seconds they were in.

She had to put the back of her hand into her mouth to stop the ridiculous giggles. There was a wobble in her knees which felt mad.

Some fingers on her arm. Deano. She'd recognize the force any day. A steadying influence, forcing her to keep calm. His fingers stopped the giggles almost immediately.

Don't act like a kid. Don't wreck this. It's important to impress.

'You said there was a study. Where is it?' Adam's words were quiet but demanding.

Clearing her head felt like sifting through wads of sticky cotton wool. 'Um . . .' Racking her brain. 'Through there.' Then a sickening thought which blew like fireworks behind her eyes. 'What about an alarm? Places like this—'

'Jinx has hacked in,' Deano interrupted as he made for the kitchen door. 'Follow me, T.'

She did; as they all did, trooping in a line. Tiptoeing even though there was no need.

The study was a shadow of shelving and desks and brief-cases. Books and papers cluttered up the surfaces. Her eyes skimmed over everything, although they weren't as trained as the boys' eyes. They knew what they were looking for within seconds. Laptops and high-tech gadgets. They seemed pretty pleased with their finds, laughing as they piled them into a bag which she'd not noticed Bulldog carrying.

It took three minutes, if that. Three minutes where she stood wide-eyed at the expertise.

'Where now, Tess?' It was Adam, his eyes glittering. She could feel Deano waiting for her answer by the door. She hadn't realized she was going to be asked so many questions.

'Um, maybe the bedrooms. I think Stephanie's mum's got jewellery and stuff.'

'Great. Hurry up, we've not got long.'

Deano took the stairs two at a time and she was jostled up by the others so her legs didn't need to do any work.

'Which one?'

She grimaced, tried to think. But it had been a long time and she couldn't properly remember. She stood on the landing feeling like a six-year-old. 'I don't know.' It was a pathetic wail. But she felt Deano's strong fingers again.

'Doesn't matter. We'll try them all.'

A small dawning of a memory. 'Over there's Stephanie's.' She pointed to her left.

Deano split them up. 'You three try that one; me and Tess'll go in here.' He nodded at a pale door ahead of them. Again it felt good to be singled out. To be accompanying the leader.

They were in the master bedroom. The air was cool with a faint hint of perfume. It smelt of adults and importance. Deano used his gloved-up hands to rifle through some drawers, where he found items which he passed back to her. Jewellery boxes, small cubes of padded fabric which contained classy stuff. Her own hands were in gloves – just as she'd been told. There was no time for opening, they'd do that once they were back in the mill tomorrow. She knew this part of the routine. She'd seen it happen before.

Deano glanced at her wide eyes and laden hands. 'They sell for a packet on eBay. Take them through to the landing, Bulldog'll stash them.'

She did as she was told, pleased to have something to do. After a couple of minutes Deano seemed happy. He came back to where she was standing, touched the side of her face and spoke softly. 'You've done well, Tess. My kind of girl.'

The waves and ripples in her stomach from those words made it all worthwhile.

She'd done good.

His fingers left trails and thrills all down her cheek.

'Let's go and see what the others've found.'

She tripped after him, feeling adrenaline soar and buzz.

But then, on the landing where they were grinning like fools, there sounded a high-pitched alarm which scarred their faces with horror.

'Fuck, what's that?' This from Deano, who suddenly looked unsure. 'What the fuck's that, Jinx? You said you'd fixed it.'

Jinx looked like he might crumble and die there and then. 'Shit, I dunno. Maybe they had a separate delayed one for upstairs.'

The siren was screaming around the house. A poltergeist of noise. A banshee of high-pitched racket.

Oh My God. Oh My God. Oh My God!

She could feel the tremors of anxiety snake up her body. She didn't know if she was screaming. She wouldn't be able to hear it even if she was.

'Run!' somebody said. She felt harsh fingers jab at her back as she almost fell down the stairs. Boxes and boots fell out of Bulldog's bag, so that she tripped up and fell each time. And each time, she felt Deano's hands lift her back up before she'd properly fallen.

'No! No! No!' was all she could say.

Why, oh why had she agreed to this? Right now it felt like the biggest, loudest scream of a mistake. The biggest mistake of her life.

They collided with each other at the bottom of the stairs. All of them. The smell of fear and sweat hit her hard. Someone stood on her foot. Someone pushed her head into someone else's shoulder. They were jostling into the kitchen like a crowd of deranged boy-band fans. There was no working as a team any more. They were running individually, pushing each other out of the way, making for the back door.

Deano was behind them all. Rounding them up. She could sense him, hard and fierce.

But the door was locked.

The door was locked.

The door was locked.

The fact rippled through them. Confused faces and foreheads. How could the door be locked?

'Jinx?' Deano's mouth had a shape to it which she'd never, ever seen. He had to shout over the siren.

Jinx held his head in his hands. He moved it from side to side. 'I dunno, I dunno . . . maybe there's a timed lock. Maybe it automatically locks when the alarm goes off. Maybe it just locks itself anyway.' His eyes rolled back. 'Fuck, I don't know!'

Gemma wanted to sit down. She wanted to slide down the wall; she knew it was only a matter of time before the police or the neighbours were there. Deano's phone was flashing with Tam's name on the screen as it was.

Jinx skirted the room to a window, his shoulders alert, like an animal's. He yanked at it with a hand made of white knuckles and twisted fingers. An escape route; a way out of this mess. Freedom from the noise which was killing her insides. He lifted his leg and used his upper body muscles to lift his bulk off the ground to reach a window ledge. She saw the exertion and started to worry. She'd never make that. She was crap at gymnastics.

She watched, horrified, as Jinx made the final push and disappeared over the ledge, then fled into the darkened distance, not turning his head. Almost immediately Bulldog made a grab for the windowsill, his impressive muscles straining in his neck and torso. She was never going to do it in time when it came to her turn. If it ever would.

She could hear Deano behind her, breathing heavily even under the brutal alarm. 'Tess next,' she heard him say, but Adam wasn't listening, or if he was, then he'd decided to ignore Deano. Because with a painful jab in her ribs he elbowed her out of the way. He was a coward after all.

Deano pushed her forward. She could feel tears choke in her throat. Her heart hammered under her ribs. It felt dangerous and explosive. Deano was using his own bulk to give her a lift. His hands were on her legs pushing her up higher and higher because there was no way she had the strength in her arms. Especially now, when it felt like her whole body was a pathetic lump of jelly.

'I can't,' she cried when for the second time she missed the ledge.

'You can!' he exclaimed. Like an order.

Everyone did what Deano said. That's just what happened. So with an effort which came from obedience she gave one last try. He pushed at her bum and at the back of her thighs and she held on to the ledge with fingers quivering in terror. And this time it worked. Somehow. She was on the ledge now, manoeuvring herself awkwardly, one leg over, then the next. Her knees jammed under her chin and forced out a painful breath. She watched with terror as lights in neighbouring houses began to flick on one by one. People were waking to the incessant siren. It was only a matter of time before the police arrived.

As she dropped to the other side of the window, she twisted around to see something which turned her insides out. Had her brain popping like fireworks. Had her gasping for breath in a throat made of sandpaper. Had her knees sagging and billowing.

'What?' She was unsure if she said the word out loud, but it was there, behind her eyes. The biggest question in the whole wide world.

Standing in the doorway of the pool house in a towelling bathrobe, tying up the belt like she'd been naked seconds before, and with Simon Luton at her shoulder – her best friend's boyfriend – was Stephanie Hughes.

She was supposed to be in New York!

Gemma pulled up her hood and hid her face in her hair. She turned quickly to Deano through the window; he was busy using his fingers to strain up. When his face looked at hers, and then in turn at Stephanie, it transformed. A waxy question mark of its own. She didn't want to think about what he was thinking.

I didn't know. I didn't know!

But the twisted lines on his face told her a different story. Deano was angry and confused and maybe scared.

She'd let him down.

*

It was a blur then. A cloud of slow motion and speed-ups with nothing at normal time.

There were police sirens now. Haunting her in the distance. Some primeval gut instinct made her step into the shadows of a nearby tree. That was all she could do.

Deano was sitting on the ledge of the window, neither in nor out of the house. Stephanie was in the pool house doorway like a frightened pigeon who had just had sex. Even frightened she looked beautiful. Her hair glimmered in the moonlight.

'What the—?' Simon Luton was adjusting his disgusting jeans, bewildered by the sights and sounds around him.

And it was then that Gemma saw what was in Deano's hand. A black hard thing. A dangerous thing. Something which shocked her and made her hold her throat. The gun.

He was waving it around like she remembered from a few weeks ago. If only he didn't. His face was twisted, looking at Stephanie.

'No!' she shouted. But he wasn't listening to her at all.

Stephanie had seen it too. She was running then. Running round the side of the garden, her towelling robe flapping like a sail. Her hair was behind her in a stream of long waves. Running round pots of flowers, hopping in bare feet off the patio. Fear and alarm from the waving gun and the siren made her lopsided and unbalanced. It was as if she was drunk.

And then a bang. A loud explosion of a blast which ricocheted off walls and guttering.

From the shadows of the tree Gemma fell to her knees. *No, no, no.*

The noise hit Stephanie's back so that she made a perfect arch with her spine. She screamed and spluttered and flung her arms up high. She lost her balance so spectacularly that she flew to the floor in a horrible twist, bashing against a rusting wheelbarrow nearby. The noise of the fall was as terrible to hear as the gun itself. Her face smashed against the side, scraping flesh and hair in a bloody mess. She dropped to the floor then; her awful dead weight adding to the force against the gravel.

Stephanie crumpled like a rag doll. A bloody, silent, messy thing with arms and legs sticking out at abnormal angles. Her frame crushed in a tangle. The echo of the gun was still ribboning through the air.

The police sirens were everywhere then. Closing in on the house from every available angle. Gemma saw Deano stagger clumsily off the window ledge and fall badly, but his eyes caught hers. 'Run, Tess!' he shouted over the noise of the alarm. Over the silence of Stephanie on the floor. Over the frozen figure of Simon.

Like a long-forgotten mantra, his words kicked into her stomach. Everyone did what Deano said.

So she ran. Ran like the wind, like a mad girl, like a frightened fox being chased by a group of hounds. She didn't look back. She wouldn't.

Sophie

On Saturday morning she makes her mind up to see for herself. Tye's mum's revelation has been confusing her, so she decides that the only way to find out is to take a look at a rehearsal. She knows they've started to rehearse on Saturday mornings now that the production is only a few weeks away. If she can slip in at the back, then she can maybe get a better idea.

When she gets to the hall she finds it easy enough to walk through the doors and stand at the back in the shadows. It's a funny atmosphere seeing kids from school out of school uniform, looking fuggy and tired so early in the weekend.

The room smells of trainers and crisps. Mr Ryan's at the front, pacing at the stage, in jeans and a Foo Fighters hoodie. Sophie doesn't know who she's looking for. There's nobody there who she can imagine Tye falling for. She recognizes a cluster of boys in a corner as some of Tye's friends: Stuart, Ewan and Gurpreet. *Summer Nights* is blaring from the speakers and six girls are on the stage going through their moves.

She squints from the back and searches out any likely character. There's a girl with crazy ginger curls, another with a lavender pixie cut, and the rest have blonde waves which bounce as they dance on the stage. Sophie knows them all, except for one girl sitting on a bench who seems short and skinny and definitely not Tye's type. She looks again at this girl. Maybe the fact that she's not Tye's type might be the key. She's eating crisps and licking her fingers, staring at the action on the stage. When she gets up from the bench to talk to Mr Ryan, Sophie recognizes her as a girl in her science class. She's convinced Tye would have told her if it was someone she knew.

Disappointment lodges between her ribs. Was this a waste of a Saturday morning lie-in?

She stays for the song and then thinks about leaving. She's getting nothing done here and it's annoying. It's so frustrating. She wishes with all her heart that Tye had the courage to tell her, it's not like he knew the disastrous kiss was going to happen. It's upsetting to think that he's fallen into a coma and with it he's taken the one and only secret they'd ever had.

From the back of the room she feels the gaze of two lads who play T-Birds. She gives them a short smile and nods at the door to show them she's on her way. One of the boys has spiky red hair and the other has eyes which seem to burrow under her skin; it's a bit like being unpeeled. He's struggling to open a family bag of Sensations; he grins ruefully at Sophie and rolls his eyes at his uselessness, and she has to give a small smile back. He looks at her again and this time she senses a curiosity, maybe even recognition.

He takes some steps towards her and for a moment she has this mad idea that he might want her to open the crisp packet. She even takes her hands out of pockets in readiness. The music has stopped and Mr Ryan's barking orders about throwing voices and not turning backs to the audience. But Sophie's not really concentrating because the boy is now centimetres from her.

'Do I know you?' He has a rich voice with an accent which isn't from round here.

She jams her hands back into her pockets. 'No, I don't think so.'

An explosion of music makes him jump. She notices he has bony shoulders and a long tanned neck where ripples of emotion hum through.

He nods and widens his eyes, 'I do. You're Tye's friend, aren't you?'

At the sound of his name she feels the sadness slide in. She finds she can only nod. The boy puts the crisps to one side and puts his head at a sympathetic angle. 'How is he?'

And then, like the last piece in a jigsaw, a dawning so bright rises through her. She looks at his hair. She looks at his height. She looks at his eyes, how curious and worried.

Of course. How could she have been so stupid?

Here, in front of her, is the very reason why Tye hadn't told her.

The boy sees her confusion; he hesitates. The crisps rustle gently against his leg. The flush of realization rushes through Sophie like a waterfall. Banks are burst with the information. She has flashes of Tye. Of this boy kissing Tye. Of Tye, who right now is lying flat in a hospital room with only a small machine informing the word that he is still alive. It shouldn't be like this. It shouldn't.

Her words come out in a shudder. 'He's still in a coma and it's the most horrible sight in the world.' She feels her eyes fill with tears and then spill over. She's amazed at herself: she's very private about crying. The boy has nice eyes and there's a kindness in them which shines. She's momentarily proud of Tye, she can tell already that he's made a good choice with this boy. He lifts a steadying hand to her arm and she feels a warmth through her sweatshirt. It's nice to be able to share the sadness.

'I was going to go and see him. I can't tell you how much I've wanted to. Only . . .' He grimaces and moves his hand off her arm in a shrug of uncertainty, '. . . only I wasn't sure what people might think . . .'

She nods slowly. 'You should. He'd like it.'

The music is now blaring over their shoulders so it's impossible to speak. The boy looks desperate and she starts to feel sorry for him. He glances over to the door, tilts his head, shouts in her ear. 'Wanna go outside for a minute?'

She nods.

In the fresh air, with the thrum of the music through the windows and a haze of rain which has come from nowhere, she feels a low buzz of cheer. Here is Tye's secret. Maybe the mood is contagious, because the boy grins at her and attacks the crisp packet all over again. He pushes the packet towards Sophie as an offer. She shakes her head. He shrugs his bony shoulders and delves in deep with hungry fingers. She waits as he eats his first handful.

'I'm Jordan, by the way. Did Tye tell you about me?'

'In a roundabout way.'

Jordan grins again. He crinkles up his eyes at a remembered image, 'Yeah, he's pretty cryptic, isn't he?'

'Especially those last few weeks.'

He looks at her with a steady gaze. 'I told him to tell you. He needed to tell someone. It's the craziest bastard of a secret to keep. Take it from me, I know.'

'Um.'

'He didn't have to tell the world . . . just you.'

The tears come from behind her eyes again and she brushes them away with cross fingers. 'It's so sad.'

She feels the hand again in exactly the same place on her arm. It's nice.

Suddenly the door flings open and Mr Ryan pokes his head round its frame. He has angry lines either side of his mouth. 'Jordan Kray, get yourself in here this minute. We've wasted five minutes looking for you.'

Jordan raises his eyebrows at her and she finds she can grin back. 'Gotta go.'

'OK,' she speaks quickly – already he's starting to turn – 'but come and see him, please. I know he'd want you there.'

He nods. 'I will.'

And he's gone, through the door, a blur of black T-shirt and hair.

Gemma two years ago

Turns out getting away with it was hard.

They got away. Deano, by the skin of his teeth. Naturally fast, he'd scarpered round the back of the house, past the crumpled-up Stephanie heap, past the wide-eyed, open-mouthed Simon. Into the farmyard at the back; lying low in some outbuildings and waiting.

But he'd been spotted. Identified. The notorious Deano was now in hiding.

A close call, and his friends weren't happy with Gemma. They weren't happy at all.

Having to go to school and pretend it hadn't happened was the hardest thing she'd ever done. The corridors were alive with Stephanie and Deano and Simon. It was the only conversation topic for weeks on end.

Slowly, over the course of the second day, when gossip was still at a ridiculously high level, she managed to piece together snippets of information which began to make sense. Tempted by an empty house while her parents were in New York, Stephanie had chosen to stay at home. To spend the time with her best friend's boyfriend in secret. She'd told her parents that she had an important exam she wanted to revise for. And they'd believed her, proud of their daughter's studious attitude.

And she'd have got away with it, had Deano and his crew not chosen that day of all days to burgle their house. Someone had let slip that the house would be empty. They'd somehow managed to key into the first alarm, but hadn't known about the second. Always a security-conscious man, Stephanie's dad double-locked everything and had instilled in his daughter to do the same, so that even when she used the pool house she was to set both alarms. The alarm had disturbed her session with Simon, and the gunshot, although not aimed at Stephanie, had frightened her into a fall down the side of a rusting wheelbarrow which had ripped at her skin and scarred her face, possibly for life.

Stephanie wasn't set to return to school for the rest of the term.

Deano was in hiding and didn't blame her for holding him up. He'd sent her a text.

But his mates weren't quite as charitable.

Walking home from school after the fourth day of rumour, intrigue and whispers, she skirted the corner by the bus shelter with her brother.

'This shooting's really bothered you, hasn't it?' He hitched his bag from one shoulder to the other. His bag was always heavier than hers; crammed full of art materials and textbooks.

She grimaced. Just the word 'shooting' sent a spasm to her throat. 'She's gonna be scarred for life.'

'I didn't know you were such a big fan.'

She scowled. 'I'm not. She's a rich selfish bitch who was doing the dirty on her own best friend.' Gemma pressed her fingers to her throat. 'I guess it spooked me, that's all.'

'They say it's only a matter of time before they find that Deano kid. And when they do, he'll blab. Apparently there were a load of them in his gang.'

She pulled her sleeves down over her wrists to hide the tremble which was beginning to spill on to her skin. It was difficult to say anything. She'd not slept properly for three nights now and her eyes were itching with fatigue. She had mushroom-coloured circles under her eyes and eczema blotches behind her knees and elbows. It was ugly. She didn't feel pretty any more, and she knew her brother was on to this. He had a nose for her unhappiness just as she had for his. It was difficult to hide anything from him. Always had been. Always would be.

A figure emerged from the shadows of the bus shelter and called out her name – only not her normal name. 'Tess!'

A hot lick of shame. She felt a pulse in her neck that she didn't know she had. Swallowed. 'Um, yes . . .' To her bewildered brother by her side: 'I'll catch up with you.'

He gave her a look which she wouldn't try to read. He crumpled his forehead and trudged reluctantly ahead. There was no way she wanted him to hear this.

It was Bulldog, then Tam, then from out of the corner of the bus shelter strode Adam. Without Deano they looked random and cluttered.

It was Bulldog who was blustering the most. His Afro wobbled, and there was a red tinge underneath his darker skin. 'What the fuck happened?' He stepped too close to Gemma.

Panic spiralled around her body. 'I—'

She watched as the others clustered around her, far too near, so she could smell their tobacco breath and cheap lager. Adam was the tallest. He towered over her and jabbed a finger at her collarbone. 'You said she wouldn't be there. What the fuck was that about? Were you trying to set us up? You stupid, stupid bitch.'

'I wasn't trying to set you up.' Tears billowed and welled behind her eyes. Tears which she used every ounce of discipline to force back. It couldn't stop the tremble in her thighs and wrists, though. And her voice was horribly high. 'Why would I have been there if I was trying to set you up?'

Like a huddle of confused cows they shuffled around her, not sure how to take the question. But Bulldog wouldn't let it lie, his lips a twist of scorn. 'You should've let him go first. You held him up, and now he's hiding out.' He carefully placed his trainer on her foot, pressing hard so that her toes curled and squeezed. They hurt. He knew it. He watched her face, waiting for the pain to spill over. She tried to stare him out, but the twinge was now shooting up her shins.

Carefully, so he had her full attention and so she had to hold her breath through the ache, he pressed harder. 'That girl

– that Stephanie kid . . . she's not the only one who'll get hurt. Her pretty little face – all cut up. 'He nodded at her; nicotine breath on her skin. 'Yours'll be the same if you let anything slip. You say one word . . .' a further press and a step closer from the others, '. . . and we'll be on to you, and it won't just be your face that gets messed up.'

Adam pressed her collarbone with his finger again. 'You get that?'

She nodded. There was nothing else she could do. She wobbled another nod at them and took a step back. They didn't follow her, but their eyes were stuck to her like superglue.

'OK,' she managed.

She tried another step, then another.

Let me go.

It felt like the tensest game of chess which she didn't know how to play.

Then she was running. Running away from their shuffling and their threats. Her hair was in her eyes, but it didn't matter. All that mattered was getting away. Running hell for leather down the road and round the corner.

To her brother's confused eyes. The eyes which had seen everything. The ears which had pricked up and had heard it all. The threats, the story, the information. Like a body full of data, he now knew it all.

'So how did you get the black eye?'

Issy flushes hotly, moves her fingers to the eye and presses. It still hurts a bit, like a reminder under her fingertips, but she'd thought the bruises had faded. In the mirror this morning she thought she could see a haze of greenness, but that was all.

'Netball. I ran into the shooter.'

Sophie smiles and shakes her head from the other side of the hedge. 'You should stop playing that game. You always seem to get injured.'

Issy laughs in what she hopes is a light way. 'I like it. And miss says that I'm quite good at it.'

It's a Saturday morning at the end of March. Sophie and her family have been back in their house for almost a week now and Issy likes the idea of them all being back to normal. It's a comfort to see the orange blocks of light from their windows at night time. And to hear the music coming from Sam's bedroom. She's missed the rattle of the shed, the slam of the dustbins and the constant chatter and harmless shouting whenever the kitchen door opens. It's good to have them back, and she wants to tell Sophie this without sounding silly.

She'd popped outside this morning to empty the bin. Nobody seemed to be doing this any more and the kitchen was starting to smell. Nobody seemed to be in the kitchen very much these days, either. Meals weren't being made and food wasn't being shopped for. There were squashed-up tea bags on the floor round the bin.

After the black eye her mum said she should stay at home because she didn't want people asking questions. So Issy did that. It was a bleak, lonely week when nobody said anything to her and nothing got done. Most mornings she was alone downstairs. So she'd taken to watching *Jeremy Kyle* and drinking the milk before it turned sour. She didn't seem to have much appetite for anything else. Not that there was anything to eat or drink in the cupboards anyhow – unless she liked vodka. There was plenty of that.

Dave would shamble downstairs around lunchtime, rubbing his face and forcing his eyes open; they were usually pink and sore-looking. Issy would sink into the corner of the sofa, hoping he wouldn't notice her. Her mum would come down later, wearing a dressing gown which was starting to smell and with bare, veined feet which Issy wished she'd cover with the lovely patterned tights she used to wear not so long ago.

Dave would come into the lounge slurping and slopping his coffee on the carpet, barking questions at her head.

'Where's your mum? Where's the lazy little bitch?'

At those times Issy shrugged and got frightened, waiting for Dave to leave the room before hunting round the house. Both times she'd found her mum, curled up like a mouse, in the cupboard under the stairs, blinking and cowering, mixed in with the fleeces and coats which they all wore when they went on days out like they used to.

Today she'd heard Sophie's back door open as she dropped the bin lid down. She crossed her fingers and hoped and prayed that it was Sophie, biting hard on her lip in the process.

The hopes and the prayers were answered, because as she stood very still by the grimy bin she heard a questioning 'Issy?' And she knew from the lovely voice that it was Sophie. She swung her head round and smiled, feeling the unfamiliar cracks in her cheeks. It had been a long time.

'Hello.' She'd felt almost shy.

They'd moved to the gap in the hedge, Sophie gingerly, as she was only wearing socks on her feet. Stripy rainbow colours, Issy noticed. They'd not seen each other for a while, not since Sophie had returned.

Sophie smiles and fiddles with a bud on the hedge. She presses it between her finger and thumb, and Issy sees brown ooze stain her fingers. 'So, what you doing this weekend?'

Issy gets worried by the question. Feels her fingers flex. 'Um . . . nothing very much. Homework, I suppose . . .'

Sophie groans. 'Tell me about it.' But her lips twitch mischievously and her eyes start to glint. 'Tell you what, though . . . how about you and me go down to the bakery and get ourselves a couple of cream cakes and scoff them on the way home?' She grins. 'Nothing like a good skive now and again.'

Issy thinks about her homework, already done. Already packed neatly in her bag at the bottom of her bed. She feels elated at the vision of her and Sophie, walking on the pavement, licking the cream off a doughnut and laughing together.

Then suddenly she thinks about money. Gulps so it hurts. Her fingernails press into her palm. 'Um . . . I've already spent my pocket money this week.' The lie fills her chest.

Sophie brushes a hand to one side, flicking the hedge as she does. 'Oh, don't worry about that. My treat. I've still got some left from the sympathy cash grandma gave me when I was in the hotel.'

Issy allows herself a small lift. 'Oh, OK, then. If you're sure.' She makes to step through the gap in the hedge, but Sophie tilts her head towards Issy's house.

'Don't you want to tell your mum? Won't she worry where you are?'

Issy steps back, suddenly remembering that this is how it used to be. 'Oh, yeah, sorry.'

'I'll go and grab my money and put some shoes on. Meet you back here in five minutes.' Sophie's already running, her hair swinging like it always does.

Issy doesn't know why, but she opens the back door. Perhaps she thinks the noise is proof that she's going out. But she knows it's pointless. She knows that her mum and Dave won't notice where she is. They won't worry at all. Dave is on the sofa, sweating, sleeping off last night's vodka, his toenails yellow and thick. And her mum is hiding somewhere in her dressing gown. Issy checked under the stairs this morning, but she wasn't there, so she thinks she might be in the new place. The new place she found yesterday: at the bottom of Issy's wardrobe, curled up under the bridesmaid's dress which Issy wore this time last year to her cousin's wedding in Poland.

The bakery is busy. Lots of Saturday-morning people buying fresh rolls, French sticks and cakes. Sophie and Issy queue up behind a woman in woollen tights which have wrinkles at the ankles. Issy fingers her bruise and feels small next to Sophie. There are a lot of people. Many more than she's been used to at her house. These days, with her mum in hiding most of the time, the house seems empty.

'Can't choose between an eclair or a doughnut.' Sophie has a line between her eyes where she's trying to decide. She draws a finger along her lips. 'What do you want?'

Issy eyes the trays of pastry and sugar and cream. Her stomach does hungry hurdles. She hasn't eaten anything today. But really she doesn't mind. Really she could stand next to Sophie all morning, in this bustling bakery, feeling safe, breathing in warm bread like a cushion. She lifts her shoulders, widens her eyes and turns up her palms shyly.

'I don't mind.'

Sophie looks at her face and smiles. 'In that case I'll get a selection.'

*

'I wonder what you have to do to work in a cake shop,' Issy says. They're sitting on a bench down the road from where they bought the cakes. Sophie's slipped into the newsagent's for cans of Coke and Issy is fidgeting with happiness. She takes a large bite of the custard slice, which hurts her mouth because she has to open it so wide. She giggles when some of the custard squidges to the side, dropping on to her hand like a wet frog. The icing on the top nudges her nostrils. She hasn't held so much wonderful food so close to her face for so long. Her senses get dizzy.

'Connections, I reckon. I bet if you knew somebody who worked there they'd put in a good word.' Sophie looks to the shop. Her eyes narrow. 'But I wouldn't want to. I'd end up being the size of a house. All that temptation.'

She snaps her lips and lays her doughnut to one side. Issy feels foolish. She's already finished her custard slice. Sophie grins and nudges her knee against hers. 'You polished that off pretty quick. Want another?'

Like jewels, the leftover cakes sparkle up at Issy. There's no way she can turn this down. Her stomach is still cheering her earlier choice. She smiles shyly.

'If you're sure?' She eyes the cream doughnut with its equator of blood-red jam.

Sophie shoves the box under her nose, then whirrs it around in a circle. ''Course.'

They eat in comfortable silence. People pass by in the March sunshine. Issy allows a small bubble of hope to rise inside her. Perhaps this is the start of the nice time beginning again. Now Sophie's back. Now cream cakes are on offer.

Now the bruising's gone down. Perhaps her mum will wake up with the sunshine and argue with Dave again. Maybe she'll get dressed today, if Issy encourages her. Maybe wear that skirt with the leaf pattern. Maybe wash her hair. Hope fills Issy's throat. Maybe Dave will get another job and they could go to watch a film on Sunday afternoons, like they used to.

'You OK, Issy?' Sophie speaks ahead of her.

Issy nods, her mouth crammed with cream doughnut, her tongue on fire.

'Only I thought you looked . . . kind of thin . . . earlier on. A bit pale, maybe . . . you are eating, aren't you? You know . . . properly . . . You've not gone all anorexic on me, have you?'

Like a pebble in a pond, the thought drops in, that this might be the reason why Sophie's invited her along. Her head fills with hot blood. Ashamed. She shakes her head violently. 'No. I'm fine. Look how I've eaten two cream cakes. I wouldn't do that if I had an eating disorder, would I?'

Sophie smiles. Tips her head back and swigs her Coke. 'S'pose not.' She presses the can so it makes a clinking sound. 'Only, I know how Year 7 can be a bit difficult. How everyone's getting used to each other . . . and how some girls can be a bit . . . mean.'

Issy thinks of the girls in her form. Of how they all wear the same hairstyle. How they all laugh behind their hands. How she and Briony ignore them and get on with their schoolwork. How this usually works, but not always. 'They can,' she whispers.

Sophie looks at her quickly. 'They're not hurting you, are

they? I mean physically.' She grimaces. She's finding this awkward, Issy can tell. 'The black eye, I mean . . . they didn't do that, did they?'

Issy's words crinkle up with embarrassment. 'No. I'm not getting bullied.'

'Cos if you were . . .' Sophie's voice is a bit fierce, 'then there are a lot of people you can tell, you know?' She smoothes down her jeans which don't need smoothing, holds her fingers up one by one. 'There's me, for a start. You could always tell me. But also there's your teacher, or your head of year, your mum,' she cocks her head, 'or even my dad if you wanted . . .' There are now five fingers in front of Issy's face. Five people she could tell.

She's made a promise to her mum.

'I did it in netball. Remember?'

Her head feels hot. The sugar and cream starts to congeal in her stomach. She catches a glimpse of the fourth cream cake in the white box – a snowball. It makes her feel sick.

'Shall we go back?' It's a blurt of a sentence. She looks up at Sophie as they stand up. 'My friends aren't bullying me. I know how to deal with them.' She can say this without lying. They start to walk. They talk about nothing much. It's what she likes about Sophie.

Sophie tells Issy about her plans. 'I'm going to spring a surprise on Tye. I'm going to take in a friend of his who was in *Grease* with him. I'm going to meet him after his rehearsal and take him to the hospital.' She goes a little pink, and twitches her fingers together. 'You know I'm seeing the driver of the car – in the accident – Harry?' She coughs to clear her throat.

'Well, I think maybe I've been neglecting Tye. And that's no way to treat a friend. I feel really guilty, you see.'

Issy glows from this adult conversation. Feels as tall as Sophie. She tries not to look like she's surprised or shocked or disapproving. Again there's that little nag over what Sophie's said. But she ignores it at the wonder of being treated like a teenager, like Sophie.

'He'd want you to be happy.' Glad to move the subject away from black eyes.

Sophie nods. 'I guess. We've got to keep it quiet because Dad will go apeshit if he finds out and Tye's parents wouldn't speak to me ever again. After all, he did nearly demolish our house and almost kill Tye. So we've been meeting in secret.' She looks quickly at Issy, her worry line reappearing between her eyes. 'You won't say, will you? I've not told anyone – not even Maisie yet. You'll keep it a secret?'

Issy nods confidently. ''Course. I'm good at secrets.'

Sophie looks at her sharply as they turn the corner into their road. 'You are, aren't you?' She laughs. 'The keeper of secrets.'

Issy doesn't know why, but she catches some of Sophie's laughter in the air. And she laughs too. It feels odd, but nice in her cheeks. She pictures how other people would see them. Just a regular couple of girls walking down the street having a laugh. It's nice having Sophie to herself – no Maisie, no Tye.

Issy fingers her eye quietly, feels another fizz of hope. Yes, she can do this. She gives a small skip; she's going to go back to the house. She's going to find the mop bucket which her mum used to keep outside. She's going to fill it with hot soapy water and she's going to mop the kitchen floor. Especially round the bin. And then she's going to open the fridge as wide as it will go and fill a carrier with all the out-of-date food which is making the kitchen smell. Next, she's going to open the window in the lounge to get some fresh air. She'll go under the sink and see if she can find the can of pink air freshener which her mum used to squirt round. And finally, she's going to throw away the cigarette butts. She's going to pick up each one; she's going to put them into the carrier. And then she's going to put the carrier into the outside bin and see if her mum can tell her when to wheel it round to the front. If this fails and her mum can't remember, then she's going to keep an eye on her neighbours. See when they put theirs out, and then she'll do the same.

And her mum will be so surprised. So grateful for how hard Issy's worked, that it might remind her of how to stand up to Dave.

Yes, she's going to do that as soon as she gets home. She'll clean the house and make everything better. She gives herself a small shake. A smile. And then she could always offer to go to the Co-op for her mum. Get some bread and maybe some cheese. Her mum likes cheese on toast. She could do that easily enough. Her throat widens at the wonderful thought.

Yes, that's what she's going to do.

'T.' It was a hiss. Next to the post office where she'd just been to buy cigarettes. He was at the side of the shop, leaning against the wall with a lazy grin on his face which swooped at her insides. He was scruffy and dirty-looking with his hood up and some grime in his fingernails. But the look in his eyes, like he'd been waiting for her for a very long time, cut through.

'Deano.'

He grinned again, stepping back into the shadows of the alley between the post office and the Co-op. Pulled her to join him, his eyes like magnets. 'Where've you been for the last few days?'

She found herself stepping into the darkness with him. He smelt of the woods and a bonfire and a smaller scent of lager. 'Oh, you know . . . school and friends and stuff. I'm kind of trying to act normal. Like last month didn't happen. That's what we're all doing, isn't it?'

He nodded. Eyeing the cigarette pack in her hands. Distracted. 'Gi's one of those.'

As she unwrapped the cellophane and pulled open the pack she looked at his clothes. They were slept-in and damp. 'Where've you been sleeping?'

He shrugged and pulled on the cigarette like he hadn't had one in a very long time. 'Around . . . 'ere and there . . . Tam's, when his old lady works nights. Bulldog's sometimes. Otherwise the mill.'

'You must be knackered. All this hiding – it can't be nice.'

He shrugged again, breathed a plume of lavender-coloured smoke through his nose and tilted his head to one side. 'Naaah, it's OK. We need one more job and I'll get enough money together to move off for a bit. Till all the shit's died down.' He placed a finger on her wrist. A tattooed finger. She could feel the heat even through her school blazer. 'I miss you, though. You don't come to the mill any more.'

Ribbons of goodbad feelings rippled under her ribs. 'Um . . . I don't think Adam and that lot like me any more.'

He sucked air through his teeth, pressing his finger harder on her wrist. 'Since when have you taken any notice of them?'

'I thought they were your friends?' She was confused by the finger. Entranced by the half-smile on his face. After all that had gone on, he still wanted to see her. She still seemed to matter.

He used his other hand, the one with the cigarette, to smooth down some of her hair. He'd never done this before and she was bothered by the effect it had under her ribs. His cigarette was dangerously close to her face. She could feel the heat. Like her whole face was warming up under his gaze. 'Yeah – but so are you. You're special, T. Don't forget. I missed you.'

Her heart hovered; it was hard to breathe.

He stepped closer. 'I'd kiss ya, but I'm not sure you'd want that. I've bin outside for a long time.'

His eyes were hard and burning and deep and magnetic. She couldn't process his words and his look at the same time. It was enough to deal with the cigarette at the side of her face and the tattoo fingers still on her wrist. Maybe she swallowed. Maybe her knees wobbled a bit. Maybe she closed her eyes for a fraction of a second. Either way she didn't say no. She was certain of that.

So he leant closer and put his lips on hers.

And it felt nice. And warm. And outdoors tasting. And cigarettes. And lager. And rough at the side of her mouth. And a nudge of his tongue. And she found that she could kiss him back.

Quite easily.

He leant back and smiled against the wall, taking a drag of his cigarette. His eyes were all lazy again. Thinking about something else.

'Who were those girls you were with just then?'

She'd been walking home with Lizzie and Kirsty from her form. She found it difficult to remember their names with the taste of him still on her lips.

'Girls from school. My tutor group. I'm meeting them in the park. I said I'd catch them up.'

'Why din't they wait?'

She frowned, bewildered by the question. 'We . . . we don't do that kind of thing . . . it's only two minutes away.' Her head was full of fog.

'Friends wait for each other. In my book.'

She didn't know what to say to this. But Deano wasn't finished. 'I was watchin' them as you walked up. Can't say I'm that keen. Think maybe they're not your real friends.'

She felt herself blush. She couldn't understand why.

He rested his head against the brickwork and washed his eyes all over her face. 'They laughed a lot, 'specially when you were in the shop. Think it may have bin 'bout you.'

A taste of something horrid flooded on her tongue. She couldn't take her eyes away from his. He'd glued them somehow. It was true, they did laugh a lot, and sometimes she wasn't sure what at.

'And I din't like the way they left you in the shop. That's disrespectful, if you ask me.'

'Um . . .' She found she was pressing a knuckle against her teeth. 'I don't think it's like that.'

He raised his eyes and sniffed, leaving four disapproving seconds before he spoke again. 'Whatever.' He tossed the cigarette to one side, where he stabbed crossly at it with a heel. 'I'm just tryin' to help, that's all. Maybe suggestin' that they might not be right for ya.' He shrugged again. 'Just sayin'.'

She swallowed again, confusion filling her lungs. She couldn't take her eyes off his. His finger was still on her wrist.

He laughed then and lifted the finger to her lips. Nodded at her mouth. 'You liked that, din't ya?'

Maybe she lowered her eyebrows as a yes.

And then he stepped back. Quickly, suddenly, so that there was no touching from him whatsoever. 'I'd best go.' He scanned his eyes over her shoulder. 'Too many people round 'ere.'

'When will—?' They were panic stutters. A shameful question. She shouldn't really ask.

He was cross with her, she could tell. Nobody questioned Deano. Nobody tied him down. He scowled over his shoulder, already halfway out of the alley. 'I'll find ya. I'll be watching ya. Don't forget.'

And then, just as he slipped into darkness she heard him say, 'Maybe we should go out one night. You and me, yeah?'

The very thought gave her lightning strikes behind her eyes.

Sophie

Sophie has her head in the coats. They tickle and graze her cheeks as she moves. The satin of a lining. The scratch of tweed. She can only just breathe. The back of her head rests against her dad's gardening fleece and she's standing on what she thinks might be a stray glove.

Harry has his thumbs pressed into her hips, his right leg nudging between hers. She can feel the sinews and the bones of his neck with her hands. Then the softness of a vein with a steady pulse against the pad of her palm. Her own throat clicks and swallows with every kiss.

He'd met her at the end of her garden path after school, all brave and jubilant because his plaster was finally off. He did a ridiculous little dance and pointed at his leg, which made her laugh. It made her forget how he was risking so much, standing there in broad daylight waiting for her.

'Look, no plaster.' He waved his hands like a conductor. 'No crutches.'

She grinned and reached for her keys, all too aware that Sam could turn the corner any minute – or, even worse, her dad could come home from work early. 'How does it feel?'

A smile split his face. 'Like heaven. Like I'm ten stone lighter. Like I take up half the space I used to.' And then he eyes her carefully, making her stomach swoop like a flock of starlings. 'Like I have the freedom to do whatever I want with my hands . . .' a rise of his eyebrows, a lowering of his voice, 'which is why I wanted to come and see you.'

She sniggered and dropped her bag by the front door. 'Well, you'd better come in, then.'

He was on her even before she'd shut the front door behind them. Taking her by surprise with his mouth and his warm breath and hands. He was right, it was like his hands had suddenly gained a new freedom. They moved all around her. Over her skin, over her school uniform, over her hair, over her mouth. And all followed by his kissing.

Sophie gulped, feeling like one gigantic pulse of her own. 'Um . . . my brother . . . Sam . . . he's likely to come home any minute . . .'

Which is how they ended up in the downstairs cloakroom, the one room downstairs with a lock; the room with all the coats.

They kiss for a long time. The ferocity is a shock. His insistent fingers burrow beneath her shirt. It's nice.

After a while, with pink cheeks and surprised eyes, he pulls away. 'Oh. My. God,' he says. 'Sorry. You OK?'

She laughs, her own eyes flickering away. Embarrassed. Her hair is attached to her dad's tweed jacket, his smart one. It spreads behind her. Some coins in a pocket shift with the movement, sliding softly over each other in the fabric. Like bells.

She nods. 'Yeah.'

There's the faint smell of cigars. Which is weird because no one in the family smokes. But it's definitely on one of the coats. And also the smell of a bonfire and grass. She sifts her face between one hanging garment and the next. She feels like a kid for a minute. But then Harry's fingers on her hips remind her that she's not.

He's grinning. 'Sorry, don't know what came over me.'

She smiles and pushes him gently away. 'It's just that Sam's due back any minute now and . . .'

Which is when they hear a key in the lock. *Please be Sam,* thinks Sophie. She can manage this so much easier if it's Sam.

Harry takes his fingers off her waist and steps quietly back. Holding his breath and watching her carefully, his eyes are ablaze with unsaid words.

'Sam?' she yells from behind the door, as the front door slams shut.

A stamping sound and something dropping on the floor.

'Sam?' she yells again. Her eyes hold Harry's.

'Yeah.' A muffled, bored answer from her uninterested brother. He's probably already checking his phone. She pictures him standing in the hallway, head bent, scrolling down the screen. Makes her voice deliberately indifferent.

'Just checking.' She moves her eyes from Harry's, afraid that she might laugh. 'Just checking you aren't some serial killer.'

'Not today, I'm not,' Sam answers, still not really concentrating. 'Can't guarantee I won't be tomorrow, though.'

Sophie rolls her eyes at Harry. Mouths *He thinks he's hilarious* at him. And he replies with a slow grin and fingers which smooth her hair off the coats for her.

She yells again. 'Won't be long.'

They hear Sam's footsteps go through to the kitchen and Sophie makes a quick calculation. A creature of habit, Sam is likely to grab himself a drink from the fridge and rifle through the cupboards to find some biscuits. Then, if he does as he always does, he'll take the packet upstairs, along with the drink, put on some music and skim through his laptop pretending he's doing his homework. Banging shut his door in the process, a very definite sign to his younger sister not to disturb.

As if in confirmation she hears the hiss of the fridge door and the click of the kitchen cabinets. She places her fingers on her lips to Harry, who looks like he wants to make a break for it, suddenly realizing how much trouble his rash behaviour could result in.

'Hang on,' she whispers. 'Wait for him to go upstairs.'

Obedient, his skin now paler than two minutes before, Harry nods.

The sound of heavy trudges on the stairs follows shortly. She's pleased Sam's so predictable. When they hear the bedroom door close and the beat of some song throb on to the ceiling, Sophie grins with mild hysterics. 'OK, it's safe now.' Her voice shakes with laughter.

He squeezes her shoulder and unlocks the door. They poke

their heads round the doorway into the empty hall. They scuttle silently over Sam's school bag and shoes and reach for the front door in double-quick time. They're both shining with laughter. It's like they're in a sitcom.

They sidle round the corner, by the side wall, where nobody can see. There's a bit more kissing, finishing off what was started in the cloakroom. But it's more half-hearted as if, out in the open, they're suddenly shy again. Harry sighs, moves away slightly, leans back against the wall, drawing up his knee so the flat of his foot is on the brickwork. He bites a nail. Sophie wants to tell him to stop.

'What's up?'

He pulls a face, moves his tongue around his nail. 'I'm just annoyed.'

'At what?' Sophie's getting worried.

'That we can't be open about this. That we have to hide and stuff.' He sighs and places his foot on the ground in a small stamp. 'I've really wrecked things, haven't I?'

She tries to be light, rubs his shin with her foot. 'You wrecked the house, but you didn't wreck us.'

He shakes his head, irritated. 'What kind of future have we got where we have to lock ourselves in toilets away from your dad?'

Sophie leans on the wall next to him. She lightens her words. 'It's only been a few weeks, Harry. Give him time. Maybe he'll come round in a while. When Tye wakes up then everyone will feel a lot better about things.'

He shifts his back against the brickwork and looks carefully at her. 'Have you ever thought that he might not?'

She winces at the words and gives her head a violent shake. 'He will. He's a fighter. And he's got a lot to fight for.' She sighs. 'And then everything will sort itself out and we'll be allowed out in the open.'

He rolls his eyes and looks at her from under his fringe. 'You reckon?' His lips are uncertain.

'Look, Dad'll start to feel better once the house is back to normal as well. At least we've got the telly and the carpet now. And once the plaster's completely dry it can be decorated. Dad's already got the colour charts. You might even have done him a favour. He wanted it redecorated ages before the accident.'

Harry looks unconvinced. He stares at his chewed nails crossly. His words are quiet. 'The date for the court hearing's come through.'

A plummet in her stomach. 'Oh.'

They don't look at each other. But the mad kissing in the coats seems suddenly days ago.

Harry shifts on his legs. They're probably still a bit sore, Sophie thinks. He shoves his hands in his pockets to protect his nails from his teeth. He gives his head a quick shake. He sniffs. 'Yeah, three weeks' time. Happy Easter! You lot will be getting chocolate, I'll be getting a prison sentence.'

She pulls in a breath. 'What? You won't go to prison, surely? Tye's alive.' She kicks the brickwork.

He pulls down one side of his mouth. 'It's possible, apparently – although admittedly not very likely, seeing as this is my first offence. They say it depends on the judge and how sorry I am, and of course whether Tye stays alive.' He looks at her and grimaces. 'Best-case scenario is a hefty fine, apparently,' he adds. 'And I lose my licence, obviously. God, it was the worst decision I ever made.' His words shake in the back of his throat. He closes his eyes and leans his head back against the wall so that Sophie has a blank face to look at.

She likes his face. She's liked it since the moment she set eyes on him in the car, behind the wheel, in her lounge. It's wide and pleasant and his cheekbones are prominent, especially for a boy. His pale hair is soft and stringy over his ears, and his eyes – when he's laughing or angry – flash bolts of blue, like a small electric storm on his face.

She reaches out and touches his cheekbone. It's cold.

He turns his face away. 'Sorry.' All the happiness from earlier drains right away. 'I'd better go. I promised Gemma I'd help her before she goes to work.'

Sophie resists the urge to sigh; to whine that yet again, Gemma's manipulating him. It's like she has her fingernail pressed into Harry's forehead and he does whatever she says, even from a distance. Like he's on a remote.

'What does she need help with?'

Harry looks coy, stares at his toes. 'Oh, it's her turn to make tea but she wanted to go to work, it's a special gig apparently, so I said I'd do it for her.'

'Held at gunpoint by your sister?' Her words form sarcastically in her mouth but he doesn't seem to notice. Instead he shakes his head and replies.

'Bad choice of words there. Gemma hates guns. Hates them with a passion. Switches films off with any form of shooting.

Won't even look at a toy gun without wincing. She's strange like that.'

Sophie clamps her lips underneath her teeth and nods slowly. 'No offence, but she's a bit weird, your sister.' She stops herself from finding all the other adjectives she could use for his twin. She holds her breath. Harry gives a wry smile.

'She goes through phases. She's not so bad now. A bit obsessed with the job at the NEC, but quite calm. She made some friends a while back who weren't good for her. Getting her into bad stuff, stuff she's regretting now. I think she's moved away from them now. Reckon this job – it's kind of good for her. Gets her away from them. Maybe focuses her a bit? I dunno, she's a bit weird, yeah. But she's my sister and most of the time we get on. You should have seen her when she was sixteen. She was seriously loopy then. Drove Mum and Dad crazy. Between you and me I think she went boy mad. I think that's when she might have started seeing blokes, blokes a lot older than her. Sometimes it's like she's got a screw loose, and then other times she's the wisest person I know. And now Dad's left, she's got nobody apart from me to turn to. She was a proper "daddy's girl". They did loads of stuff together. She could twist him round her little finger and she loved every minute. Now he's too obsessed with this new girlfriend. Reckon she feels a bit pushed out.' He shakes his head. 'God, sisters!'

Sophie smiles. 'We're a cool breed.'

A small bang above them makes them jump. They both look up. It's the bathroom window being pulled shut. Sophie makes out the darkness of an arm. She can't remember whether the window was open when they got there. Forces a thought to the back of her head.

Harry gives her his lopsided smile again. Steps towards her. Leans his head into her neck and lifts her hair. She hears the word 'Sorry,' whispered under her ear, like velvet.

It feels better.

Once he's gone, Sophie is listless. She drifts around downstairs, not wanting to go upstairs to think about homework. Her skin is still hot and jumpy from Harry's hands. His question about Tye gives her shivers. She wanders into the kitchen, where she looks around for a note: often her dad leaves instructions for her and Sam to put something in the oven or to get something out of the fridge for tea. Jacket potatoes. Preheat the oven. That sort of thing. Only today there's nothing. Just a sour smell from the dishcloth and one of Sam's farts still hanging in the air. Sophie turns up her nose, pulls open the fridge door and grabs some juice.

Her thoughts are a mess. She's not sure that what she said to Harry is ever going to happen. The way her dad talks about him, it's as if he's some kind of drunken, violent criminal who bashed their house up on purpose. It's hard to hold this image of him up against the real Harry she knows. The sensitive, quiet, guilt-ridden boy who still can't look at the house without wincing. Who she can't believe was stupid enough to drink and drive. To be honest it doesn't quite add up. In the last few weeks, when she's really got to know him, he's never once shown any sort of recklessness or wildness which would make him crazy enough to drink and drive. Quite the opposite. He's been the one to be sensible; to rein in his wild sister; to hide behind locked doors so that they can't be seen by her brother. It doesn't make sense. And she can't help thinking that Gemma has something to do with it. Could she have somehow forced him to drink and drive? Was this yet another favour which Harry was prepared to do for his sister?

She takes her drink up the stairs, dragging her school bag behind her. She has six biology revision questions to do and she's babysitting later on. So she doesn't have much time.

It's a shock when she opens her door.

There, in her normally quiet, deodorant-smelling, untidy room is her brother. He's on her bed, his back upright and his face a twist of thunder.

'What are you doing here?' They both hate their rooms being invaded by each other. They've set strict rules which they both abide by: *Don't enter without permission*, *Always knock* and *Never go in when it's empty*.

Her shoulders ride high with the question.

'Waiting for you.' His eyes are bright with accusation.

'Well I'm here now, aren't I? So get out!'

He sits firm, her quilt crumpled around his legs. His fists are balls of angry knuckles. 'How could you, Sophie?'

Hot guilt in her throat. It slurs her words. 'How could I what?'

'How could you see that idiot? How could you be seeing the dickhead who crashed a car into our house and nearly killed your best friend? You got some kind of death wish or something? Dad'll go mental!'

Sophie closes her eyes. So he'd heard. He'd been in the bathroom all the time they'd been outside at the side of the house. He must have heard every word. Every kiss.

Sophie flushes at the thought.

'He's not a dickhead.'

Sam's lips twist. 'He was drunk, he was driving, and he smashed up Tye and our house. In my book that's dickhead behaviour.' He shudders with obvious disgust. 'And now I find him here, sneaking around, hands all over you.' He shakes his head. 'God, Sophie, that's some bad taste.'

Sophie takes a step back, banging into the bookcase. 'It's not like that . . .' She has this image of Harry's fingerprints on her skin, under her shirt. Showing up in ultraviolet light like she was being scanned for evidence. It gets hard to breathe then.

'Seriously, Dad will never ever forgive you. There's no way he'll allow this.' He looks all self-important sitting there on her bed. She hates him with perfect clarity.

She grips on to the bookshelf behind her. 'It's not up to him who I see and who I don't see, and it's certainly not up to you.'

Sam laughs then. Shakes his head, looks at her with withering sympathy. It isn't nice and it makes Sophie angrier. 'We both know that he can make it very difficult for you.' He stares hard. 'What the hell were you thinking? Of all the boys in the world you picked the worst one. Are you going all revolutionary on us? Trying to make a point? 'Cause it's a crap point and it's going to wind Dad up the wrong way. And what about Tye? How do you think he'd feel?'

'Shut up!' She puts her hands to her ears, hating every word.

'Dad will never forgive a drunk driver after what happened to him, we both know that!'

'He doesn't have to know.' It's almost a whisper.

Sam coughs up an ugly laugh. His fists squeeze tight on her quilt. 'You want me to keep this a secret? You must be joking. I'm with Dad on this one. I don't normally give a shit who you're seeing. But even *I* draw the line at drunk criminals.'

The words are horrible in her bedroom. They don't belong. Hot tears swell behind Sophie's eyes. She gulps them away. She won't cry in front of Sam.

'Get out! Just get out. I hate you in my room and I hate you, full stop.' She lunges for the door handle, surprised at the shake in her fingers.

Sam fixes the snarl back on his lips and stands up off her bed. She immediately feels better. It was bothering her that he was on her quilt like that.

He takes a slow walk to the door. He flicks her hand away off the handle. He smells sour as he brushes past her.

'I'm not keeping this secret, Sophie. Either you dump him or I tell Dad *exactly* who you're hanging round with.'

Her fingers quiver. She yanks them behind her back. 'Get out, I said.'

He steps on to the landing and laughs. 'You're playing a stupid game. And it'll end in a mess. You watch.'

Sophie hates how he marches across the landing like a head teacher. Nose in the air, hands in a perfect prayer position behind his back. She visualizes running at him and pushing him, face down, on to the carpet.

She likes the picture, so she holds on to it.

She turns round, walks into her room, slams the door so it vibrates in its frame and jams her forearm into her mouth. From here, with her teeth sunk into her sleeve, she can scream out the fury which has been suffocating her insides for the last five minutes.

And then she stands in front of her mirror, at last letting the tears slide down her cheeks.

They slide for a good ten minutes.

Things got worse.

Every day there was something to upset her. Every day there was the continued talk of Stephanie and her scarred face. It was always inevitable – she was the richest, coolest girl in school with a wardrobe to die for and the glamour to go with it. Her story was never going to fizzle out. In fact it was quite the opposite. The gossip rampaged and gained momentum: she was a hero. She was running to Deano to wrestle the gun off him. She was fighting to keep the family silver. She was only in the pool house with Simon because he needed to talk. She was being entered for a bravery award. There might even be a blog.

And every day there was one of Deano's gang to greet Gemma. To remind her. To watch over her so that she'd always know. There would be someone in the bus shelter, smoking, watching, sending her messages with the looks on their faces or the set of their shoulders. Sometimes all four of them were there, sometimes just one.

Then Deano's gang noticed her brother. And this was easily the worst. Her lovely, innocent brother who would never have got himself into such a mess; who had never got into a fight in his entire life; who wouldn't harm a fly. Her brother: the thinker, the artist and the sensitive one.

It was a day in week five of the shooting aftermath. A day when everything was shrouded in a haze of rain which gave everything a grey sheen. The sort of rain which drenches you without you really noticing.

She spotted them before her brother. They were all there this time. All four of them: Adam, Tam, Bulldog and Jinx. And they were waiting for her. She knew they would be. It would be like this for the rest of her life.

Only this time they moved forward as one. A well-choreographed line which took her by surprise.

And this time they weren't looking at her. This time their eyes – all of them – were seeking out her brother.

The four of them jostled forward, brave in their numbers. They were each wearing the same uniform of skinny jeans and hoodies. Bulldog's Afro glistened and the rest had hair which stuck to the sides of their faces. She was pushed to one side almost immediately by Tam.

'Ow!' was about all she could manage, standing there in the gutter.

'Something y'need to know.' Adam's finger was centimetres from her brother's nose, so that he had to pull his neck back. Harry didn't say a word, but his jaw was set in that determined stubbornness Gemma had always hated.

'Harry,' she said urgently – wanting to warn him of the danger they were in. She had a fleeting thought of the gun. Surely Deano still had it.

Harry didn't even look at her. His eyes were fixed horribly on to Adam.

'What?' Adam's finger was getting closer.

'Your sister – she's not as innocent as she looks.'

There was a small pulse in Harry's throat – other than that, nobody would know how difficult this was for him. He didn't look at her.

'My sister's got mixed up with a shitty gang. She knows she's made a mistake.'

Tam sniggered, a high, horrible hyena laugh. 'You've got no idea.'

Harry straightened up, looked from Adam to Tam. She'd never seen him look so strong. 'So tell me, then. Tell me something I don't know.'

Adam's finger wavered very slightly. There was a hesitancy in his wrist which was reassuring. 'She was involved in that shooting. The shooting at that girl Stephanie's house.' He stepped back, waiting for the information to filter through. To shock. To surprise. To horrify.

It didn't. And she was wide-eyed with gratitude. Her quiet, nervous brother was standing up to these idiots like she'd never been able to.

'I know.' His words were quiet so that the others had to strain to hear. 'I know.'

It set them back. They weren't rehearsed for this. They'd thought he'd be amazed and horrified. Gemma watched as they glanced at each other, unsure of their next move.

Adam collected his thoughts before the others. 'Well, she'd better watch herself, cos one word from us and she's in the shit.'

The thought jabbed at her, like it had been doing for the last five weeks. She needed their silence just as they needed hers.

Adam continued. 'She needs to keep her mouth shut, otherwise *she* –' and here he returned the finger to her brother's forehead, '– and now *you* – are gonna get everything you deserve. She let us down. No one does that to Deano. No one sets us up.'

Harry kept his voice quiet underneath Adam's louder threats. His next words shocked her.

'And where were you lot? Where were you all when the police turned up?'

'What the fuck's that s'posed to mean?' She could tell Bulldog was angry. His chin wobbled and his eyes were wide livid circles. Harry was crazy. Harry was absolutely crazy to be doing this. Gemma's heart battered under her ribs.

Harry placed fake-casual hands in his pockets and lifted his chin. 'It means that while you continue to intimidate her, she's got every reason to go to the police and tell them everything.'

There was a small, hesitant cattle shuffle in the group of four as his words sank in. One of them, she wasn't sure which, blustered something like, 'If we go down then we take her with us.'

To which Harry, even braver now, forced a smile. 'She'll get off. She's younger than you lot. She was being used and manipulated by some older and well-known bullies. If she goes along with the police and gives them all your names they'll protect her. Haven't you seen those cop shows on TV?'

There was a split, poisonous second where horror spilled on to Adam's face. 'Shut up, rich boy,' he blustered. Bulldog's fingers flexed into a fist and Tam flushed red.

She could see the signs. See that things were going to go wrong. That these boys were itching for blood now. That their plans had gone wrong and they weren't in the mood for forgiveness.

'Harry.' She touched his arm. 'Harry, shut up. I think we should go now.' She could see the blood. She could hear the gunshot. She could see the scarring on Stephanie's face. Even in hiding Deano would have some influence. Gemma wasn't stupid. She knew how these things worked. Her brother's words, although thrilling and shocking, scared her too. She knew these boys wouldn't let someone like Harry have the last word. She could almost smell the bloodshed. 'Please, Harry.'

He shook her hand off. His eyes were glowing with something she'd never seen before. He was quiet. He was shy. He was artistic. He wasn't the type to get into a stand-off with four legendary psychos.

'What are you doing, Harry? Just come, will you?' She hated how her voice wavered in the late-afternoon greyness. She saw how it made Bulldog brave. How her weakness made him strong.

In the end Harry wasn't ready. She watched in horror as first Bulldog, then Tam lifted fists as high as their heads. As they slammed them first, then second into her brother's face. She heard the crunch of cartilage and saw a smear of blood spread and bloom over his cheek. His body folded in half and he grunted as air was pushed from his lungs.

Gemma screamed and shook, images of the gun flooding her head. The remembered sensations of repulsion and terror smacked at her insides. She was rooted to the spot, her limbs vibrating.

Her brother was on the floor now. In the gutter with the brown slime of leaves. Curled up in an attempt at protecting himself. Adam had an ugly laugh on his mouth and he was getting ready to kick the soft part of Harry's waist.

She screamed again, making her own siren of alarm, and this time it worked. This time a shopkeeper hurried out of the newsagent's a few metres down the road, yelling about calling the police. His words were such a relief that Gemma found her legs working again. Just enough to move to her brother; just enough to stretch to his arms in order to help him up; just enough to act as a barrier while Adam decided what to do with the foot. It hung in mid-air, wavering.

Thankfully, Adam chose to scarper with his mates,.

Harry was all soft. All moaning. All bloody. He didn't look like he was ready to take on four psychos any more.

There was a brown leaf sticking to his cheek like a leech.

It made her cry as she peeled it off.

Twenty minutes later, as she was dabbing at his wounds with TCP-scented cotton wool in the utility room, she found his eyes. 'Thank you,' she whispered.

He grinned and winced at the cotton wool under his eye. 'S'OK.'

'I didn't know you could be like that.' She dropped the cotton wool into a bowl and took a dry one from out of the pack.

He smiled then and shrugged his shoulders. 'Neither did I?'

And then they laughed together. Maybe it was hysteria, maybe it was fear. But his admission had them giggling like they were seven years old all over again.

The small TCP-smelling room echoed with their childish laughter. It was nice.

She saw Deano the very next day. By chance he'd invited her to a party. Said to get dressed up and sparkle. And when he met her at the postbox at the end of the village she could see that he'd made an effort too. He smelt of aftershave, and he'd washed his hair so there was a wave in it at the back of his neck and something like a quiff at the front. He had on some clean skinny jeans and a pair of trainers she'd not seen before.

As she walked up to him she felt the familiar jitters of good and bad, like he was an addiction; a poisonous, glorious drug; a guilty secret. He looked her over approvingly, then nodded.

As they began to walk up the hill to the bus stop she plucked up the courage. 'Your friends, Deano . . . they don't like me. They keep trying to scare me and my brother . . . every day on the way home from school.'

She felt like a little girl.

He shrugged. 'S'a free country. I can't call them off, they're not my dogs.'

'But they're really intimidating.' She had to skip a bit to keep up with him.

He rolled his eyes and slowed down for a minute. 'Look, they're just protective of me. They don't want it to 'appen again.'

She felt a sob in her throat. 'I didn't set you up.'

Another shrug. 'Just walk home a different way.' He stepped forward again, past the glitter of an oil spill on the road. 'Look, let's get to this party. It'll cheer you up.'

He walked really fast.

The party was at a house on Elms Road, an estate on the edge of town with a reputation. Lots of money and no questions asked about where it had come from. It was a house party. A proper one with beer in the fridge and music in the front room. She was surprised that Deano went to parties like this; it was a far cry from the mill. But he seemed at home as the door opened for him and he grabbed the hand of a man who was around the same age as her dad.

Turns out that Deano knew everyone and everyone knew Deano. It was bewildering. Men of all ages (there didn't seem to be many women) clasped his hand or cuffed his neck or slapped his back like he was an old friend.

They stood in the kitchen by the fridge for most of the night and man after man greeted Deano. She'd never realized he was so popular. She'd thought it was just the gang at the mill. He was admired, everyone liked him – they were even nice to Gemma. It felt good – to be with Deano – to have these men act attentive and smiling while she stood at Deano's side.

And to be fair to him, he never left hers.

He smoked all night and drank beer after beer. Kept handing her the odd one, reminding her from behind his tattooed fingers to be nice, his voice slightly strained. But she was always going to be nice. She wasn't that sort of girl. She'd been brought up to be nice.

The men were older than Deano. All smarter and drunker and smearier in the face. To be honest, she wasn't that keen on them. She didn't like the way that they looked at her and she didn't like some of the things they said. But it seemed to matter to Deano that she kept smiling. And when he leant a thigh against hers, or squeezed her waist, it helped.

Besides, it didn't matter. She knew about middle-aged men. Her dad was a walking mid-life crisis. She knew how to make them smile and make them laugh. It was what she'd been doing at home for a while now. Harry always told her she could wrap their dad round her little finger. This was much the same.

She wondered if Deano would kiss her on the way home. Like he'd done in the alley by the post office.

And he didn't even mind when it was time for her to go home. When she'd really had enough of the standing and the smiling. They stood at the postbox while he lit up a fag. The street light shone on his forehead. His good looks made her swallow.

'You did well there. My mates thought you were a stunner.'

She could smile at this. 'Thanks.'

'They said they'd like to see you again.'

She'd prefer to see him on his own, maybe at the mill. But if it pleased him and put him in a good mood, then maybe it was worth it. 'OK.'

'There's another party next Friday. Wanna come?'

She frowned. 'It's Lizzie's birthday. We were going to Zizzi's.'

He sent the cigarette through the darkness like a dart. 'Suit yourself.' He inhaled and drew away from her. 'She's a bitch and you'll find that out eventually.'

Another step back, so that it started to hurt her to breathe. He hadn't kissed her yet. She didn't want him to go. Not yet. Not without some kissing.

'I'll see what I can do.' In a rush. A blurt.

He nodded slowly, looking down at her top, her waist and then her legs. She felt a glow. 'Wear that skirt again, yeah? And maybe do your hair a bit different. Sort of *up* or something.'

She could feel a blush rise up her neck. She'd spent precisely forty-five minutes on her hair that night.

But it was OK because almost two seconds later, while she was still thinking that thought, he stepped closer and lowered his face against hers so she could smell his cigarette scent and feel the heat off his skin on to hers. His lips were the only thing that touched her. And it made all the hours by the fridge with the dodgy men worth it.

Deano was kissing her under a street lamp with warm breath that took away her own.

She'd definitely put her hair up next week.

*

Sometimes, when she allowed herself, after a time when she'd been greeted by Deano's gang with their vicious taunts and laughter. When there was nobody in the house, when she couldn't find a way of releasing a surge which pulsed under her skin, she gave in to something she wasn't proud of.

It involved a match, the ends of her toes, the patio and a lot of vinegary pain. It didn't last long, but the relief was always immense. Like something ugly sliding off her back which had been grabbing her and slowly strangling her for days and days and days.

On those days, and the days after, she allowed herself to wear shoes.

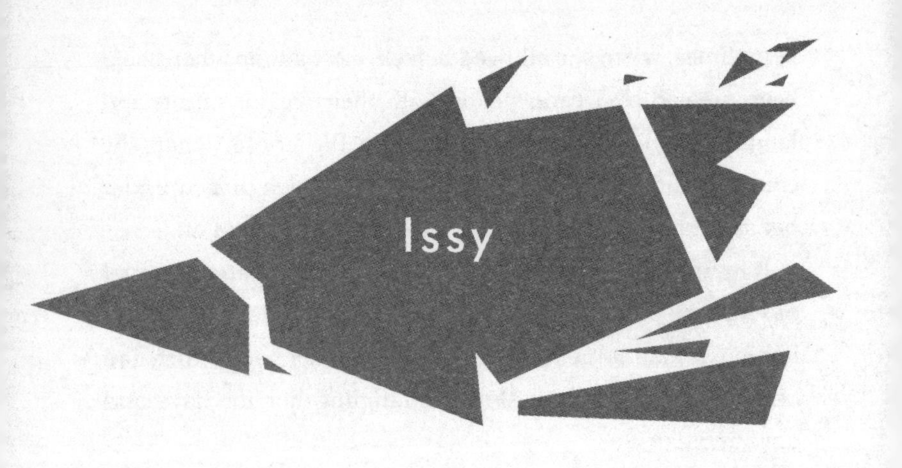

Issy

Issy's plan doesn't work, though.

She finds the carrier, finds the mop and bucket. She empties the fridge of the out-of-date stuff. That only leaves a bottle of vodka and a jar of meat paste, but this doesn't matter. She's going to replace it with food from the Co-op.

Dave walks in while she's mopping the floor, scrubbing around the bin. His face is pink and he looks like he's just woken up. Issy holds her breath. She wonders if he'll notice the fresher smell.

He sticks his head in the fridge, bending his knees, which click. Then he wants to know where his cheese is.

Issy tries to say that it had some mould on it; that she would replace it while the floor was drying, she was going to the Co-op.

Only she doesn't have time.

Because before she knows it, Dave has her right elbow tight in his hand. She's pulled off her feet, pulled away from the mop, which spills on to the floor so her socks get wet. She's told she's a stupid bitch. Some of Dave's spit lands on her eyelid when he says 'stupid'.

And then she's yanked across the front room, tripping on her tiptoes, her feet getting muddled up with his. Her arm socket hurts from where he's pulling her arm. She's learning to say nothing, though. Learning that complaining will only result in another black eye. And she doesn't want that. She wants to go to school on Monday.

So she swallows the shout. Swallows down hard.

She feels, rather than sees, Dave opening the triangle door.

And there's a surprise then. As he swings her full force, as she's crashed into the dark space of the under-stairs cupboard with a kick up the bum to prove his point, she finds that she's not on her own; that her mum's already there.

She falls on to the jumble of her mum's legs. Gulps back hot tears and feels her mum's damp arms wind round her.

They stay like this all day.

She decided she'd take him by surprise. Give him a treat, make him laugh. She remembered his kiss, what it felt like to have a fuss made of her by someone as renowned as Deano. Remembered how it felt when he said he was proud.

So in the end she gave in to these feelings and cancelled Lizzie's meal. But she'd not tell him. Instead she'd take him by surprise. Watch his eyes and his face light up when she walked into the party wearing the same skirt and her hair up like she'd been practising in the bathroom for the last three days.

It would probably make his day.

She thought about the kiss she'd get when they were walking home.

She rang the doorbell. The door was almost immediately opened by a drunk man who swooshed his eyes from the tips of her toes to the hair which was stacked high on the top of her head. There was sweat in the lines above his eyebrows.

Blasts of music hit her in the chest, but she remembered this from the last time. 'I'm here to see Deano. He's a friend.' She had to shout over the noise of the R&B.

The man with the sweat lines nodded like he knew. 'Any friend of Deano's is a friend of mine.' He opened the door wide for her to step in. Gemma pushed herself out of the first room and into the quieter yet crowded corridor. Scrambling over legs and party shoes, she found the kitchen through all the smoke and grabbed a bottle of something to make her feel better. She took a couple of swigs and started to look around for Deano. Her heart was banging under her ribs. She couldn't wait to find him. She knew he'd be pleased to see her.

He wasn't in the kitchen. Refusing to be nervous, she took another drink and skirted the bunches of men. She squeezed through bodies smelling of aftershave which hung in a cloud around them.

Not many women. Not many women at all.

She spotted him over her shoulder. He had his back to her, but she felt a cushion of relief somewhere inside. There were the beginnings of small curls at the back of his hair again. It felt nice to see them. He was deep in conversation with a big man who was giving Deano some money. The man looked an unlikely friend for Deano: a smart suit and a handkerchief in his top pocket. She couldn't imagine Deano with a handkerchief.

Deano's head was upright and straight and when he looked down at the money he shook his head. The big man scowled and reached again into his pocket for his wallet.

Gemma took another drink from the bottle in the doorway. She couldn't move at the moment, jammed as she was between two scrawny men who were slurring their words and jabbing fingers into the air. The big man offered more money to Deano and this time he seemed to accept, though it was difficult to work out what was going on from the back of his head.

She was about to push herself forward. Elbow the man with his jabbing fingers out of the way. Move forward to Deano, tap him on his shoulder, make his day. He was talking, the men around him standing with grins and cigarettes. They nodded in enthusiastic agreement. Like he was saying stuff that they liked. That they liked a lot. One of them moved on to his toes, sniggering, then rocked back on to his heels.

Gemma pressed forward, widening her elbows to make space. His voice and words began to make sense to her ears.

'Thinks she's a duchess, she does. All posh and rich.'

The man passed a hand over his sniggering mouth, nodding like an eager dog. 'Useful, though. Good at contacts . . .' he passed a wink at the man next to Dogman, who moved a slow nod up and down, 'and as fit as Megan Fox. Wants my hands all over her. If you know what I mean?' He winked at Dogman, who looked like he might be slavering. 'Gagging for it . . . honest to God . . . reckon she's a firework waiting to happen.' He slicked his fingers through his hair, lapping up his audience. 'I'm biding my time, though. Keepin' 'er guessing. Don't pay to give her everything at once.'

An actual giggle now from Dogman, who was beside himself with respect. 'Yeah?'

Deano nodded. 'Slowly, slowly catchy monkey – reckon she might come in very useful if I play my cards right. Reckon y'might all get the benefit if y'get what I mean. She's a beauty, there's no denying . . .'

Watching, mesmerized, from the doorway, she stopped where she was. Just for a second or two, to get a breather.

Deano shook his head, his foot against the door, his skin shining, and nodded. 'Patience, that's the key . . . reckon she'll be worth every poxy minute once I've finished with her. Eating out of my hand, you just watch. Maybe out of yours too.'

A sweat had broken out all over Dogman's forehead and nose.

Gemma stood there for a moment, frozen to the spot. She felt a wave of sick coming up her throat and started to panic that she might throw up there and then in the corridor. She crept back into the shadow of the man standing in front of her and started to ease herself out of the place. There was shouting and music blasting in her ears and she could hear a girl shrieking with laughter. She pushed herself out of the front room, knocking people's drinks and treading on feet. Some girl with prawn-cocktail breath shouted 'Oi!' in her face, but she didn't listen. She just turned her head and made for the front door. She needed to get out through that door in ten seconds flat. That was the target that she'd set.

The man who had opened the door in the first place saw her trying to turn the handle. 'Going so soon?'

'Yes,' she mumbled, fumbling with the handle. She gave it a shove with her bare knee and forced her way out.

She stood in the front garden, with the stars and the cold and the quiet. Breathed for the first time in minutes, resting her hands on her legs.

Gulping cold moonlight air, she fixed a thought into the centre of her head.

She never wanted to see Deano again.

On Thursday morning Issy decides she's going to tell someone. It's been bugging her and she wants to say something.

She gets out of bed like she has been doing for quite a while now: quietly, without waking anyone up. She's getting good at it. If there's nobody around then she can slip out to school before anyone realizes.

The uniform is a problem. Now nobody does any washing, her school clothes are getting scruffy. Yellow patches under the arms of her shirts, scuffs on her skirt and a stubborn yoghurt stain on her sweatshirt which no amount of scrubbing with a tea towel can get rid of. But at the weekend, when her mum was hiding somewhere and Dave was asleep on the sofa, she managed to wash three of her shirts in the bath with some old bubble bath which she got last Christmas. They drip-dried all Sunday on an airer behind the shed and although bubble-bath-scented, at least they're now clean.

She's getting good at leaving the house without anyone realizing.

She walks past the newsagent's feeling hungry. She has bags of time, so she can stop and buy something if she wants. And today she can. Because yesterday she'd had the foresight to watch Dave carefully when he got in from the pub. He'd been purple-fleshed and sweaty and had banged into the wall three times. But from where she was hiding, behind the curtains in the lounge, she'd seen him empty his pockets of his phone and money. He'd put them into the pottery bowl her mum used to keep on the coffee table for potpourri. It's been empty for quite some time now, ever since Dave tried to eat from it, thinking it was a bowl of snacks after the pub.

Last night he'd drained his hands of six pounds thirty-three in change. It landed with a clatter in the bowl and Issy stood behind the curtain silently urging him to fall asleep.

She was in luck. He'd fallen into snores before the news had finished, and she'd crept out from her hiding place, picking out three pound coins between her fingers.

And they are now in her purse in the side of her bag.

Skipping into the shop she buys a carton of apple juice for thirty-six pence and a packet of bacon-flavoured crisps at sixty pence. Two whole pounds left for dinner. The thought thrills her insides.

She doesn't see Sophie or her friend Maisie at school all day, despite keeping her eye open, and it's disappointing. Especially now she's made her important decision. Instead she has to stand on her own because Briony's away. Lunchtime without Briony seems to go on for ever. Even with a stomach full of cheese pie and chips.

At the end of the day Issy lingers by the school gates for two reasons. Firstly because she is hoping to catch Sophie, who's never out early, but also because these days there is no longer any point rushing home. There's no Mum to sit at the kitchen table with, to chat and discuss her day; no smell of cooking as she walks through the door; no clearing of the table to start on her homework. Her mum used to be very strict on this: *Always do your homework as soon as you get in – then you can relax and enjoy the rest of the evening.*

Now there's an empty, sour-smelling house with her hot, shivery, silent mum curled up in a cupboard somewhere, and Dave either in the house brooding or out of the house threatening to come home at any moment. The prospect makes Issy want to stay at school for as long as possible.

She leans against the damp school sign, letting the rest of the school drift by, their voices high with the rush of freedom. It's lonely watching everybody else laughing and talking, *wanting* to go home.

She searches the faces, expecting to see Sophie soon. But it doesn't happen. There are rehearsals going on in the hall. She can see figures on the stage. One of them is a tall dark boy who is a friend of Tye's. She's seen them together quite a lot. It's nice he has a friend other than Sophie. It makes Issy sad to think of Tye. He should have been there. He was going to be an actor when he grew up. Now he might not grow up and Issy feels sorry for Sophie because of this.

It's embarrassing to stay much longer. She feels small and awkward standing there, by the sign, when absolutely everyone has left. So she makes reluctant steps off the school premises towards home. She'll have to postpone her revelation until tomorrow. She's disappointed, having boosted herself up for the talk. It's a bit like being a deflated balloon.

She decides on a detour round the park. There's warmth in the air and a small scent of spring. Someone somewhere has cut a lawn. It's a nicer thought than home.

At the bottom of the park is a storage container. It's a rusting green cuboid, ugly against the olive of the trees behind it. It holds sports equipment for the rugby and football teams who play there once a week. There are scratched-out words scarring the green; Briony and Issy live in fear of having their names found in the paintwork. Some of the things written there are far from complimentary. They tend to do a weekly check.

Today, Issy decides, is one of those days.

She skirts the container, passing her finger along the scratched paintwork, rough under her skin, studying the words carefully. Nothing new today.

Her leg still hurts from last week. If she walks for too long it starts to give way. There's a bruise like a purple world map on the side of her thigh; it hurts if she puts pressure on it. It's because of her leg that she stumbles on some loose stones. Just a small stumble, but one that slackens her grip and sets her head round the back of the container, where she wasn't thinking of going. She gives a short yelp.

Right in front of her are two figures wound round each other, up against the side of the container. They're tangled.

His hair colour gives it away. It's pale blond; Sophie's boyfriend's pale blond. And the person he's wrapped around – her shoes give her away – is Sophie.

Issy can't see their faces because they're locked on to each other, attached at the mouth. She sees no hands but the hands are there, moving around under their clothes like kittens under a blanket. Their feet are in a neat row. It goes Harry first, one way, then Sophie's two the other way, then Harry's at the end. Four soldiers.

There's a noise coming from Sophie's mouth. It makes Issy blush. She thinks about running back round the corner – it would only take three steps. But it's too late. Her yelp has disturbed them. Their hands wrench free from under the clothes like they are burning. Sophie spreads her fingers wide and Harry shoves his hands in his pockets. His mouth glistens with an embarrassing moisture. They both have exactly the same shade of rose pink filling their cheeks. Issy flushes too.

'Oh!'

'Issy!'

'Oh!'

Issy follows the wobble of Harry's Adam's apple as he swallows. His eyes skitter from Issy to Sophie back to Issy again.

Sophie's shoulders flop. 'Thank God!'

'Ummm . . .' Harry flexes his fingers in the pockets of his jeans.

Sophie shakes her head, smiling. 'Don't worry. Issy won't say anything, will you, Issy?'

Issy moves her head slowly from side to side. 'No.' But

she's not quite sure what it is she shouldn't say.

Cheered and suddenly confident, Sophie grins, then looks down at her top. Adjusts it with a slight smile. Harry doesn't look so sure. He takes in a breath and his chest rises under his shirt. 'Even so,' he looks down at his pockets, 'I think I'd better go. I promised I'd meet Gemma at four.'

Sophie narrows her eyes. For some reason Issy thinks Sophie isn't pleased about this. But she nods once and gives a tight smile with just her lips, not her eyes. 'OK.'

'Same time tomorrow?'

'OK.' Sophie's voice is quiet again.

It's a bit awkward when he's gone. Very silent. A little bit sad.

'The thing is, I really like him.'

They're walking back. At last Issy has someone to walk with. It makes her feel inches taller. Especially as it's Sophie. They're taking the shortcut back, through the woods, over the little bridge. Issy glows with how she's being spoken to. Like she's sixteen, not eleven.

She nods her head, plucking at a branch which has new green buds on it. Sophie seems to have a lot to say.

'Only, Dad and Sam, they hate him. Sam went crazy when he found out that I was seeing him. Threatened to tell Dad. Said that I had to dump him or else he'd blab.' She whacks a tree with a stick that she's picked up. Bits of blossom haze around. A piece gets stuck in Sophie's hair; Issy doesn't think she realizes. She doesn't say anything, because it's pretty.

'I feel so shit about Tye,' Sophie sighs. Issy sighs too. It seems to be the right thing to do. 'But anyhow, it's not up to Sam who I see and who I don't see. He's not in charge of me. He's horrible when he wants to be.' She looks at Issy like she's suddenly remembered she's there. 'God, you're so lucky you haven't got a big brother.'

Issy's doubtful. She fiddles with her own stick and feels a little bead of disappointment at the back of her throat. Right now an older brother might be what she needed. She gives a quick shake of her head. She doesn't want to think of that. She wants to enjoy the shine of walking through the woods with Sophie.

Another deep sigh; it looks like Sophie can't get enough of the woodland air. 'And I don't want to split up with Harry, he's by far the best boyfriend in years.' She gives a shy look. 'He's really nice. Sort of sensitive but in a good way. And I like being with him and I know he's into me. He makes me happy despite everything, Issy.' There's a small wobble in her voice when she says this. Issy nods because she's sure she's meant to.

They walk through the bit in the woods where the trees suddenly stop. Where there's a great pool of sunshine. It hurts Issy's eyes for a second, so she screws them closed, and then opens them wide. There are a few star specks at the back of her eyes, but it feels better. She notices Sophie doing the same.

She would love a sister like Sophie.

Sophie strides through the sunny patch, back into the gloom towards home. Issy has to use longer strides than she's used to, to keep up. She worries about her leg.

'So, we've decided to keep seeing each other. On the quiet.'

She gives Issy a steady gaze. Issy smiles warmly back. She's good at keeping secrets.

'I won't say.'

Sophie nods. 'I thought not. You can see he's great, can't you?'

Issy nods again.

'I mean, he's got his faults and everything. He's a bit of a worrier and he gets bossed around by Gemma. Now *she* gets on my nerves. I don't get why he puts up with her, she's a proper psycho. But apart from that, he's brilliant.' She sighs again as they come to the edge of the wood. 'Dad makes him out to be some kind of drunken yob. He's not – he's really nice. But I feel so bad about Tye.'

Issy nods again as she takes her turn over the stile on to the pavement in the crescent behind Sophie and Issy's road. The top part brushes against the bruise on her thigh. It reminds her of home. There's another drop of disappointment in her throat. It would be nice if she could do this whole walk all over again.

She wants to keep Sophie talking. It's lovely. 'Why do they think he's a drunken yob?'

Sophie screws up her forehead, looking irritated for the first time. 'Because of the car crash, of course. Because he'd been drinking when he drove the car into the house. Remember?' As if Issy could forget.

And then, like a flash of something golden, Issy suddenly remembers the decision she made this morning. The thing that had been bugging her for some time. Now would be the best time. Now would be so good. She could lay the sentence down in front of Sophie like the best ever present. And Sophie would be so pleased. So grateful. She might even invite her in for a drink before she has to go home.

The words are a tumble in her mouth before she can even think about it.

'But that's just it . . . Sophie . . . I mean . . . that's just it.'

Sophie's face is a crease of a frown. 'What do you mean?'

Issy peers up at her, her lips straining to get the information out. 'It wasn't him . . . It wasn't him who was driving . . . I was looking, you see. I was watching from the window. And it wasn't him. He wasn't driving . . . it wasn't Harry. It wasn't him, Sophie . . . it was Gemma.'

The piece of blossom in Sophie's hair detaches itself in a small breeze and lands between Issy's feet. Issy watches Sophie's incredulous stare with a heart that threatens to explode at any minute.

'What are you going to do?' Harry asked her.

They were sitting in his room. An evening when their mum was out and their dad was downstairs in front of *Top Gear*.

'I have a plan.'

He lifted a pen from the cluster in a basket on his desk. There was always a pen in his hand. He used the fingers in his other hand to sweep hair out of his eyes. Hope swam in their blueness. 'The police?'

She shook her head. 'No, I can't do that. I'd get implicated. They'd take me down with them. There's no doubt of that.'

'Come on, please. It was a mistake. A stupid mistake. Your first time. They'd let you off.'

She felt familiar tears well up behind her eyes. Tears which could come spilling out at any moment these days. 'I can't go through it. I just can't. I'm not strong enough for a court case and things like that. I'd be crap at standing up and telling the truth or defending myself. Besides – there's Deano. He's not like the others. I couldn't grass him up. He's got this sort of hold over me and it scares me shitless. One minute all I want to do is please him, the next he scares me to death. It's doing my head in. I don't know what to do. I need to get away.'

He flung the pen back in the basket, letting a sigh move the hair off his face. 'You wouldn't have to grass him up if you didn't want to. Besides, you're the strongest girl I know.'

'Not at stuff like this.' Her voice was horribly childlike. She pushed the heels of her hands deep into her eye sockets.

'So what, then? You're going to hire hitmen to get back at them? Knock them off one by one, leaving you and Deano to live happily ever after? Is this the kind of thing you do now?'

'Stop being horrible.'

Another deep sigh. 'I'm not being horrible. It's just . . . sometimes some of the things you do these days take me by surprise.'

She tucked her knees under her chin. 'Don't be like that. Don't be another one who hates me. I couldn't take that, I really couldn't. I've got no one any more. Don't be another one.'

He lifted himself off the chair at his desk and sat beside her on his bed. The soft sag in the mattress felt comforting. Nowadays her brother was the only one who could make her feel reassured. Everyone else, it seemed, was busy being suspicious of her or just downright angry. She knew she wasn't helping matters. Knew she'd become prickly in other people's company. Knew the tension coiled up inside her was making her impossible to like. Nobody knew her like her brother. He was the only good thing.

'I don't hate you, you idiot,' he said. 'I'm just worried about you. That gang – Deano's gang – they're watching your every move. Whatever you do they'll be there. I've seen what they're like. They'll never leave you alone. Not until you tell the police. It'll get them off your back. Please, Gems, please think about it.'

'No!' Her chin smacked on to her chest.

'What then?'

'I'm going to go away.'

'Where? Away from me?'

She nodded.

'When?' She hated the stutter in his voice. Hated the hurt which was flooding his eyes. It was the hardest thing to say.

'After the exams. I've done the research.' She watched as a horrid understanding prickled at her brother's eyebrows. 'I've been offered a job next year. Small City have offered it to me – you know, that band I was telling you about? They've got a world tour. They could be big. They're being called the next big thing. It's flattering that they've asked me, and it's my chance to get away. To escape. Away from all this.' She swept her hand round the room and the window. 'Away from Mum and Dad and their arguments. Away from Deano's gang. Even away from Deano. I'm just so confused. Away from the stupid kids at school. Away from Stephanie's face – you know I saw her last week, in the shop? She looked awful. Apparently she doesn't go out much any more – she's lost all her confidence. I hate her guts but I don't wish that on her, I can't deal with the fact that I was a part of it. The guilt, Harry. It's shit.'

'Away from me?' His voice was as soft and as a sad as a small pebble on a shingle beach.

She placed her fingers in his so they laced together, a weave of pale fingernails and knuckles. 'You could come too. We could work together.'

He winced. She knew the university he wanted to go to – in England. The one he'd picked out from the brochures and pamphlets. The one with the high-tech art department and its shit-hot reputation. She knew this was all he'd dreamt of for a very long time.

There was a silence then which inflated to fill the room. So that she found she had to pile it with words. 'You could take a year off and I could start all over again. We could do the job together. It's only roadie-ing and sorting out the tour. But it'd be brilliant, they're really nice people and it'd be a fresh start. I'd not get myself into bad situations. Be happy all over again. Only – only I can't go with a criminal record. There are countries which wouldn't let me in. Some are really strict. I need to steer clear of Deano's gang. Keep my head down and get my A-Levels. Then I can go. Escape it all. With or . . . without you.'

Her brother lifted his fingers from hers and placed a nail between his teeth, something he'd not done since he'd kicked the nail-biting habit at seven. It wasn't good to watch. But she saw him lift his chin in his clever brave way. He nodded at her just once, then looked away. 'I get that. I understand.'

Sophie doesn't know how she gets through tea. Her head is brimming with the knowledge. Fit to burst like a balloon full of water.

Her dad's made a lasagne – supposedly her favourite. And he insists they eat together like they do on the adverts. Only it isn't smiley and golden like TV. Sam is as moody as anything, checking his phone under the table every five minutes and interrogating her in between. Where has she been? What did she do between school and home? Like it's his right to know everything about her. He's letting her know that he's suspicious about Harry. He isn't thick, she knows that. But he's doing it right under their dad's nose and he's proving a point.

Her dad's in a foul mood. Let down by the decorators, yet again.

Sophie's pleased when she's allowed to skip pudding in order to finish her homework.

*

She has no intention of doing her homework. It can wait until midnight if that's what it takes. For now she has to deal with the chaos in her head and decide what to do. She lies on her bed, with her school books by her side just in case someone comes in, and she goes over Issy's information.

Can Issy be trusted to be right? Could she be lying? Was she perhaps mistaken?

But Issy was determined. She said that she'd been in the window for some time. Said that she saw exactly who was driving and she was one hundred per cent sure that it was Gemma in the driving seat and Harry by her side. And Sophie has to admit, she's seen Issy in the window on many occasions. It's her place. She's a lost little thing who is obviously lonely. The window was a place where she'd stand to watch the world go by and keep an eye on people. It can't be much fun in that house. She suspects that Dave isn't a great stepdad, and Issy's mum seems pretty quiet these days.

So, if it was true, what on earth is Harry doing taking the blame for his sister yet again . . . only this time wrecking his life in the process? Her head's jammed with it. It starts to hurt.

She makes a decision. Slams her fists into her quilt and stuffs her feet into her trainers. At the front door she shouts, 'Won't be long!'

'Where are you going?' Sam's at the lounge door like a greyhound.

'What's it to you?'

Her dad hovers out of the kitchen, a tea towel in his hand. 'What about your homework?'

'I need to get a book from Maisie. I can't do my work without it.'

Sam raises an eyebrow. He smirks. 'Yeah, yeah, yeah.'

'What's that supposed to mean?' Sophie could happily strangle him, the way she's feeling right now.

Sam looks at his dad. 'And you believe her . . .?'

Her dad twists the tea towel. 'Why shouldn't I?'

Before Sam can answer, because her hands are now shaking with the need to get out, Sophie interrupts. 'I'll be an hour at the most.' She pats her pocket. 'I've got my phone.'

Sam's angry. She can hear it in his voice. She won't look back. He shouts at their dad. 'It's the oldest trick in the book. Surely you don't believe her.'

Her dad's voice begins to rise, 'If she says she's going to get a book, then I believe her. Sam, what's your problem tonight?'

Sophie slams the door behind her, letting the argument rise without her. She can still hear their muffled words as she leaves the garden path. Sometimes her family are seriously annoying.

She pounds the pavements, taking two slabs at a time. She'd run if she could. She's so angry, she's bursting with it.

Past the Co-op. Past the newsagent's. Both still open. Past the garage.

To the bus stop. If she cuts through the alley she should just catch the seven-ten.

The bus is packed with old people on their way to bingo. She swings on to the front seat, where she can mooch alone without someone asking her how she is. She draws her knees up under her chin and stares out of the window.

She feels like crying. She misses Tye.

It's only three stops into town. Hardly enough time to get her thoughts together. Instead they hurtle around behind her eyes, making her dizzier and dizzier.

She'll admit to being in a state when she stands to gets off. In the doorway, while she's waiting for the bus to stop, she stares at her reflection in the glass of the door and feels unsure. She looks a sight. Hair a bit wild from her rush. A stain she'd not noticed on the front of her sweatshirt. Trackies she only usually wears to slob around the house. And no mascara. For the first time she wonders if she's doing the right thing.

Harry's house is lit up. Six windows throw gold light on to the driveway. Three cars on the drive. One wheelbarrow stacked with gardening. Loud music coming from the window directly in the middle. Shadows floating through the frosted glass of the front door. A shout of laughter. A sneeze. The scent of cooking mixed in with a fragrance from a tree by the third car.

She swallows at the front door again, remembering the last time that she was here. Feels the same nerves. She really wants Tye. Good, steady Tye, who makes her brave by just being there.

But it's anger that makes her press the doorbell. Anger that quivers in her finger. If Issy's right, then Harry's been lying. And if there's one thing Sophie hates, it's being lied to.

She gulps as the doorbell cuts through the family noises seeping through the glass of the front door. A ten-second wait, then the haze of a figure.

Let it be Harry. Please let it be Harry.

Gemma opens the door, her eyes wide and pool-like, her hair cleverly tousled. Another five seconds as her eyes wash over Sophie's trackies, the stain on her front and her wild, spectacularly messy hair.

Embarrassing.

'Oh, it's you.' Looking at Sophie like she's a piece of shit.

Sophie feels a tremble in her thighs. She's never known anger like it. Her fingertips pulse with it. She shoves some hair off her face. She hates this girl in front of her. Can't stand her lying, manipulative ways. And how dare she look at her like she's something she's scraped off her shoe?

'You were driving, weren't you?' There's a crack in her voice.

She's momentarily proud at the way Gemma's pink cheeks turn pale. At last Sophie's said something to affect her. Finally, a reaction.

Gemma steps towards the driveway, her bare feet curled over the step, her face suddenly tense. 'What?' Her hands have drawn the front door closed behind her. She doesn't want anyone to hear this.

A spark of power flashes behind Sophie's eyes. 'You weren't the passenger in the crash.' She raises her voice a fraction. 'You were the driver.'

Gemma widens her eyes so that Sophie can see a small trace of panic. She frowns, then leans back against the front door. Gazing at the stain on Sophie's sweatshirt, she shouts, 'Harry! Someone's here to see you.'

They stare at each other for the few seconds it takes for Harry to bound down the stairs. Sophie feels her backbone bristle. She watches as Harry's familiar frame joins his sister's at the door. It hurts to think that only a few hours ago she was feeling the satin warmth of his skin under her fingers. Now she wants to scream at him.

'Oh, hello.' He grins, friendly and a bit surprised.

Gemma twists round to look at him, her face suddenly ugly. 'You need to talk to Sophie. She's saying some crazy things.'

Harry's face crumples in bewilderment. Sophie fiddles with her fingers, suddenly awkward.

'What?' His forehead is divided by three puzzled lines.

Gemma points a shaking finger at her and repeats, 'She's saying some crazy things. Will you talk to her?'

Sophie puts him out of his misery. She doesn't care. Right now she wants to scream it off the rooftops. 'I know.' She swallows. 'I know that you weren't driving. That you were a passenger. That you've been covering for your sister all this time. That you've been lying to everyone, including me.'

Harry's Adam's apple shoots up, then down again. He blinks four times. He fires a look at his sister, then back at Sophie. In any other circumstances Sophie might feel sorry for him. But not at the moment. Right now she wants answers and she doesn't care how she gets them, or who she hurts in the process. She presses her foot on the step next to Gemma's bare foot and speaks clearly. Crystal clear. 'Isn't it a criminal offence to lie to the police?'

At this, Gemma lifts her hands wide, fingers spread, and

shakes her head at Harry. 'Will you take her somewhere to talk to her?' Her nose crinkles up, her forehead concertinas.

Sophie hates the way Harry does as he's told.

Every bloody time.

He puts a hand on her shoulder. It's hot and nervy and not at all warm like it was in the park a few hours ago.

'Get off.' She shrugs him away. 'Don't touch me!' She's cross to find tears blurring her vision.

He lifts his hand away. 'Sophie.'

'What?' She rounds on him, her voice shrill in the evening air. 'What have you possibly got to say to me that isn't a complete lie?' Her knees wobble. Her chest heaves.

He looks at her, his eyes a chemical mixture of sorrow and pain and blue electricity. 'Sophie, please come inside.'

'No!' It's a shout.

'Ssshh,' Gemma hisses. 'Just be quiet.' She yanks the door wide with tense, dramatic arms and takes hold of Sophie's wrist.

Harry takes hold of the other.

'No.'

'Please.'

'No!' Louder again.

Gemma looks really agitated now. Harry covers his mouth with his hand like it's him who's making the noise. He drops his head. 'Look, Sophie. If you come in I promise I won't lie. I promise I'll explain . . .'

Gemma's eyes are on fire. 'What?!'

Harry shakes his head.

At last, Sophie feels a small drip of curiosity. She exhales.

Shakes off the hands, lifts her shoulders. 'I'll come in on one condition.'

Gemma rolls her eyes. Harry nods. 'What condition?' His voice is gentle. It makes her want to cry.

'You have to be completely honest about everything. And I mean *everything.*'

Harry nods quickly, avoiding the looks from his sister, whose face is now thunder.

Sophie gets bundled up the stairs. Literally. There's no other word for it. Harry's behind her and Gemma's to her side. She feels like a prisoner in hiding. She wouldn't be surprised if a blanket was thrown over her head. She can hear laughter from the kitchen, and the pleasant chink of some glasses. It sounds all warm and like a party. But being jostled up the stairs like this, she couldn't feel less like a party guest.

Harry puts his hands on her waist. She can sense the hesitation. She pushes them off.

At the top of the stairs she gets led to the right. She steps on a carpet so deep it's as if she's walking through soft grass. Harry moves forward and pushes open a door. Gemma shoves her inside so that all three of them hover in the doorway to what is obviously Harry's room.

It's large and glowing with soft light thrown from a desk lamp in the corner and a table lamp next to his bed. In one corner is a space which he obviously dedicates to his art. There's an easel, some paint pots, giant sheets of paper and two impressive-looking tins full of every colour of pencil. Then there's his bed, made-up and plump-looking with a guitar-shaped cushion propped up on the pillows. Opposite, under the window, is the desk with the lamp and three towers of books. It smells warm and comfortable, of soap and fabric conditioner. A bit like Harry. It's relaxing, but the tense twins either side of her make her feel far from relaxed. She glares at Gemma. 'Will you leave us alone?'

Gemma widens her eyes as if to deny her, but Harry puts his hand on her arm to interrupt. 'Yeah, go, Gemma, leave it to me.'

'But—'

'Please.'

Sophie rolls her eyes.

Gemma folds her arms crossly. 'OK, but be careful. You know what you're like.'

Sophie feels like stamping on the delicate bare feet right next to hers. But Harry ushers her out, placing gentle hands on his sister's shoulders.

There's a silence when she's gone. Just some heavy breathing. And it's only after a bit that Sophie realizes it's coming from her.

Harry points to the bed. 'Sit down.'

'I don't want to sit down.'

He closes his eyes. 'Sophie.'

Tears glaze her eyes again. They make her throat swell so her words are thick. 'You lied to me.'

He steps back, against the windowsill, pulling his hand over his face. 'What's made you suddenly think this?'

She steps forward, her foot a heavy thump. 'Don't you dare deny it.'

He holds up his hands. 'OK, OK, OK, I won't lie.'

'It makes perfect sense. I didn't get it. I knew you weren't the sort to drink and drive. God, you're so careful about things. And then, when she said you weren't driving, then it all slotted into place.'

'Who said?' His chin lifts in interest.

'It doesn't matter. All you need to know is that there's a witness to the crash and they told me. And as soon as they said it, I knew.' Tears twist her voice. 'God Harry, you lied and lied and lied. To me, to the police, to the nurses, to absolutely everyone. You made me feel so bad, seeing the boy who put Tye in a coma, and all the while it wasn't you, it was your sister. I can't believe it, I simply can't believe it.'

She watches the ripples in Harry's throat. He looks over her shoulder. She can see the whiteness of his knuckles where they're gripping on to the windowsill.

'How the hell could you?' Her breath wobbles out of her. 'Why are you protecting your sister? Why do you always do everything she says? Even if it means that it wrecks your life? That you can't see your supposed girlfriend? That you might end up in prison? That you have a criminal record, for life? What kind of sister is she, to get her brother to cover for her? She's a bitch. A manipulative, scheming, selfish bitch who would happily see her brother in prison rather than own up to something that *she* did.'

Harry looks miserable. He slides down the wall so that he's sitting against the radiator, his head in his hands. 'I'm sorry. I didn't want to lie to you. Not to anyone, but especially not to you.'

'But you did.' Her words are suddenly slow. 'You put

your sister before everything. Including me. I felt so guilty for no reason.'

'I know.'

'I stuck up for you to my family. They said some horrible things and I stuck up for you.'

'I know . . . and I'm sorry.'

'But I don't get why.'

There's a slice of silence in the room then. It cuts through the air.

At last, after about a minute, Harry lifts his head, and with eyes so heavy they look painful, he speaks to her. 'I can't tell you.'

The anger starts to rise up in Sophie again. She feels the flush in her skin. 'Why can't you?'

'Because it's complicated. Because there are other people involved.'

Hands clenched tight, Sophie starts to shout again. 'And all these *other people*, they're worth it, are they? You're putting all of them before you and me, are you? They're really worth all the lies and the fact that we have to hide away from my family?'

'I hated that.'

She shakes her head. 'But you could have done something about it all the time! All this for your sister who has done nothing but make me feel like a piece of shit ever since you – no, sorry – since *she* crashed into our house.'

Sophie's been so rooted to the spot that her knees have started to ache. Harry pushes himself up off the floor. Takes steps towards her. Reaches out his hand. His face is a twist of distress. 'Sophie, I didn't have any choice.'

She bats his hand away with her wrist. 'And you still won't tell me why?'

He shakes his head, a glum look in his eyes. 'No, look, I know you think she's a bitch. I know you think she doesn't deserve it, but she does, I promise. Really, for a whole year, she's done stuff which you wouldn't believe. Stuff that I can't tell you about. She got herself into a shitload of trouble, and now she can't get into it any more.'

'What trouble?'

He lowers his head. 'I can't say.'

He's centimetres away. She can feel his heat. 'Then we're finished.'

'Sophie—'

'I hate liars, Harry. More than anything I hate liars. My mum spent two years lying to my dad while she was seeing someone else. I saw what lying does to people. And now I'm staring at another liar right now and he won't give me one single stupid reason. So we're finished.'

He exhales so that a part of his fringe blows up. His hands fall dejectedly by his side. 'I did it because it involves other people as well. Not just Gemma.'

Confusion. 'Who?'

'I really can't say. But trust me, Sophie. I didn't have any choice. I'd have done anything to have told your family that it wasn't me. To have let the police know that I was a passenger. But . . . but . . . Gemma needed me to say it was me and I agreed, to protect her. Now that's all I can say. But you have to *trust* me.'

'Trust!' Her lips curl around the word. 'You have to be joking.' She feels her knees shake. And she knows she has to get out of the room quickly now, before she really loses it. 'I wouldn't trust either of you as far as I could throw you.'

She chokes on the words. She hates how they make her feel weak. So she rattles the door handle until it springs free. She makes for the stairs, and hopes and prays that she can get down them before all the tears which are welling up begin to spill out.

She runs. Stumbles. And manages to stifle all but one sob before she reaches the front door.

She knows Harry is behind her.

She needs to get to the front door quickly so that she can get out before she has to touch him. She doesn't trust herself.

The evening smells of smoke and the cold hits her when she opens the door. She's very quick to close it behind her. Quick to replace the look of horror on Harry's face.

Issy

It's been a bad day. Right from the moment she got up.

Dave wouldn't let her go to school. Said she was getting above herself and that she should stay at home with her mum who needed her. That her mum was under the weather and should be looked after and that he couldn't do it. He had other fish to fry.

What the fish were Issy couldn't tell, except that it involved going to the Co-op to get vodka and watching *Jeremy Kyle*. Then nipping to the Co-op to get cigarettes and watching *Loose Women*. Yelling at Issy's mum, when she finally came downstairs, to go back upstairs because it was all she was fit for. That she should clean herself up a bit as she was stinking the place out.

And all the time Issy kept her eye out. For a foot to trip her up. For a cigarette which might land on her arm. For a swear word with spit on it. For his face to get redder and more swollen. For one wrong word from her or her mum. For there to be nothing that he liked in the fridge. For the bottle of vodka to slowly disappear. For bits of cash which he might not notice. For her mum to have a speck of life in her eyes. For some clean clothes from anywhere. For the chance to have a long warm bath. For her mum to put her arms around Issy and tell her everything was going to be all right.

It's been a long day.

Her mum won't change out of the clothes she's been wearing for a week now. It's a tracksuit she got from Next two Christmases ago. The hems are frayed and the knees are baggy and faded. It's meant to be royal blue but the cuffs, knees and elbows are more lilac now. Issy thinks she might be wearing it because it's the only thing with a hood. It's always pulled over her head and Issy guesses it's protection from the hair-yanking that Dave's started. She looks like she's hiding in that hood. Also it's warm.

But it's started to smell. And, sadly, so has her mum.

That hurts to think about.

Three times Issy tried today. Three times when she was sure Dave was either crashed on the sofa or engrossed in daytime TV. Three times she enticed her mum into the bathroom with a bath full of warm water and soap; a set of dry clean clothes on the side. But each time her mum stood wide-eyed and scared like she thought she might drown.

Issy doesn't think she's heard her mum speak for about a week now.

Just mouse noises whenever Dave goes anywhere near.

And now, in bed, tucked under her One Direction quilt at half past nine at night, she's started to hear something.

Something she doesn't like.

They're downstairs, in the living room. She can hear the mumble of the TV. Dave's voice interrupts every so often, all slurred and old-man-sounding. Each interruption brings prickles to Issy's skin. She wishes Dave would go to sleep. Wishes she could creep downstairs to watch over her mum. But he's sent her to bed. Saying she was getting on his nerves with her questions and dull expression. So her mum's downstairs on her own with him, and this brings Issy a sweat of fear every time she thinks about it.

Another shout, and this time a noise from her mum. A mouse-squeak, but loud. Loud enough to be heard from under Issy's duvet. It gets too hot under there. She flings the quilt aside and chews on a fingernail.

Draws her knees into her chest and lies on her side worrying.

Listens out for more.

Some more squeaks, then something heavy moving.

An angry bark from Dave.

It's too difficult to lie in bed now. She finds herself hovering at her bedroom door. Another fingernail chewed down. Her feet are cold and she takes it in turns to place one on top of the other. But her cheeks are on fire with alarm.

She stands for some time. Knees bent, arm on the door handle, her ears pricked for sounds.

Her mum's mouse noises get louder. There's a sort of 'nooo' wail, and maybe something Polish. It makes Issy realize how long it's been since she heard it. Then a giant crash and some massive English swear words from Dave which make Issy jam her hands over her ears. She squeezes her eyes tight and tears spill out. They're hot on her cheeks. She hears a mouse noise coming from her own throat.

Her knees quiver.

A yell from her mum then. Big and scared and high. 'No, Dave!'

'Shut up!'

More furniture being moved and a door being banged. Issy tries to picture what's going on. She can't make out which door it is. Something gets thrown against something else and something shatters. A scream. It hits the inside of Issy's stomach and rolls it over and over and over.

She can't stay in her room any longer. She has the sudden memory of the cooker. Of how blue the gas flames are. How strong and hissy they sound. How the smell is toxic, especially when skin goes near it. How strong Dave is when he's drunk vodka. How her mum's arms are weak . . . and how they're covered in burn marks.

She hopes it wasn't the kitchen door.

Please.

She pads down the stairs in her bare feet and pyjamas. Her hand over her mouth, her fingers pressing into her cheeks, making dents.

She can hear a scuffle in the lounge. Squeaks and yelps and a smack. Sees shadows on the wall. Giant, ugly shadows. An angry pointed nose. Oversized fingers pulling at her mother's hair.

A small grunt from her mum.

Through the banister she sees him pulling at her mum.

Yanking her off the sofa and reaching for the kitchen door.

When he reaches it, with outstretched fingers and one final tug at her mum, it all gets too much for Issy.

She doesn't think. It's reaction. All blind and unthinking movement. Like her body is taking charge.

She suddenly doesn't care if she gets seen. She doesn't even care if he swears and yells at her. She's ready if he does.

But he doesn't. He's far too intent on dragging her mum towards the kitchen.

So she's suddenly free. She may be in her pyjamas, she may be barefoot, she may have absolutely no access whatsoever to the back door, because that's where he's heading. But she's free and unseen and pumped up with adrenaline.

So she goes to the front door, in the lounge. It's never used. The key is already in the lock.

Issy's fingers fumble and shake at it. It's stiff from being unused, and her hands feel stupid and small against it. She gives a little yap of frustration. Hopes she's not heard.

She looks quickly behind but sees only shadows: the tangle of her mum and Dave as they move into the kitchen.

It's cold and raining outside. Her feet and the hem of her pyjamas are wet within seconds. The cold makes her gulp in surprise. She's shivering before she even gets to the front gate. Her pyjamas are thin and too small.

The image of the cooker's flames propels her forward into the dark, cold night.

Through the gap in the hedge.

Towards Sophie's.

Four orange rectangular windows of light and relief and hope.

There are sobs in Issy's throat now which won't stop coming. One after the other, after the other, so that she has to gasp for breath. There are sharp bits of grit on the path to Sophie's back door, so she has to do a sort of hop. Her feet hurt and the rain is stinging her scalp.

The material of her pyjamas is so wet that it clings to her shoulders and her tummy and her thighs.

The wetness on her face could be tears or rain.

The wetness on the soles of her feet could be blood or rain.

Mud gets squashed between her toes.

And all the time she can imagine the hiss of the gas. The heat of the blueness. The smell of burnt hair and skin.

Sophie's back door will be open. But if it's not, Issy knows where the key is. Like the night of the crash. *It'll be all right,* she tells herself over and over. Even says the words in tiny shivers.

It'll be all right. It'll be all right.

Her chest heaves as she reaches the door. She's not even noticed the dark. Her hand rattles on the door handle. Her hand is shaking like it belongs to someone else. Issy looks at it like she doesn't recognize it.

She twists. Trips and falls on to the doormat. It hurts her tummy. It scrapes her shins.

But her head is up and she searches the room.

Please let Sophie be in.

Sophie and her friend Maisie are at the kitchen table. There's some soft music in the corner. Sophie has red eyes like she's been crying. They both turn in alarm.

From the doormat, shaking and struggling with the words, Issy says, 'I'm sorry if I've made the floor wet. But I think I need your help.' A gulp as loud as the words themselves. 'I think Dave is trying to kill my mum.'

Gemma the day of the crash

'I'm not coming, Gemma. They don't want me there.'

He's hunched over his easel, a bright orange crayon in his right hand. He's got a scowl as dark as a weapon on his face. She's sitting on his bed, cross-legged and pouting, pulling at her toes. 'C'mon, Harry, please. You can be my plus one. I'll drive. I won't leave your side. We only need to be there for a bit. It's Rajit, for God's sake, his parties are legendary.'

He dabs at the paper, jabbing in a way she knows will be creative and wonderful. 'Legendary for rich, spoilt kids who don't think twice about cracking open a case of Daddy's champagne. We don't mix in those circles any more. You know we don't.'

'I need to go. That Jayden Holt-Smythe's going and he's definitely got the hots for me.'

He waves his orange crayon in the air. 'So go. But don't involve me. He's a prize wanker.'

She flops back on her brother-smelling pillows and crosses her legs in the air. 'Please, Harry. It's just an hour out of your life. A measly hour and I promise I'll never ask again.' She dips her head. 'Besides, it'll keep me away from Deano.' She sees Harry stop with the orange crayon. 'I've been really good. I've avoided him for ages now. It's been horrid. It's nearly killed me. But I've done it. And now I need something else to distract me. Some*one* else, maybe.' She hates how her voice still quivers when she says Deano's name.

'You've definitely stopped seeing him?'

'Yeah. You must've noticed how I've avoided all the places where he used to find me?' She presses her fingers against her mouth. 'He was like an addiction. But I've done it, Harry. I've done it.'

He sniffs and she spots a small notch of resignation in the slope of his shoulders and pounces like a cat. 'C'mon, man. I'll make tea every night next week. I'll even put the bins out.'

He widens his eyes. 'Do you even know where they go?'

'I can learn.'

He closes his eyes and rests the crayon back on the tin. 'When is it?'

'Tonight.'

He folds his fingers and sighs. 'An hour?'

'If that.'

'And you'll drive?'

'Yeah. You can drink your way through the whole hour while I try to twist Jayden round my finger.'

'Jesus I can't believe I'm doing this!'

She jumps up and winds her hands round his neck, resting

her head on his. 'Thanks, little bro. You're the best.'

He shakes his head. 'I'm a mug.'

'But a brilliant mug.' She flexes back upright. 'OK, so I've got an hour and a half to make myself look irresistible while you create art.'

He's back to frowning and shaking his head as she rushes out of the door.

She drives, he navigates. A place neither of them have been. All country lanes and hedges; a level crossing; an open, star-filled, inky sky; scents of fields and fresh water through the air vents; nothing but the occasional car rounding a bend with dazzling headlamps.

Gemma feels the fizz of anticipation in the pit of her stomach. She's heard so much about these parties. How there are bouncers and temporary Portaloos; how there are marquees and fire pits; hired DJs and no neighbours to enforce music curfews.

The place is teeming with people. Laughter and teeth and phones and so much bare skin. It's hard to imagine it's not summer. Nobody's feeling the cold. There are silver trays of glasses filled with wine and buckets of ice-laden lager. She watches as her brother lifts one from the ice and drains it quickly. She's never seen him drink so fast. It makes her realize how much he doesn't want to be there. There's nobody she recognizes. Yet. It doesn't bother her. She's getting better at being on her own these days. (Although she'd quite like to be barefoot.) She leads the way.

'Where the fuck are we going?' she hears him grumble

behind her.

'In search of some fun, remember?'

There are more pungent scents now: weed and wine and sweat. The music's pounding. It batters her insides and thrills her bones. Even Harry's getting buzzed up now. Flashing lights create flickers in his eyes as Gemma tugs at his arm and yells, 'C'mon, dance.'

Harry grimaces and raises his eyebrows. 'Really, to this?' But he shrugs and agrees to be pulled into the thick of the heaving, weaving people who smell of warmth and perfume and shampoo.

She's a good dancer. She knows it. So's her brother, although he'd never admit to it. A girl starts to swoop around him. Gemma can see the signs of attraction. This girl obviously likes the way her scruffy-looking twin dances and dresses.

She moves slightly back to let the girl in.

One step.

Then two.

Until she's now in a completely new group of strangers, equally laughing. Equally moving.

She floats to the music some more. Three more tracks, until she's so thirsty she goes in search of a drink. True to her promise, she finds an orange juice. She doesn't need alcohol to have a good time. The music and the heat and the laughter are intoxication enough. She slips her shoes off. Slides them into her bag. Feels better for that.

She finds herself smiling. It feels unusual and good. She's proud of herself for finally pushing Deano from her life. She's not thought of him since she got here. That's good.

It's while she's grinning and weaving around that she feels a pair of hands clamp around her waist and a wet kiss at the back of her neck. 'You came, Gorgeous Girl.'

It's Jayden. He's laughing, with teeth all straight and gleaming. He's wearing black skinnies and a shirt which is plastered to his chest. It's black with tiny robins dotted unevenly over the fabric. She finds she'd like to place a finger on each small bird to feel the heat and the hardness beneath. It's a relief to feel these things for somebody other than Deano. She allows herself a glow of hope. Of celebration.

'I did.'

'What do you think?' he says, nodding at the action around them.

'It's awesome.'

He nods, pushing fingers through his damp hair. 'His parties are famous.'

'I know. I've heard.'

He studies her then. She feels his eyes bathe over her shoulders, her hair, her breasts and her legs. It feels OK.

'Who've you come with?' he asks.

She nods at Harry, who has succumbed to the girl. 'My brother.'

Jayden nods again, then raises his eyes. 'Does he know Cassie?' This is obviously the dancing girl.

'Don't think so.'

Jayden smirks. 'She's crazy, that girl. Does he know what he's letting himself in for?'

She smirks with him, then shrugs. 'It doesn't seem to be

bothering him.'

He lifts his palms in the air and laughs. 'Good for him.' He studies her again and puts two fingers into her hair, pulling down a strand. 'He's your twin, right?'

She nods.

'You into danger, then? Like him?'

She knows a challenge when she hears one. She's heard enough of them from Deano. The words frighten and fascinate her like a barbed-wire knot. This sort of test from Deano used to make her feel older, dangerous and thrilling. Now she's not so sure. But it's important to play the game. It *has* to work. She *has* to move on.

'There's nothing better,' she laughs, pressing a finger on a robin. Feeling a heartbeat underneath. There's a split second when she's sure he's about to kiss her. When they study each other's lips. But he doesn't. Instead he glances at her glass. 'You want another?'

'OK.'

He grabs her hand. 'C'mon, then. Let's go outside. There's loads of drink outside.'

He leads the way with fingers which are wiry and strong amongst hers.

It's much cooler outside. The chill blasts against her dress, taking her breath away for a second or two. Jayden saunters over to a bar piled high with drinks and cupcakes. He walks like a strolling giraffe. It's easy to stare at the way his shoulders fill his shirt. He points at a bottle of orange, raises his eyebrows. She nods and can't keep her eyes off him as he ambles back, an orange in one hand, a beer in the other. He frowns as he hands over the orange.

'I'm driving,' she explains.

'Oh!'

He looks at her feet then, noticing the lack of shoes. 'Aren't you cold? Won't they get muddy?'

She grins a lopsided, knowing smile. 'Nothing wrong with a bit of mud.'

He laughs into his beer. 'I like you, Gemma Stone. I like you a lot.'

They stand for a while, drinking each other in, with the muffled music pulsing through the canvas of the marquee. He has a small indent in the centre of his jaw and an S-shaped scar just below his ear. It's hardly noticeable unless you're up close. And it's interesting to see that she is. That somehow she's centimetres away from his skin and that he smells warm and glorious, of fresh leaves. It's new. It's brilliant and it's not Deano. That thought hums between each rib bone.

'Gemma Stone,' he says as he drags a thumb down her cheek and moves a step closer so that there's now nothing in between them. His head is bowed so that she can't see the scar.

But then there's a screech. 'Jayden!' And hands and high-pitched laughter. A group of six or seven girls has rounded on them, shouting Jayden's name like he's in some boy band. Gemma gets elbowed and jostled out of the way so that suddenly she's on the edge of the group and there are now three girls between her and Jayden's mouth. The robins get smothered in fangirls. Someone stands on her foot so a shot of pain spurts up the front of her leg.

There's not much she can do. It's important not to look like you're desperate or waiting for some dregs, or that you don't know what to do without him.

So she starts to step backwards. She'll head back to the marquee again. Or maybe to the toilets.

She smells the scent of a cigarette in the air around her. Maybe she could scrounge one? It'd be a good way of spending a few minutes while Jayden gets rid of the girls . . . if that's his intention . . . which she's not entirely sure about.

And it's while she's thinking this that she hears a voice from the past. A voice which has haunted her for a long time.

A voice which she never wanted to hear again.

Deano.

A dark, powerful voice. The sensation in her stomach rolls like a giant wave. It's toxic. Poison of the sourest taste. Acid. And within seconds she's back at the V-shaped tree with his fingers in her bra and the tremble in her knees. She's by the pool house with Stephanie's screams and an unnatural arc to her spine. She's at the last party watching him boast about the power he has over her, offering her up like steak.

She wants to run. To scarper. To flee the suddenly nightmarish noise of laughter which doesn't feel good any more.

But he's seen her from the folds of his canvas cave at the side of the marquee. He's seen her, and he's been there for a while. His face tells her this without saying a word. He waves his cigarette and laughs.

What the hell is he doing here?

'T!'

This confuses her for a second. But then the memory floods in like a tidal wave. A tsunami of horror.

Run. Walk away. Hide. Ignore him.

But he's cleverer than that. He senses her urgency to run. He steps out of the shadows and makes a grab for her arm. She tries to twist away but his hand is firm and slimy on her skin.

'Long time, no see.'

She stands still like an animal stuck in a trap. She won't look at him. She can't. The feeling of his fingers on her arm is like five poisoned darts, clamping her to a standstill. And his voice . . . it's almost hypnotic in the way it controls her.

She shakes her head, moving her hair so it draws curtains around her face. 'Um . . .'

'You owe me an explanation.' His voice is sarcastic and laced with the wrong kind of danger. There's no trace of the softness she sometimes used to find.

'What?' she manages to say in a voice too thin for her. It's like his fingers are around her neck.

He pushes his fingers down on her skin. She can imagine their tattoos, and the bruises she'll have tomorrow. 'You vanished, out of the blue. Disappeared in a puff of smoke. Just when things were gettin' good.'

She feels trembles skid up her arm and down her spine. She shakes her head too quickly. 'No. Noooo.'

He steps on her toes. She's not even sure he realizes. But the pain is excruciating. (Although there's a horrid little sigh in her stomach which thinks she might deserve it.) 'I don't think that was very nice. Not for someone as well-brought-up as you. Avoiding me like that. When I've done so much for you. Sticking up for you and hiding out for you. Ungrateful, I'd call it. Ungrateful and not very nice.' He looks ugly now. His eyes flash spite. She wasn't sure how she'd ever seen kindness or good looks. His fingers press harder. 'You can make it up to me now, though, if you want?'

She doesn't like the dangerous battering of her heart.

He pushes a finger on her lips, so it presses against her teeth and misshapes her mouth. She can taste tobacco and it brings on old familiar feelings of fear and danger and excitement. Feelings she doesn't want to feel any more. Feelings she's been running away from for a while now. Stirring up emotions she never wanted to experience again – not with Deano.

His voice softens slightly. 'You used to like this.'

A swoop to the space under her ribs.

But then he steps back as if to dismiss her, and his voice gets poisonous again. 'Or else . . . a posh girl like you . . . do Mummy and Daddy know exactly what their daughter's been up to? Do they? Maybe I should pop round and see ya . . . maybe see your parents too . . . a few words in the right ears . . . I've done my research, T . . . or should I say *Gemma*? I know where you live.'

At least this breaks her stillness. The thought of Deano at her house. The quiver of fear gets the better of her and she glances at his face through her hair curtain. 'I don't know what you mean.' Then braver: 'What are you even doing here?'

He shrugs his shoulders, grins but doesn't loosen his grip. 'Seems we both share friends in high places.'

She thinks about the scent of weed she's been smelling in patches of the party. Of the larger-than-life laughter which is probably a result of something stronger than alcohol. Things start to slot into place.

Kids like these need dealers like Deano.

He watches her as the information slides into her understanding. He's no friend of these people. He's just a market-seller trading his stock. He's a lousy, stinking drug dealer and his grubby fingers are on her skin. He can't have the control he used to have. She can't let him. But his fingers are clamped shut and his mouth is a line of iron.

'So, do you want to make it up to me or not?' His words are a twist.

She remembers the way his lips felt on hers. Swallows at the thought.

'How?' She hates her feeble whisper.

He eyes a small bag at his feet. A bag she'd not noticed before. 'Help me get rid of these. Sell them – to some of your rich friends.'

She tries to pull her arm away. 'No!'

He slowly shakes his head. 'Oh, Gemma. When are you going to learn? You can't avoid me for ever. What you did back at Stephanie's house . . . that's like a memory. A memory which won't ever go away. That's priceless information, that is. And I reckon that puts me in charge. That information . . . it only needs a quiet word in the right place . . .'

'No.' It's less of a whisper now. More of a yelp.

He reaches down for the bag with his free hand. 'Sell these – a tenner apiece – unless they're really rich, then you charge 'em twenty.'

'I don't want to . . .' A frightened little girl.

'You have no choice.' He scoops some small plastic

envelopes from his bag, reaches for her handbag and opens it. They waterfall into the bag as she watches with wide, horrified eyes.

He zips the bag and releases her arm, pushing her, so that she can take fast steps away from him. Away from his smell. Away from his voice. Away from the memories.

'I'll be watching,' she hears from behind her head.

As she re-enters the marquee she's shaking so horribly that she can't pick up a glass from the tray. She has to hold her breath and put effort into every muscle necessary to move bicep and tricep to wrist to finger. And at last she's holding a drink, amongst a crowd of kids who don't even notice her. Her eyes skitter to the doorway.

Don't come in, you bastard. Stay in the shadows. Stay away from me.

She drains the glass without even tasting the bubbles. Reaches out for another, finding it easier this time.

Loses herself in a throng of dancing people.

Hides under up-reaching arms. Disguises herself in folds of swaying dresses. She can do this. She can hide for ever if she really tries. She doesn't need to sell drugs. She doesn't even know how to. She doesn't need to do as he says.

Backward glances towards the entrance every few seconds.

Fear in every drink which she finds easily on silver trays.

In the middle of a dance floor you can pretend to be anyone. Dancing and weaving like she's having a good time. She can hide the trembling with a smile.

There's a guy grinding away at her back. She doesn't even mind that he's grabbing at her tits. It's a disguise. A dressing-up costume of being at a party and having a good time.

And there's always another drink.

She snatches for a boy's beer. He's got ginger curly hair and makes an expression of surprise when she does this. A real-life, cool, startled Ron Weasley type in a dishevelled white shirt. But his lips slide into acceptance as she uses her finger on his mouth to silence his irritation.

And she's not sure where the bag is any more. Whether it's there or whether it might be under the tangle of dancing feet.

Dancing and weaving like she's having a good time. She can hide the trembling with a smile.

And for a while it works. She doesn't have a bag full of Deano's stuff swinging on her shoulder any more.

But then she sees a Deano in the distance, banging his head to the beat three groups away. And then, another Deano in the doorway, hanging back brooding with some girls. And then at the bar knocking back a beer. He's everywhere. Each time she sees one, her arms falter and she feels a sock of horror. His shock of dark hair. His good looks. The certain tilt of his head. A cigarette tip flashing like a wand. There's no getting away from him. He's everywhere she looks.

And she can't dance any more. The fear gets too much.

And she wants to go home.

Without meaning to, she gasps out of the heaving bodies. Feels her way blindly against elbows and flesh, treading on toes and pushing past groans of outrage. Someone digs her in the ribs, calls her rude, but she doesn't give a toss. She just wants out.

She makes it to the entrance, breathless for some air.

Where's Harry? Where's her bloody twin?

'Harry!' she yells into the darkness. Her legs wobble as she shouts. It's hard not to sink to her knees.

She's misplaced her bag. She's misplaced her shoes. But nothing matters apart from escaping from this place.

And quickly.

There are Deanos everywhere now. At every corner. At every turn.

'Harry!' Again, like it's the only word she can say.

Running wildly in the mud, searching for the blond of her brother.

Nowhere to be found.

'Harry! Harry, where the fuck are you?' At frowning groups of people.

Mud up her legs now. Doesn't know how that happened.

Hiding in a tarpaulin corner. Tries to slow her breathing. Shivering and trembling. Remembering his fingers in her bra. The waving of the gun. That horrible alien feeling. A scared, trapped animal. Stephanie's scream.

But then Harry's there.

Like he always is.

He puts his hand on her arm. 'You OK?'

Relief seeping into her lungs. 'Yeah. Only I want to go home.'

He grins. 'God, yes. Please can we? That girl has arms like an octopus. I swear I was being mauled from every angle.'

She doesn't even smile. The relief is too immense. She doesn't know what he's talking about.

'C'mon.' She grabs his hand and leads the way to where she

thinks the car is. Across a mud track, through clumps of balloons and tea lights in jars. Knocking a couple over in her haste.

'What's the rush?' He's out of breath, finding it hard to keep up.

'I just want to get out of this place.'

'Jayden a disappointment, then?'

It takes a while to even remember who Jayden is. 'Come on.' Through a gap in the hedge and then running along the road past parked-up car after car.

But it's only when they're on the road, when they've squeezed themselves through the gap and they're still searching for the car, that she hears the sound she's been dreading. There are steps behind them now. Running steps. Running, chasing steps with toxic words and a shocking determination.

She looks behind her and sees Deano running after them with a twisted face full of grit. His bag swinging off his shoulder.

NO!

He throws her an ugly scowl and hisses, 'No running away any more.'

Harry's not noticed in his search for the car. *Where's theirs? Why didn't they park closer?*

It's at the end of a long line of cars. Gemma grabs for the keys, which are in her pocket with her phone. Opens the doors and dives in.

She shrieks at Harry and he looks at her, confused. 'Hurry up. Get in!' She turns her head towards the figure following them and sees realization dawn slowly on her brother's face. 'Who—?'

'Doesn't matter,' she screams. 'Just get in!'

Harry's irritatingly slow as confusion gets the better of him, it makes him fumble at the handle. She turns the ignition and screams: the engine is sluggish and cold. It takes three goes for it to trigger. Three precious moments where Deano's getting closer. She can feel him in the night air.

Her heart's still hammering as she pulls a U-turn in the deserted road and presses her foot to the floor to crank up the speed. And it's while she does this, at the end of the U, that she hears the back door open and Deano's body slide in.

'No!' she screams, and Harry's face is a picture. His neck twists in bewilderment.

'Who?'

'Deano!'

'Stop the car then.' He turns round and yells. 'Get out!'

Deano doesn't say anything from the shadows of the back. But she can see his grim face in the mirror, and he makes sure that he fills it. And then she sees the flash of something she'd been dreading. It glints black and brown in the mirror as he waves it for her to see. It's the gun.

'Get out!' The panic makes her scream.

She puts her foot to the floor. The urge to escape this place is immense. The gun is still there and she doesn't know how to get away. She doesn't speak. She doesn't breathe. Doesn't feel she can, until she's closer to home. Feels sick at Deano's presence with the gun waving dangerously in the back of the car, but panics at the thought of stopping. While she's driving he won't do anything. She'll think of something. When she can see the lights of their neighbourhood.

'Slow down, you idiot!' Her brother's voice is a screech as she takes a country corner at breakneck speed.

'Keep going!' Deano's voice splinters the interior. 'Let's get out of here.'

They take country lane after country lane, Harry trying to keep up with directions on his phone.

'What's he doing, Gemma? Let him out.'

'Keep going.' From the back.

'Left here.'

'No, right.'

A deserted roundabout at an impossible hurtle.

'Gemma!'

She doesn't listen. She just wants to get home. To get rid of Deano and the gun in town. Push him out with her feet if she has to. To get home, bolt the door and slide into her bed.

The lights of the town in the distance should give her some relief, but she's so hungry for home that she loses her bearings.

'You're going too quickly. I don't know where we are.' Harry gets cross and chucks his phone into the footwell. It's useless.

Deano starts yelling from the back that she's going too fast. His voice is vicious. She can hear it slick on her neck.

She tears over mini-roundabouts. Hurtles round corners that she doesn't recognize. Shop lights and garages begin to dazzle her. Streets lights daze her vision. She's drunk and she finally realizes this. She's lost. She's drunk and she's shaking like an overwound clockwork toy. The gears don't work for her. She forgets where to brake. The steering wheel's got a mind of its own and the inside is too hot. Harry and Deano's arms are gesticulating in the space around her. They jerk like puppets with the dark of the gun in the mirror. The heater's blasting an unforgiving heat which brings her out in a sweat on top of the sweat from the dancing. Her arms jolt wildly and she hears Harry scream. She has no use of her legs and then they seem to wrench of their own accord.

Someone's screaming and it could quite possibly be her.

Toxic words blaring from the back. Right into her neck like small sharp daggers.

The heat.

And then an explosion.

A wall.

And a blood-curdling bawling which definitely isn't from her.

Shattered glass on her dress, down her bra, in her hair.

She gives in and joins in with the screaming.

Sophie

'It's incredible that it was happening under our noses and we didn't know.'

She and Maisie are walking out of school with the floods of other kids at the end of the day. Maisie's been there for the last two days, since Sophie split with Harry. She's been a good friend.

'So what happened when I left?' Maisie shifts her bag higher on to her shoulders.

'Not much, really. The police came, of course, but you were there for that. Then they took Dave away from the house. He was yelling and everything. Swearing at everyone – even Dad. He looked completely off his face. Then the policewoman took Issy back into the house to get her dressed and dry.' Sophie looks quickly at Maisie. 'She must've been freezing – I didn't even notice, did you?'

Maisie shakes her head. 'Not really. I remember she was wet, though.'

'And then ages later, when we'd all gone to bed, I saw them walk out together. Issy, her mum and two police officers. Her mum looked dog rough. All bent double and shivery. I wouldn't have recognized her if she hadn't been with Issy. God – that's awful. How come I didn't know anything? I overheard Issy telling the policewoman that it'd been going on for weeks. I mean, I thought she was getting thin and I kept telling her that she was looking tired, I wondered if she was being bullied at school, but . . . God . . . I didn't know she had to face all that at home. For some time.'

Maisie nods. 'It's been a mad couple of days.'

Sophie pulls a face. 'Yeah. First Harry, then this.' She'd told Maisie about Harry. The secret was too heavy to keep inside.

'Has he tried to contact you since?'

Sophie shrugs. Sighs. 'Three texts. Two on the night and one last night.'

'And did you text back?'

She shakes her head. 'Nope. I'm still pissed off that he'd lie like that, especially when he knew telling the truth would make it easier for me and him.'

Maisie looks thoughtful as they cross the road. 'But it'd put his sister in the shit.'

Sophie looks at her with narrowed eyes. 'God, don't start making excuses for him.'

She holds up her hands. 'I'm not. Only it must've been a pretty difficult decision, that's all. And you've said how determined his sister is.'

'Then he needs to man up and stick up for himself. I cannot believe he's prepared to get a criminal record for her. She's a bitch. I mean, what kind of sister lets a brother take the flak like that? There's something totally weird and screwy about Gemma. I hated her before, but now I hate her even more. She's supposed to have this soft side, but I've never seen it. I reckon it's all in Harry's imagination. And I'll never forgive him for making me feel so bad for no reason.'

It's a warm, sunny afternoon with touches of spring now obvious. Blossom and green leaves and spring flowers bounce in the breeze. It could be a scene on an Easter card.

'I think she's a bit screwed up, that's all.'

Sophie toes at a stone. 'She just didn't want to lose her licence. She likes that job at the NEC too much.'

'I thought you said there were other people involved.'

She nods. 'There are, apparently. But he wasn't prepared to tell me any more, so I didn't seem to have any choice.'

'And you're sure all this is worth it? 'Cause you look bloody miserable to me. And I know he was really into you.'

Sophie winces. It hurts when she thinks about it. She softens her words and slows her strides. 'And I was really into him. It's horrible to think that it's all ended. I can't see me finding anyone else like him for a long time – if ever. But you know I hate liars. And his relationship with his sister was doing my head in.' But the words sound hollow. It's still really difficult to imagine not seeing him again. There's an ache in her stomach that's been there ever since she walked out on him two nights ago. 'And at least I can stop feeling guilty about Tye now.'

But it's Harry's eyes she sees when she tries to go to sleep. All betrayed and dragonfly-blue in the darkness.

A group of noisy kids wander by. A football is being kicked around, the soft thud irregular and easy. Sophie glances up. They're mainly the football kids in her year, along with some stragglers. She likes them. A couple of Tye's acting friends are there too, red-cheeked from running. One of them – Jordan Kray – sees her and smiles a smile just for her; they've made a date for his visit, his brown eyes crinkle with it. Then he notices Maisie next to her. 'C'mon, Maisie. Come and join us. We need you.' Maisie plays for the school football team. There have been rumours about scouts seeking her out.

She shakes his head and nods over to Sophie. 'Naah. Better not.'

'Suit yourself.' He grins, gives another flash of knowledge to Sophie, then jogs on after the rest of the group.

Sophie frowns. 'You didn't need to say that. You could go and join them, you know. I'm not exactly brilliant company right now.'

Maisie shrugs. 'I'd only embarrass them with my shit-hot passing skills and swift left foot.'

Sophie has to laugh.

Three roads from theirs, Maisie slows down. She squints in front of her. Almost stops. Sophie, who's distracted by the nearby shops, is trying to calculate whether she's got enough cash on her for a can of Coke, so doesn't take much notice.

'I fancy a drink—'

'Umm . . .' Maisie interrupts, looking awkward. She shoves her hands deep into her coat pockets.

'What?'

She nods in front of her. At the bench. 'Maybe the drink can wait . . .'

Sophie follows her gaze with puzzled eyes. And there, so that her heart hurtles dangerously and her breath gets caught in her throat, is Harry. Sitting on the bench in his school uniform, waiting.

'Oh, God.'

Maisie fingers her fringe anxiously. 'That's him, isn't it? Perhaps I *will* go and play football after all.'

'Oh God, I don't know if I can do this.' It's a bit of a wail.

Maisie rolls her eyes. Gives a small grin. 'Sophie, a word of advice. You've been as miserable as anything this last couple of days. If nothing else, give him the chance to explain. He deserves that, surely. Doesn't everyone?'

Staring at the slumped figure on the bench, she sighs. 'I guess.'

She suddenly wants Tye again. It keeps happening like this; she wants his arms right round her, so that she feels tight and warm and soothed. It's good breathing in Tye. Like hot chocolate.

Maisie touches her arm. 'It'll be OK.' And then she's off in the other direction. Kicking at an imaginary ball with impossibly athletic legs.

Harry's not seen her. Instead he's watching a couple of lads approaching from the corner. They're older than him, rough-looking with twisted faces. They spot Harry, sitting on the bench. Sophie's too far away to hear, but she sees them say something to him. Sees their ugly laughter, their toxic hand gestures, and the way Harry screws up his face in distaste. Whatever is said isn't pleasant. Harry looks horribly uncomfortable.

There's a bark of laughter from one of them and one more comment. She sees Harry cringe, but then he flicks the Vs, his face miserably creased up.

They pass Sophie, their bodies still rattling with poisonous laughter. It's an ugly scene to have witnessed.

She bites on her lip as she gets nearer. He spots her and his face gives a weak smile. He sits up, squares his shoulders.

'Hi.'

'Hello.'

'Thought I'd see you here.'

She smiles lopsidedly. 'Pretty inevitable seeing as it's on my way home.'

'My detective skills are on fire.'

She smiles again. He looks at the space next to him on the bench. Taps it with the palm of his hand. 'Will you join me?'

She drops her bag on to the pavement and sits down. The wood is warm from the sun. It's nice. 'Who were those lads, just then?'

He rolls his eyes. 'Just twats who Gemma knows.'

'What was their problem?'

He sighs, looks straight ahead at the passing traffic. 'It's a long story.' Gives her a quick glance. 'Do you want to hear it? I mean, it might explain a few things. And I've been thinking about it, and I guess you deserve to know.'

There's an anxious line between his eyes. His fingers twist on his legs. This is hard for him.

'OK.'

He thinks about something, then reaches in his bag. He brings out a Creme Egg. It wobbles in his hand. 'I got you chocolate.'

She smiles. She takes it from him, but doesn't open it, enjoying its weight in her hand.

He sighs again, stretches his legs before him and then fills his cheeks with air. It's like he's about to begin an interview. 'Um . . .' He clears his throat. 'OK, so you have to promise you won't tell a soul.'

'OK.'

'Those idiots, just then – they're part of a bigger crowd who've been intimidating Gemma. I don't really want to go into too much detail because it's not fair on you if you get to know things you shouldn't. But,' he inhales here and chews on his nail, 'she got into some pretty dodgy stuff. Stuff which could have her and those lads up in court and arrested. There was a kind of criminal incident where she got away and those lads, they blame her, they say she set them up and they've never let her forget it. For a while they never left her alone. Made her life hell.'

Sophie leans her thigh against Harry's, feeling his warmth. 'So why did you have to pretend to be driving?'

He shifts on the bench. 'Because . . .' His fingers tremble slightly. 'Because the only way she thinks she can get away from them properly, away from their blackmailing and their bullying, is to leave the country. She wants to go abroad – with this band who've offered her a job. It's a world tour. Apparently they're going to be big. It's the only way she thinks she can be free of them.' He fidgets his legs. 'And it's not just them, it's their leader – the bloke in charge. She had this kind of dodgy addictive relationship with him. She knows it's wrong and she needs to get out. And I agree.'

She frowns. 'So what's stopping her?'

'A criminal record would. If she got caught drink-driving or the police found out she was involved in the incident I can't tell you about, then they'd never let her into some of the countries she wants to go to.'

A lorry pulses by, pumping out grey diesel fumes; the noise is suddenly too loud for Harry to carry on. They wait patiently, breathing in diesel. The Creme Egg sits gently on Sophie's still hands.

'Does that sound stupid?' His voice wobbles slightly. 'Does it sound weak?'

Sophie tilts her head. 'No – not really.'

But Harry hardly hears her, he's so intent on his misery. 'She's really screwed up, Sophie. Everyone thinks she's this really cold character who doesn't give a shit. Just cos she's confident and attractive and can twist boys round her finger, they all think she's tough. But I know different. I know that actually she's completely messed up and scared to death. That she thinks her only chance of happiness is to run away.'

'You're really close to her, aren't you?'

'Yeah. She's been there for me all my life, sticking up for me and cheering me up when nobody else can. I used to get bullied all the time when I was little and she always helped me out. Sorted out the bullies, kept them off my back. She's my twin sister and she fights my battles; at eighteen that's just embarrassing. So, pretending I was driving in the crash . . . it was time I stepped up . . . time I grew a pair . . . time I did something for her. Only it turns out that now, maybe I'm stronger than I thought. That maybe I can do stuff for her now. And that makes me feel good.'

Sophie's eyes widen.

The line between Harry's eyes gets deeper. He shoves his fingers under his legs. 'I was wrong to lie to you. Wrong to keep up the story. But I didn't have a choice. I was already committed. Within seconds of crashing into your house I'd made a decision I couldn't get out of.' Ripples of tension rise and fall in Harry's throat, like waves. He chews on a nail. 'And I've already told you more than she'd like. But right now, I think you deserve it, and I'll explain that to her.'

Something bleeds slowly into Sophie. 'I think you're stronger than you realize.'

He nods. 'Yeah – and that's a bit of a surprise. Kind of funny really.'

A group of cyclists swishes by, a blur of bright Lycra and voices. They remind Sophie of a swarm of wasps.

She thinks of her own brother. About their arguments, about their banter. How she hates him sometimes; how they do stuff to deliberately annoy each other. She can't imagine Sam ever sorting out her problems, just as she'd never get herself a criminal record for him. They love each other, they're family and everything. But that kind of dramatic behaviour doesn't happen in their family.

But then, they're not twins. And there's something hard and special and a bit brittle between Gemma and Harry.

'So you lied for her?' Her words are as soft as she can

make them.

'So I lied for her,' he repeats.

'Those boys. The ones who were here – are they still intimidating her?'

'Not so much. I think they're still around, still making their presence felt. But after I stood up to them and explained that they needed her silence as much as she needed theirs, things quietened down. They're not around these days. Sometimes she can be quite normal now. Sometimes she even has a laugh.'

'And the leader bloke? Does she still see him?'

'No. Not if she can help it. I think the crash scared him off. She knows better these days anyhow, knows he's pretty destructive and bad for her. But it took the night of the crash to finally make her see that.'

At last his hands are still. His breathing almost back to normal. As a watery sun slides out from behind a cloud, and as yet more late-afternoon traffic hisses by, Sophie feels the side of her thigh press warmly against his.

It's quite nice, all of a sudden, to notice that the full length of her arm is beside his, sucking up warmth through his school blazer. That the bones of their knees are knocking against each other and their calves pressed gently together. It's nice not to have noticed. Nice. Warm. Sort of comfortable, sitting there, squinting in the sun.

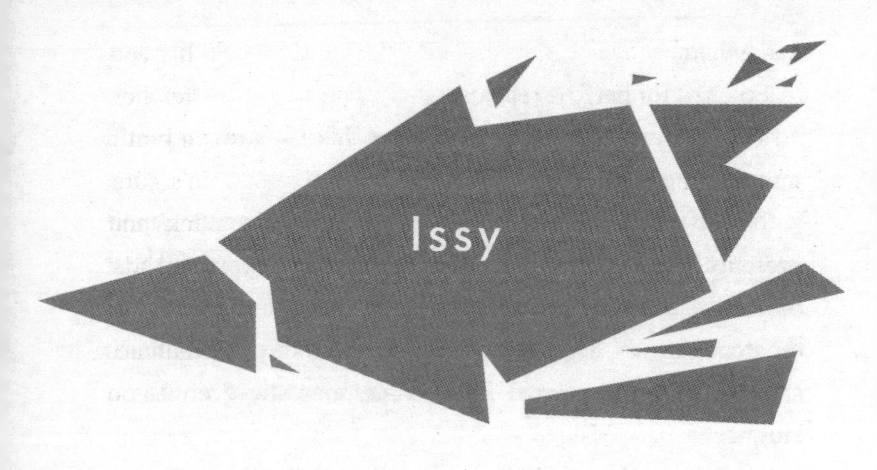

Issy

There are six bedrooms, five families and three bathrooms. There are two lounges, one kitchen and a back garden with a climbing frame and two swings.

It's the noisiest place she's ever lived in.

It's safe.

There are no men.

There are CCTV cameras everywhere.

And there's a lady called Pat who looks after everyone. Issy likes Pat. She likes her big worn hands which look like they can deal with anything.

It's a women's refuge and it's the weirdest place she's ever lived in.

It's breakfast time and she's sitting in the kitchen with her mum and another child called Lincoln. He's eating Cheerios, making a slurping noise. Her mum won't eat anything, but Issy has found she's starving and is on her second bowl of Coco Pops.

They've been here for two weeks now and Lincoln has sort of attached himself to Issy. He wanders around after her, asking for pushes on the swing, asking if she'll make him a sandwich, that kind of thing. She doesn't mind. He's cute, with scruffy blond hair, freckles spread across his cheeks and eyes which dart every time the door opens. Issy understands. She recognizes the scared feelings when a shadow appears at the doorway. Sympathises with the need to stop a sentence midway through and hold on to your belongings, until you are sure it's safe. She feels it in Lincoln's fingers as he grabs on to her leg sometimes. She's familiar with the panic of fingers. He must be about six years old, but she's sure he's seen more than the average sixteen-year-old.

She wishes her mum would eat. But she won't. Just mouse portions. These go with the mouse noises she didn't stop making for the first week. Pat says Issy must be patient. That her mum will eat when she feels ready. That she's still feeling very nervous.

It took four days for Issy and Pat to persuade her to change out of her Next tracksuit.

When she did it was a shock.

Issy doesn't want to think of the sight of her mum's body. Of the bruises and the burns and the bare patches on her scalp. So she doesn't.

Pat says it's one step at a time. First the clothes. Then the talking. Next the food. Then finally letting Issy go. At the moment Issy's mum won't let her out of her sight. Even when she's pushing Lincoln on the swings, Issy's mum will sit silently on the bench, gently playing with her hair. All the while watching, watching, watching.

It doesn't bother Issy too much. It's nice to have a mum who loves her so much. It's nice to be protected. Every night, despite there being two beds in the room, Issy's mum curls her thin body against Issy's and they sleep together, hot and quiet. It seems to make her mum feel better. So Issy doesn't mind.

But she misses school. She misses Briony. She misses her lessons. She misses glimpses of Sophie and Tye. And she'd really love to go back. She's told Pat. She's told her mum. She's told everyone who asks.

But her mum goes all quiet and squeezes her lips together when she mentions it, and Pat sighs and blows on the cup of tea which she's always holding.

But today it's Pat's morning off, so there's another lady in the office called Claire. So Issy decides she's got to have a go on her own.

'Mum, will you eat that toast?'

Her mum widens her eyes like she's only just seen the plate in front of her. She pulls a face.

'C'mon, Mum, just half a slice.'

'I like the jam,' grins Lincoln, who already has three Cheerios stuck to his cheek which he doesn't seem to know about.

Issy's mum pushes the plate towards him. 'Here you go.'

Under the table Issy spreads three fingers, counting. The first three English words of the day. Yesterday her mum managed twenty, and Issy's hoping that every day the number will go up. She'll tell Pat tomorrow. She's even written the score down in a notepad which Pat gave her on the first day here.

They weren't allowed to bring very much. On that first night, when Dave was arrested and they hunted the house to find her mum, Issy and the policewoman collected together the few things which they thought might be needed. Her mum wasn't in a fit state to help when they eventually found her in the bottom of the airing cupboard. The policewoman asked about chequebooks and birth certificates, about tenancy agreements and identification. But Issy didn't really have much idea. So instead she opened up the bottom drawer of the chest in the lounge, where she knew her mum put important letters, and let the policewoman sort through. After five minutes the policewoman seemed satisfied with a collection of papers and they were put in the suitcase along with everything else that they were allowed to take. So pens and paper weren't really a priority.

She likes the pad of paper. It's new, like her new life.

Lincoln chews carefully at the toast. His eyes check with Issy that it's OK. Her mum glazes over with a faraway look, not really noticing. There's a baby crying upstairs and the noise of some post coming through the letterbox and clattering on to the hall floor. The baby's probably Lincoln's sister. She seems to cry a lot. And the post won't be for Issy or her mum, as nobody knows that they are there. That is one of the conditions. That's why they are allowed to stay there. But sadly, it also means that she can't go to school. And she really does want to go.

Instead she sits quietly with her mum whose eyes are still far away, and Lincoln the six-year-old, who has finally found the three Cheerios stuck to his cheek. He peels them off carefully with chewed-down fingertips. He places them into his mouth, one by one.

'Guess where I've been?'

Pat's back. They're in her office. It's the afternoon and she's got a cup of tea on the desk. Issy's mum has one too, only she's not drinking hers. Pat wanted them to come and have a chat. Issy doesn't mind. She was bored of drawing a plan of the building with Lincoln and a girl called Sunita. They were getting the colour coding all wrong, and besides, Lincoln's drawing wasn't very good.

Issy answers because it doesn't look like her mum's going to. 'Where?'

'To your school, sweetheart. I spoke to your head teacher.'

Issy can feel her mum's fingers tremble on her arm.

'He seems to think you are one clever young lady.' Pat smiles. There's a piece of wobbly skin under her chin.

Issy's tummy tingles. It's a nice feeling, but awkward.

'He wants you to go back. He has a plan and I think it's a really good one.' She clears her throat, and Issy thinks what's going to be said might be very important.

'He suggests that Issy comes to school after everyone else gets there and then leaves before everyone else,' Pat says to Issy's mum. 'We'd get her there using our transport and she'd always be escorted by one of our staff.' She smiles. 'It might even be me.'

Issy thinks of school. Of Briony, of glimpses of Sophie. Of English, of Design, even French. Her stomach makes swooping movements. She thinks of playing netball, the wind in her hair, the freedom of it. But she catches sight of a solitary tear moving down her mum's cheek and she doesn't like the look of it. Her fingers cling on to Issy's sleeve.

Her mum wheezes a bit and Issy knows that she's trying to get together some words. Pat has taught her to wait. There are the sounds of a small argument in the kitchen. It's Sunita and Lincoln. They're not very good together.

'What about Dave?'

Issy counts the words again. They bring the total to eleven because she'd said, 'what's that on your top?' earlier when Lincoln had spilt some gravy on Issy's T-shirt.

Pat sighs over her tea. 'He won't go anywhere near the school, Nina. He doesn't know where she is. For all he knows she might well be in the depths of Cornwall. Besides, there's an injunction, you know that. He'd be stupid to break it. He knows that it won't do his court case any good if he tries to find either of you. He knows that he'd be locked up straight away.'

Issy thinks about this. To be honest, she doesn't know where she is herself. She doesn't even know if it's the same town that she used to live near to, when she lived at home. The journey was far too stressful to notice where she was going. She doesn't remember much about the drive here anyhow. Just how much her mum was shaking. So badly that it made Issy feel sick. She remembers that the policewoman tried to be kind. That she'd given Issy a Creme Egg but that Issy couldn't eat it because of the sickness.

'Nobody apart from the head will know Issy's address. And

Issy's too sensible to tell anyone.'

Fear jams up Issy's eyes. She watches her mum start to shake again. Her body wracks next to Issy's.

Pat gets up and comes round to her mum. She kneels down in front of her and wobbles a bit on her knees. A small 'eegh' sound comes out of her mouth. She lifts one of her mum's hands off her lap and folds her own around it. 'Don't let Dave win. Don't let him take away Issy's education. He's already done enough to the pair of you. Don't let him take this away from her too. She's really clever. She deserves to do well. Don't let him win.'

'What about me?' her mum whispers.

Issy's too full of hope to even count these words. She watches Pat carefully. 'You'll stay here with us. You can pack Issy off every morning and you'll be here for her when she gets back home. You can learn to be her wonderful mum again, like before all this happened.' She shifts on her knees. 'We can have a few sessions together, you and me, to get you back to normal. To get you more confident and ready to take her home when all this is over. When he's locked up for good.'

Issy bites her lip. 'Mum?'

Her mum turns to her then. She stares at her properly, right into her eyes so that Issy feels almost bare.

And then she gives a small nod. Just a gentle drop of the chin, but a nod all the same.

Quickly Issy throws her arms around her mum's shoulders, feeling the thinness and the bones, which she is starting to get used to. She begins to cry herself then. And then she feels Pat join in the hug from behind her so that she's sandwiched between the two of them. There is a lot of gasping and it's very hot. It smells of perfume and of tea and there are tears in hair and muffled around words. It lasts for a long time.

But more than anything, it's lovely.

'Do you want a lift?'

The shout makes her jump. She's been thinking of Tye over and over. How she could wake him up. How it feels like time's running out; how she can't bear the thought of all the things he's missing out on. How she wants him back, to talk to, to laugh with, to tell him about Harry. Because if there's one thing for sure, it's that Tye would like him. That he'd approve, unlike everybody else, who thinks their relationship is in bad taste.

She's anxious about Jordan. She's due to meet him at the hospital this afternoon, to take him into the ward and let him talk. She's planned it all out: she'll stay for a while and then leave him on his own with Tye. So that Jordan can say the things which just might bring Tye to life again. It has to work. It *has* to.

The shout gives her the jitters. It's a familiar voice, and one with unsettling associations. She twists her head.

Gemma nods at the door. 'You getting in, then?'

She tries not to look shocked.

Unsure, she opens the door and chucks her bag in the footwell. As she reaches for the seat belt she sees Gemma's feet, bare with orange nail varnish, pressing on the foot pedals.

'Is it legal to drive barefoot?'

Gemma knocks back her head and laughs, filling the car with her peals. 'My bare feet are the least of our worries.' She clicks on the indicator and pulls into the flow of traffic. They're silent for a while. She's a slick driver, confident as a thirty-year-old, which is ironic considering she drove through a wall into Sophie's house. She closes her eyes at the thought. The sounds of Gemma's music system drift around between them.

'Where are you going?' Gemma asks.

'To see Tye.'

Gemma nods. They wait at a roundabout, Gemma tapping her foot. 'Is there any change?'

'No.' She fiddles with her seat belt, the black digging into her fingers. 'I'm meeting one of his friends. I'm hoping that a new voice might wake him up.' She looks at Gemma's feet. 'Where are your shoes, anyway?'

She shrugs. 'I don't wear them any more.'

'Why?'

'Cos I like being barefoot. Cos I'm not that keen on shoes. Cos unless I have to wear them, that's what I do.'

'Don't you get cold? Doesn't it hurt when you walk outside?'

Gemma presses the pedals with long slim legs. 'Sometimes. In the winter. But most days I love it.'

'How long have you been barefoot?'

Gemma looks away with haunted eyes. 'About a year.'

Sophie checks out her profile. 'Bet you get some weird looks.'

Gemma glances back. 'I don't care. I'm used to those. I don't have many friends these days, so I'm always getting weird looks.'

'Why don't you have many friends? A girl like you . . . thought you'd have thousands.'

She fiddles with a bracelet. 'I used to . . . only . . . only I kind of messed up. Started seeing dodgy people, dangerous people who scared off my real friends. I'm not sure how it happened, but before I knew it, people were leaving me. Stopped inviting me to things, stopped talking, that kind of thing. I guess I stopped fitting in.' She glances towards Sophie who sees a sadness she'd not noticed before – in the lines by her eyes, in the shape of her eyebrows. She lifts her shoulders. 'Doesn't matter, though. I've got Harry and I've got work. '

'Do you still see those people?'

She lifts her fingers against her mouth and sighs between them. 'Not now.' Presses down the indicator.

It's like a full stop to the conversation. She doesn't want to say any more, Sophie can tell. She coughs; it's easier than she thought. 'You know what? You're actually not that bad; nice, even.'

Gemma grins. Clears her throat, adjusts the seat belt. 'The problem is, people don't see that.'

Buildings blur through the window.

'You're nice when you're open like this. People need to see more of this Gemma.'

She pulls a face. 'Why?'

'Cos it's good.'

'I *am* nice – well, I was. Only I got myself a reputation and it's hard to shake off. I'm trying to break free. Trying the best I can . . . only . . . only they're not making it easy for me.'

'Who?'

'That gang I was telling you about.'

Sophie nods.

'I'm not very good at being nice. I haven't been nice for a while.'

'You have to find something you really care about, and then everything falls into place, and you can stop being so hard.'

'God,' Gemma laughs. 'Didn't know I was here to be analysed.' She draws a finger down a strand of her hair.

Sophie feels a small laugh trip through her.

Gemma fidgets on her seat. Her voice takes on a different tone. 'Are you serious about Harry?'

The surprise makes Sophie cough. 'I really like him, if that's what you mean?'

'Good.' Gemma aims a quick glance at Sophie before moving the car forward.

'Is that what you wanted to hear? I know you're not my biggest fan.'

She sees a twitch in Gemma's cheek. 'It's not that I don't like you. It's just . . . I can see Harry really likes you, and I know how girls can ruin him. He once stayed in his room for four days when he found out that this girl had been cheating on him. Wouldn't eat or anything.'

'I'm not like that.' Sophie feels her nose wrinkle. 'I've had my own share of bastard boyfriends.'

They pull up outside the park. A haze of rain has begun to form. It mists up the windscreen and Gemma flicks on the wipers. She turns off the engine and the car is suddenly quiet. She reaches over Sophie for the glove compartment. Sophie can smell the fruity fragrance of her hair. Gemma plucks out a packet of cigarettes, unopened, still shiny in its cellophane. She tears at it with fingernails the same bright orange as her toes.

A group of kids with a football troop out of the park. Their shoulders are damp from the rain and the ball looks muddy and slippery.

'I'm not very good at this sort of thing.'

'You mean honesty?' There's a strange seep of power flooding up Sophie's veins.

'Yes, honesty.' Gemma sucks on her cigarette. Her profile is near perfect. 'Do you want to hear something?'

'I'm all ears.'

She swallows; Sophie sees her fighting with the words. 'There was an incident. A bad crowd. A bad incident. Something I could have got done for.'

'Really?' It's important not to betray Harry's trust.

'Yeah – it's part of the reason I want to leave this country.'

'Oh, Gemma.'

'I know, I'm a coward, aren't I? Turns out Harry's less of a pushover than I thought. He helped me out with that as well as taking the flak for the driving. Turns out he's quite good at standing up for me.'

She flicks the unfinished cigarette out of the window and winds it up. She fiddles with the car keys; they jangle unhappily.

Sophie reaches for the cigarette pack on Gemma's knees, places it back in the glove compartment with a click. 'You know what? I think you should go to the police and tell them everything.'

Gemma hangs her head so that her hair falls like curtains around her face. 'I'd lose my job.'

'You'd get another.'

'You think I should tell them everything? Absolutely everything? The other stuff as well as the driving swap? It'd be big. I don't think I can do that. I'm not like that. I'd have to go to court. I'd have to grass people up. I may not be able to go abroad.'

Sophie screws up her eyes. 'I think you are like that, really. Harry's said as much to me. He's told me enough times that everybody's got you wrong. And anyhow, why would you need to go abroad if those people you were grassing up were in prison?' She has a sudden realization. 'You love your brother more than anyone knows, don't you?'

'He means the world.'

'Yet you've wrecked his life.'

'But I've saved it over the years too. You don't know the half . . .'

'I reckon you need to go and confess everything.'

She watches as Gemma's chin slowly rises, like she's

drawing strength. Filling up with it from somewhere. Sophie puts her head on one side. 'What other stuff, by the way?'

She sees a small flush in Gemma's cheeks. It's a surprise. 'I have secrets, Sophie. Bad secrets.'

'Tell me.'

'No.' She shakes her head.

'Everyone has secrets, you idiot. You're in good company.'

She manages a small, sad smile. 'No. I did something bad. And it's eating away.' Nervousness seeps through her clothes. She fiddles with her fingers on the steering wheel.

'If it's eating away then you need to tell someone.'

'Even if it'll wreck my life?'

'Sounds like you're wrecking your life anyhow.'

A silence as thick as treacle spreads over them.

'What if I was involved with something? What if I was a witness to something bad, something nobody knows about, something that might get me in trouble?'

Sophie sighs, watches Gemma's profile with the small lift of her chin which acts like a question mark. She decides to stay silent a while; she thinks there's more. She hears a tremble in her own exhalation.

Gemma swallows. 'It was horrible. I was there. I know what happened to someone. Something which has ruined someone's life. Something she'll be reminded of every time she looks in the mirror. It's an unsolved mystery and it's eating away. And all I have to do is explain . . .'

'So why don't you?'

She flicks a glance of blue at Sophie's eyes. 'Cos it'd get me in the shit. Cos some people might say it was my fault. Cos I could get the blame.'

'*Was* it your fault?'

She shakes her head; Sophie inhales the fruity shampoo fragrance again. 'Well, I shouldn't have been there. But I was young and stupid and there was a boy – a lot older than me – who sort of controlled me.'

Firmly now, because Gemma needs it. 'So tell someone. You might get off, if you were young. If you explained why you were there.'

She looks away so Sophie can barely hear her whisper. 'I'm scared.'

Sophie digs out a memory. 'When me and Tye were younger we were playing this game where we shoved each other in this toy box thing he used to have. We'd sit on it so that the other couldn't get out. We'd count sixty seconds and make the other one beg to be let out. It was a stupid game but we used to do it all the time. Only one time I went too far. One time I sat there for two minutes longer so that he screamed and screamed and bashed the lid. I remember sitting there giggling and thinking it was hysterical. Only, when I eventually let him out he was bright red and dizzy. He couldn't walk properly and kept falling over. His mum had to take him to hospital because he wasn't making sense and kept hallucinating.' She can feel Gemma's interest on the side of her face. 'All evening I was a wreck. Full up on my guilty secret – that I'd made my best friend go mad. And nobody knew why he went like he did. So in the end – after everyone had gone to bed and I still couldn't sleep because it was eating away at me – I sat at the end of Dad's bed and told him. Everything. In the dark. I confessed, Gemma, and it felt so good afterwards. Like a burden had been lifted. Dad texted Tye's mum and explained. Tye was on the mend anyhow, so everyone was cool.' She moves her knee against Gemma's and gets a small jerk back. 'Confess, Gemma. It's good for the soul. I know only too well how secrets can burn away and destroy things.'

Gemma pushes some hair off her face. 'M . . . aybe . . .' Then she lifts the keys back into the ignition, starts the engine so that the music suddenly fills the car. She glances over, her eyes now shining again, her fingers suddenly strong on the steering wheel. 'Well, I'd best get you to hospital. I'm not the only one who has important things to do.'

Sophie smiles a bit. Sad.

It seems that the conversation is over.

She stands at the entrance for ten minutes before she sees him. He's wearing a black bomber jacket and jeans. The haze of rain has made his jet-black hair all slick and glistening. His top half glitters as he strides towards her. Sophie totally understands why Tye fell in love.

As he approaches, though, she sees his face is folded dark with uncertainty. He steps in front of her. Sophie feels the plunge of disappointment. She knows what he's going to say.

'I can't do this.'

She presses her nails into the palms of her hands inside her pockets. 'Yes, you can, Jordan. Please.'

He sighs and pushes his hand over his face. The creak of an ambulance moving slowly behind gives him a couple of seconds. 'It's just . . . I've never done anything like this before.

It feels stupid. I'm up for a snog like anyone else . . . but talking someone out of a coma . . . that's something else.'

A flash of anger hits Sophie behind the eyes. 'Is that all he is to you? A snog?'

His head shakes and fierce sparks of rain spin from his hair. 'No. I don't mean that. He's more than a snog.' He swallows. 'He's actually bloody gorgeous inside and out. Only I guess I'm more of a chicken than I realized . . .'

A robin chirrups in some foliage behind them and Sophie finds herself searching with her eyes. She cannot allow this boy to go. There has to be a way of getting him to talk to Tye. 'Well, at least come to his room. You don't have to talk to him this time. You could just look at him through the window.'

Jordan screws his eyes shut. 'What if his parents are there? What if they see me and want to know who I am?'

'They won't know. You'll just look like a friend.'

'It'll feel like a betrayal.'

'Don't be an idiot.'

He sighs. 'Just look at him through the window . . .?' She can see him weighing things up.

'Yes, for today.' She nudges him in the arm. 'Small steps. One thing at a time.' Tries a grin. 'You'll be snogging by Thursday!'

She sees glitter in his eyes. 'Shagging by Saturday!'

It's nice to walk with him through the corridors. He smells of fresh rain and patchouli oil. His hands are deep inside his pockets and he doesn't notice the looks he gets from every direction: male, female, young and old. It's like walking with a celebrity.

He doesn't notice, but Sophie does.

He doesn't say much, but she doesn't mind. As long as he's here then there's a chance she'll get him to Tye. Maybe bringing Jordan to Tye's bedside will make up for seeing Harry.

Karma.

Maybe.

At the corridor she senses him slow down. His head gets heavier and his hands push deeper inside his pockets. She slows down with him, nodding to the nurses who are now so familiar. They look with interest at the vision next to her.

'Nearly here.' It's like cajoling a reluctant puppy.

'I can't . . .'

'Just the window.'

She feels him sigh beside her.

Through the window she spots Tye's mum and dad. As if through Jordan's eyes, she sees them from a different angle. They look gaunt and creased and very, very thin. Tye's dad seems wrong without a tie and lanyard. Tye's mum looks like she's slept in her clothes. There's a cloud of despair which seeps under the door, you can breathe it in.

She touches Jordan's sleeve where he's stopped just out of view. 'He's here.'

Jordan makes a soft step forward so he can see but not be seen. She realizes this is how he likes things. No wonder Tye fell for him. He's like a wizard of mystery and intrigue. It's hard for her not to fall underneath his spell herself. She hears a small 'ooeff,' from somewhere in his lungs, and his shoulders drop forward. Tye looks paler and flat and the opposite of Kenickie. Prickles of fear stab Sophie's wrists. It's important that Jordan still feels something.

'God!'

She fills the awed silence. It's necessary. 'That's his mum and dad.' She nods at the two adults. 'He has a brother too who keeps coming back from university.' Jordan nods beside her like he knows about this. 'And his grandma comes round every few days.' She watches the ripple in Jordan's throat.

'They don't know about . . .?'

She's quick to answer, 'Nobody did, although I think he told his mum. But I think it was early days . . . I'm not even certain Tye knew for sure.'

A flash of a memory passes over Jordan's skin so his eyes spark abruptly. There's almost a grin. 'He knew in the end. I can assure you.' His words ooze dirt, it's hard not to grin back, so she does. It feels strange on her cheeks in the hospital.

Then Jordan seems to go limp and has to prop himself against the window frame; his fingers, with white protruding knuckles, are the only strong thing about him. 'I can't . . . not if they don't know . . . it's . . .'

'Please, Jordan. Please come in. They'll think you're just a friend.' She can hear the strain in her own voice.

He shakes his head. Another nurse wanders past, her ponytail bobbing in time to her steps. 'They'll see. It's obvious. Take it from me.' He scowls at the floor. 'I don't think I can do that to him.'

'Yes, you can, it doesn't matter. His mum and dad won't mind, I'm sure.'

'I've heard about his dad, how strict he was . . .'

'Well, he never had to watch his son nearly die before, did

he? Maybe things have changed . . .' The words sound horrid and cross as they echo up the walls.

Jordan lifts his eyes and gazes at Sophie; she sees pain and fear in the irises. 'I'm sorry, Sophie. I know I'm letting you down, but I can't do this.' She can see him assembling his body to move back down the corridors.

'Please . . .'

He steps away from the window. 'Maybe another time . . . when I've got my head together.' She senses his leaving.

'Tomorrow?'

He shrugs, 'Maybe . . .' And then he gives her one more apologetic frown and begins to slide away leaving nothing but the vague hint of patchouli oil.

The tang of tears fills up behind her nose. She's letting Tye down. *She's letting Tye down.*

A cluster of medical people pass by, their vocabulary a foreign language; but it's as they do that she makes a decision. Something shifts inside. She has to do something else, and she has to do it soon.

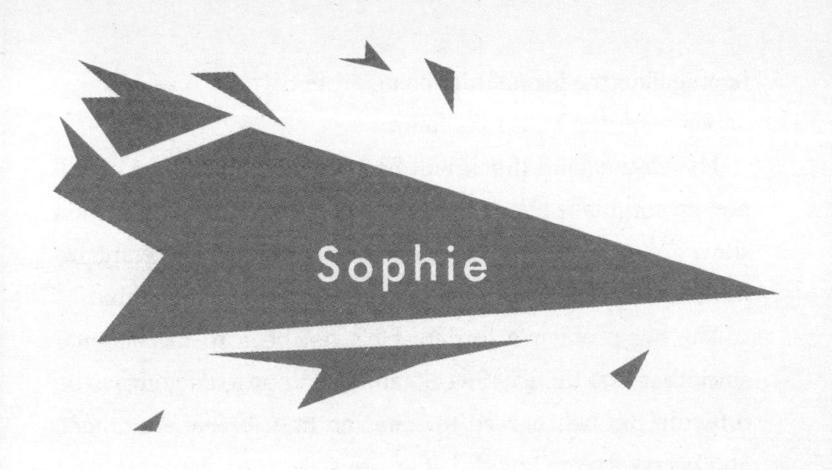

She gives herself plenty of time. It's what she does now. She owes it to Tye to put everything into this. It's the only way she can deal with the fact that she's seeing Harry.

They've been obsessed with keeping things calm and quiet in that antiseptic room of his, and it hasn't worked. So today she's playing things differently. Today she's going to fill it with people and voices and laughter.

It's been a logistical nightmare to arrange. They're all going to be there; all his main friends. Stuart, Ewan and Gurpreet from Grease, Maisie, herself, and of course Jordan if he plucks up the courage. Issy from next door has begged and begged to be allowed. It's breaking all the rules, but it feels only right that she's there. After all, if it wasn't for her, they might all be in a coma. The woman from the refuge has allowed it, as long as Sophie's dad gives her a lift back. Harry's going to be there, even though he doesn't know Tye. But he's an extra voice, and

Sophie likes the idea of him being around.

She's starting to like that a lot.

The *Grease* soundtrack will be on a loop and if any of the nurses complain about the noise and the extra people then she's got an excuse. *Grease* opens tonight, and she wants to have a party: an opening party. Tye would have loved that.

The big problem's Jordan. He's not been to the hospital since that first time last week, and she knows it's going to be difficult. But he's agreed to come, an hour before the others, and his texts seem hopeful, if anxious. Sophie's thoughts buzz with anticipation. This has to work. This completely *has* to work. She won't allow the idea that it might not. She can't bear one more day of Tye lying flat under that sheet. Her fists ball by her sides at the thought.

The morning shimmers with moist sunshine. She's going to take this as a positive sign.

But it's as she's about to enter the hospital, with several early-morning cars in the car park and two nurses talking in Spanish, that she feels the hum of her phone in her jeans pocket.

She plucks it out, distracted.

It's from Gemma.

Can you meet me?

She stands still, next to the hospital sign, leaning on the rusty pole. Punches with her finger:

I'm at hospital. Got people coming to see Tye in an hour.

She leans further in, not wanting to go into the building

before Gemma's reply. She's mildly troubled; Gemma's never asked this before. It's only a minute before a reply arrives.

It'll take less than that. I can pick you up. It's important. I need your help.

Shit. She sighs, looks at the time, frowns. She could still do it, just. If she stresses that she needs to be back in an hour. If Gemma takes her seriously. It wasn't the preparation she'd anticipated, but it would still be possible. And besides, she's interested: Gemma's never asked for help before.

She's there in five minutes. In the car. With shoes.

'Hop in.'

'You OK?'

She grimaces. 'I suppose.'

Sophie slides into the passenger seat, inhaling Gemma's mint and cigarette scents. 'Where are we going? I haven't got long.'

Gemma watches as she belts up. 'Have a guess.'

She shakes her head. 'Who knows, with you?'

Gemma gives a sad shrug. 'We're going to wreck my life.'

It's a tense drive. She doesn't seem herself. No bright laughter, no flicking of her hair. They drive fast; buildings and cars flash by, she only half recognizes the journey. Gemma slides up and down the gears. Sophie senses she doesn't want to talk. She sits back in the seat and worries about Tye.

Gemma pulls up outside the police station. Parks in a slot that's just the right size for her car. It's as if she's meant to be there. She switches off the engine and fiddles with the keys. Fishes out a tenner from her pocket. Hands it over.

'Look, if I'm not out by the time you need to go, you can get a taxi with this.'

Sophie opens and closes her mouth. She's shocked at Gemma's courage. Doesn't know what to say. 'You want me to come in with you?'

She shakes her head. 'No, I wanted you to be with me before. To show me it's the right thing to do.'

She nods. 'It is.'

She sighs again and reaches for the door handle. 'Thanks, Sophie.' She tilts her head. 'Hey, why don't you come round next week? I'll cook for you and Harry . . . and I'll promise to be nice and on my best behaviour.' She flashes blue eyes at Sophie, then a quick look down and a grimace. 'That's if I'm not doing a life sentence in some stinking prison cell somewhere.'

'You won't be. Not if you explain everything . . . I'm sure. What will you say?'

She sighs. 'That I was driving the car. That I made my brother swap with me. That I was doing it because I was running away from someone. Someone who was bad for me. Someone who had some sort of weird control over me and got me involved in things which were wrong. Criminal things. That I was involved in a burglary which resulted in the permanent disfiguration of a girl my age. That I'll never forgive myself. That by trying to escape from that life, I went and ruined some others in the process. That I messed up, but I'm trying really hard not to mess up any more.'

Sophie doesn't like her nervous expression. Nods towards Gemma's feet. Tries a smile. 'Well done.' She leans over and touches her sleeve. 'You're wearing shoes.'

She grins. 'I know. I feel like I'm suffocating. But I didn't think they'd take me seriously otherwise.'

She lifts herself out of the car, closes the door behind her. It gives a soft clunk.

Sophie watches her from the car. Her long, lean legs are clad in denim skinnies. They make stiff, lengthy steps forward towards the entrance to the police station. She hitches up her T-shirt. Elegant even when she's nervous, her whole body seems packed full of determination.

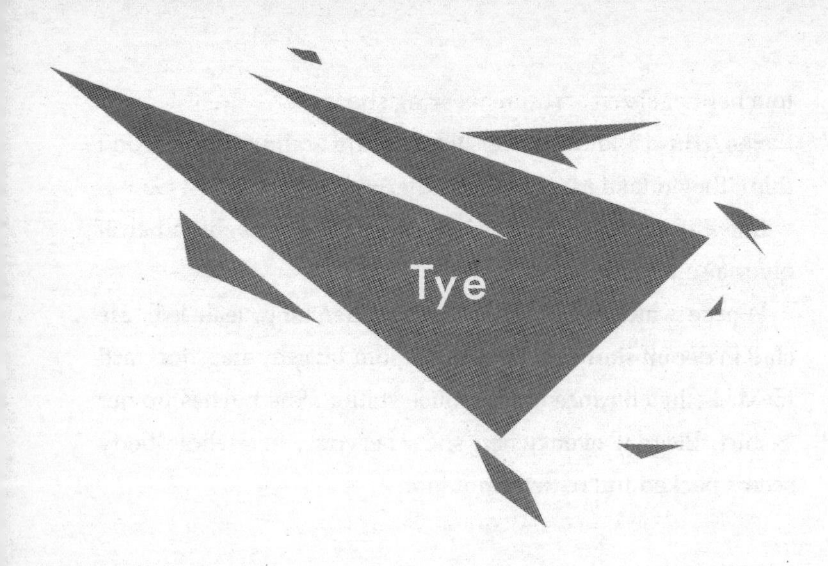

Tye

It's like warm mud.

The pleasure is intense. Like satin between his toes, in the creases of his waist, in the lines between finger joints. Lying in a wallow of mud like those giant animal beasts. He can't think of their name right now, but it'll come. He'd like to tell someone that this is the coolest sensation he's ever experienced. But right now he has nobody to tell.

He's on his own in the mud.

He's aware of people somewhere, but it's an effort to put thought into where they are. So at the moment they're a bit like wallpaper: seen but not looked at. Resident but not to be thought about.

Hippopotamus.

Slides around and wallows. Chuckles in his head but it doesn't reach his throat. That doesn't matter.

Rolls his eyes at the sound of Sophie's laugh. A babbling brook. When she was thirteen, for her birthday, they had a tent in her garden and slept over. Ate raspberries in little plastic bowls and told dirty jokes till the early hours. She was good at it, like none of his male friends. And her laugh . . . God, it was like nothing else. All tinkling one minute moving to dirty old man.

What's a bloke got to do to get some sleep round here? He shifts himself in the mud. She's a pain but he loves her: fact. He'd like to tell her, only she's not around right now, although he can bloody well hear her.

Turns over and tries to get some sleep.

The thought that some fingers are in his is a swell of a thing which trickles into his brain. He'd not noticed this before, only somehow they were always there. Something's fucking with his head.

Her laugh again, like a bloody waterfall, all gushing and force. Bells and fairy lights which he'd quite like to grab at.

Tries, from his mud bath, but it ends up hurting.

Thinks about those fingers in his. How long have they been there? Strange how he's not noticed before. Either way – he's glad they're there. Maybe they belong to Sophie. He needs to tell her everything's all right.

There's a way. With a jolt he remembers. There's a way he can find out if it's Sophie.

She has this bracelet, the one her mum bought just before she left. It has a heart which dangles and glints. She loves it. She never takes it off.

He'll maybe have a look with his fingers when he's had a little nap. The draw of the mud is too much of a temptation.

Only she's nagging with her laughter and she won't let him

sleep. It's actually bloody irritating.

So just to make a point, he goes on a hunt. Ferrets with his finger.

'OH MY GOD!'

The electric words hit him full-pelt. She's shouting it now. Three words which thunder around his head like bullets.

It's too much. He can dart like one of those gold things in a fish tank back down to the mud. Hide under a weed for a few minutes. Get his shit together.

He shouldn't have done that thing with his fingers.

Goldfish.

She's screaming words now. Something about 'he moved his fingers'. They're harsh and split at his insides. They worry him.

And then something else. The mud's not right any more. It's a bit like clay. It doesn't mould to his body now and there are clods of it instead of satin. Besides, there's a commotion up there which it's difficult to ignore.

Did he do this? With his fingers?

And then another voice. Much lower, to his right. Shit. It reverberates round his rib cage like fire. There are lips and moisture and something under his ear. Something which whacks like a wooden plank at full power in his stomach. It sends white sparks everywhere which buzz fear and alarm and silver stuff in his bloodstream.

He needs to dart back like the goldfish. Only there's nowhere to go now. The stuff down there's disappearing. He needs some time to think. What's a bloke got to do to get some peace?

The voice and the moisture under his ear (could it be a kiss?) wraps him up in a blanket of emotion. It's familiar. It's fire. It's a great big silver blanket. And the smell? It kicks at him. Patchouli oil like nothing else. He finds he can sniff.

The aroma floods his nostrils and makes him want something he'd forgotten about. But it'll come.

Sophie. He needs Sophie. More than he's ever needed her. He needs her fingers in his so he can gain some understanding of what's going on. Some basic knowledge.

So he feels again for the bracelet. Ferrets around like it's all he's lived for. He's never felt so lost.

And she's there. Like he'd hoped. Like he always knew she would be. She flicks her fingers against his and gives a small giggle.

Finds he can't breathe. Finds he's searching out with his nose for the patchouli oil. Maybe a tilt of the neck. If he can manage it. It's a strain. It hurts but the searching out is worth it.

He's frightened, he'll admit that.

Breathes it in. A cushion on his lungs sending live electric sparks to his alveoli. They inflate like a newborn baby's. It feels immense.

But then he can't breathe at all. He can't bloody breathe. That mud, that solace is now cloying and thick. Suffocating. And it's the scariest thing imaginable. He's suffocating in his own fucking mud. He needs a gasp. He needs to rise up out of it and breathe some air. His neck rockets sky high with a force he didn't think he had any more. Shit, he needs some air. He has a mouth. He's sure. He needs to open it and get some fucking air. But he's forgotten how to do it and all the time he's suffocating under the mud. His heart's thundering because he might be dying and he doesn't want to. It's suddenly important to rise above the mud and he might be beginning to die.

He doesn't want to die but he doesn't know how to stop it.

He clings on to his lifeline with the bracelet and she's clinging back too, with an urgent voice and fingers which scream importance.

He can do it. He can do it with her help if he puts his mind to it.

Thinks about the scent and the moist lips to his right. He can't think of the name of the person. But it'll come.

Gasps. Wheezes. Draws breath in a horrid, ugly torrent. Gags, but finds some golden oxygen. It's not much but it's enough. Enough to find he can draw another breath and then another till he hears some laughter to his left. Some teary, crying laughter.

And he knows it's Sophie all right. Knows because she's letting him play with her bracelet.

Jordan.

They're all there. He can see through the slits in his eyes now he's found them to open. It's been a crazy while and he's still not sure that his thoughts make sense. But he lets them slide and shift around his head and he's starting to trust that while Sophie's in his hand, everything will be all right.

There's Stuart, Gurpreet and Ewan in the corner, grinning like idiots, shifting around in jeans and sweatshirts, sipping cans of Coke and shoving chocolates down like a nurse might remove them.

Because he realizes he's in hospital. He's got that much. For a while, some time ago, it had been him, Sophie and a nurse and a doctor. They'd done some assessments with a fierce-looking clipboard and Sophie clinging on to his hand with a grin from ear to ear. Then when the doctor was happy and she'd told him a few facts, they all began to troop in. Stuart, Gurpreet and Ewan with their awkward shambling, nudging each other and rolling their eyes. Maisie, Sophie's mate, looking tearful and jittery in an oversized New York hoodie. Little Issy from next door, who apparently isn't next door any more, with giant wide eyes and her hair in a different style. Her eyes don't flit from side to side any more, and there's some meat on her bones, which she could do with. Her eyes shine on to him from her side of the bed and for some reason there floats the idea that he should thank her. He's not sure why, but maybe it'll come.

Then Jordan. Bloody Jordan. Just the name starts the thumping in his chest. He's sat there now for ages with his hand on his arm sending currents through his skin. There's no need for oxygen or saline drips when there's this live, pumping electric force right next to you, with wide full lips and a voice like liquid chocolate. His fingers tap away on Tye's skin to the *Grease* soundtrack in the background; they've got sturdy, short fingernails and a patch of softness on the end of each finger which Tye would like to kiss if there was nobody else around.

And his mum. Like a gust of wild, anxious wind she swoops through the door, her face a twist of apology and relief. How could she ever make up for the fact that she wasn't there when he woke, only his nan had a hospital appointment and she knew Sophie was going to be here? He's made her so proud. Did she know how much she loved him? Is there anything he needs? Does he feel thirsty? Is he cold? Is he in pain? Should she get a nurse for some tablets? His brother's on his way, right this moment from uni and his dad won't be many minutes now. She's wearing a strange combination of clothes which he thinks she might regret, but her face has a flush which he knows is down to him.

And to be fair to her, she doesn't bat an eyelid at the way Jordan's fingers continue a tattoo on the skin of his arm which he hopes will never go away.

Nor has Sophie, and for some reason this is important. A sensation swarms at the back of his eyes. Sophie's there at the same time as Jordan's fingers and she's OK. In fact she's better than OK. She's brimming with smiles and bursting with pride at the way Jordan touches him.

That's important, he's not sure why, but it'll come.

He's still not found his voice. The doctor said that might take some time. But he can nod, and he can sigh, and he can grin like an idiot.

Sophie's yammering about *Grease*. How it's the opening night tonight. How Jordan's fantastic in it. (He knew that.) How Issy's going to be let out for the Saturday matinee so that she can see it. (But he's not sure where she's being let out from.) How school's still boring and how everyone's signed a card.

Halfway through the yammering, a boy he doesn't know wanders in. He has a shade of pale blond hair which he's never seen before, but on closer inspection he thinks that maybe he has. This boy is introduced as Harry, Sophie's friend. The glow in Sophie's skin as she says this and the way that Harry puts his hands on her shoulders suggests he's more than a friend. It makes him laugh how she does this.

He looks around him, breathes it all in. The noise of the song and the twittering of voices. Sophie's waterfall laugh, the tap-tap-tapping of the fingertips on his arm; his mum's questions and high colour; the way she smoothes down his hair, bustling elbow room with Sophie. A fly batting against a window, flinging itself in a suicide bid at the large pane of glass. A nurse with a high ponytail dipping her head into the room then smiling at the action.

Feet that need moving. Knees that need bending. A tongue that needs to talk. A throat that needs to swallow. Hands that need to hold things; and fingers which need to caress and smooth and talk for him. But it doesn't matter right now. The doctor said it'll come. And at the moment, it's just a joy to breathe it all in. To watch Jordan speak to Sophie with a voice as thick as treacle and to have her answer him like she understands everything, gives him a wave of relief he didn't know he needed.

He doesn't understand right now, he's not completely sure. But it'll come. He's certain of that. It'll come.

Acknowledgements

I want to pass on my thanks to so many people, it's ridiculous.

To the Chicken House squad, Barry, Rachel H, Rachel L, Jazz and Kesia. The help they provide is immense.

To my agent, Anna Power, working behind the scenes, thank you. To my two early mentors, Dan Tunstall and Maxine Linnell, this would not have been possible without their encouragement.

It's been a difficult two years and I couldn't have done it without the support of my lovely friends and family. To Sarah and Sherrralyn, as ever, they're my two shining stars. To their gorgeous partners, Chris and Neil. To Kathryn with her laughter. To my village friends, Jane and John, Stefan and Lucy, Jane P and Janet. To the lovely holiday crew, Mike, Olivia, Jack, Erin and Max. Thank you, I love you all.

To my family, Rob, Kate and Owen, Mum and Dad, Jan and Bill, they've been a tremendous support. To Alister, Julie, Peter, Su, Jill, Paul, Keith and Karen. They're always there.

To Matt and Feef, Jim and Debs. They know what they've done and I'll never forget it.

Mostly, though, I want to thank my kids. Kate and Owen I am so very, very proud of you. What would I do without you? I'm a proud and lucky mum.

Huge hugs and kisses to you all. Thank you X

TRY ANOTHER GREAT BOOK FROM CHICKEN HOUSE

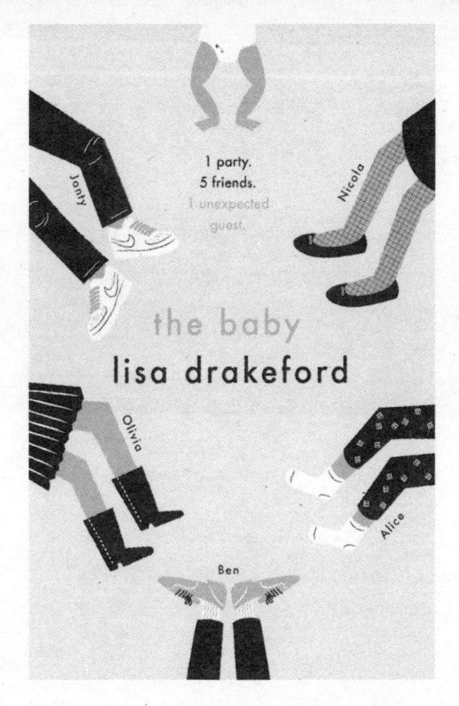

THE BABY by LISA DRAKEFORD

Five friends. A party. One unexpected guest.

When Olivia opens the bathroom door, the last thing she expects to see is her best friend Nicola giving birth on the floor – and to say Nicola is shocked is an understatement. She's not ready to be a mum, and she needs Olivia's help. But Olivia has her own problems – specifically her bullying boyfriend, Jonty, and keeping an eye on younger sister Alice. And then there's Nicola's friend Ben, who's struggling with secrets of his own . . .

'I read it in a day and couldn't do anything else until it was finished.'
THE SUN

Paperback, ISBN 978-1-910002-23-0, £7.99 • ebook, ISBN 978-1-910002-24-7, £7.99

TRY ANOTHER GREAT BOOK FROM CHICKEN HOUSE

UNDER ROSE-TAINTED SKIES by LOUISE GORNALL

I'm Norah, and my life happens within the walls of my house, where I live with my mom, and this evil overlord called Agoraphobia.

Everything's under control. It's not rosy – I'm not going to win any prizes for Most Exciting Life or anything, but at least I'm safe from the outside world, right?

Wrong. This new boy, Luke, just moved in next door, and suddenly staying safe isn't enough. If I don't take risks, how will I ever get out – or let anyone in?

'. . . the most beautiful, yet unflinching, depiction of agoraphobia I've ever read.'

HOLLY BOURNE

Paperback, ISBN 978-1-910655-86-3, £7.99 • ebook, ISBN 978-1-910655-87-0, £7.99

FACELESS by ALYSSA SHEINMEL

When Maisie is burnt in a terrible accident, her face is partially destroyed. She's lucky enough to get a face transplant, but how do you live your life when you can't even recognize yourself any more? As Maisie discovers how much her looks shaped her relationship to the world, she has to redefine her own identity, and figure out what 'lucky' really means.

Paperback, ISBN 978-1-910655-19-1, £7.99 • ebook, ISBN 978-1-910655-35-1, £7.99